THE WIND SINGER

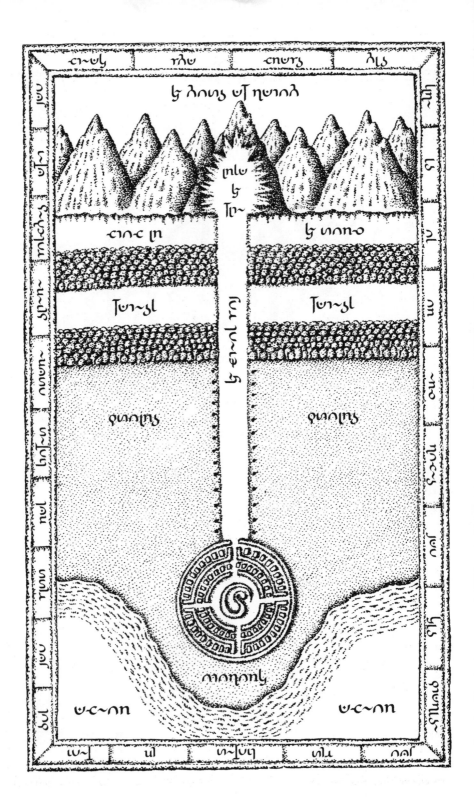

BOOK ONE in *The Wind on Fire* trilogy

THE WIND SINGER

AN ADVENTURE BY

WILLIAM NICHOLSON

WITH ARTWORK BY

PETER SÍS

Hyperion Paperbacks
New York

For Edmund, Julia, and Maria

Text copyright © 2000 by William Nicholson
Artwork copyright © 2000 by Peter Sís
First published in the U.K.
Reprinted by permission of Egmont Publishers.

Printed in the United States of America
First Hyperion trade paperback edition, 2003
3 5 7 9 10 8 6 4 2
Library of Congress Cataloging-in-Publication Data on file.
ISBN: 0-7868-1799-2 (trade paperback edition)

Visit www.hyperionteens.com

CONTENTS

LONG AGO

AT THE TIME THE STRANGERS CAME, THE MANTH PEOPLE were still living in the low mat-walled shelters that they had carried with them in their hunting days. The domed huts were clustered around the salt mine that was to become the source of their wealth. This was long before they had built the great city that stands above the salt caverns today. One high summer afternoon, a band of travellers came striding out of the desert plains, and made camp nearby. They wore their hair long and loose, men and women alike, and moved slowly and spoke quietly, when they spoke at all. They traded a little with the Manth, buying bread and meat and salt, paying with small silver ornaments that they themselves had made. They caused no trouble, but their near presence was somehow uncomfortable. Who were they? Where had they come from? Where were they going? Direct questions produced no answers: only a smile, a shrug, a shake of the head.

Then the strangers were seen to be at work, building a tower. Slowly a wooden structure took shape, a platform higher than a man, on which they constructed a second narrower tower out of timber beams and metal pipes. These pipes were all of different sizes and bundled together, like the pipes of an organ. At their base, they opened out into a ring of metal horns. At their upper end, they funnelled together to form a single cylinder, like a neck, and then fanned out again to end in a ring of large leather scoops. When the wind blew, the scoops caught it and the entire upper structure rotated, swinging around to face the strongest gusts. The swirling air was funnelled through the neck to the ranked pipes, to emerge from the horns as a series of meaningless sounds.

The tower had no obvious purpose of any kind. For a while it was a curiosity, and the people would stare at it as it creaked this way and that. When the wind blew hard, it made a mournful moaning that was comical at first, but soon became tiresome.

The silent travellers offered no explanation. It seemed they had come to the settlement with the sole purpose of building this odd structure, because when it was finished, they rolled up their tents and prepared to move on.

Before leaving, their leader took out a small silver object, and climbed the tower, and inserted it into a slot in the structure's neck. It was a tranquil summer dawn, the day the travellers departed, and the air was still. The metal pipes and horns were silent as they strode away across the desert plains. The Manth people were left as baffled as when the travellers had arrived, staring at the overgrown scarecrow they had left behind.

That night, as they slept, the wind began to blow, and a new sound entered their lives. They heard it in their sleep, and woke smiling, without knowing why. They gathered in the warm night air, and listened in joy and wonder.

The wind singer was singing.

CHAPTER ONE

BABY PINPIN MAKES HER MARK

"SAGAHOG! POMPAPRUNE! SAGA-SAGA-HOG!" BOWMAN Hath lay in bed listening to the muffled sounds of his mother bathing in the bathroom next door. From far away across the roofs of the city floated the golden boom of the bell in the tower of the Imperial Palace: *mmnang! mmnang!* It was sounding the sixth hour, the time when all Aramanth awoke. Bowman opened his eyes and lay gazing at the daylight glowing in the tangerine curtains. He realised that he was feeling sad. What is it this time? he thought to himself. He looked ahead to the coming day in school, and his stomach tightened, the way it always did; but this was a different feeling. A kind of sorrowing, as if for something lost. But what?

His twin sister, Kestrel, was still asleep in the bed next to him, within reach of his outstretched arm. He listened to her snuffly sleep-breathing for a few moments, then sent her a wake-up thought. He waited till he heard her grumpy answering groan. Then he counted silently to five, and rolled out of bed.

Crossing the hall on the way to the bathroom, he stopped to greet his baby sister, Pinpin. She was standing up in her cot in her fuzzy night suit, sucking her thumb. Pinpin slept in the hall because there was no room for a cot in either of the two bedrooms. The apartments in Orange District were really too small for a family of five.

"Hallo, Pinpin," he said.

Pinpin took her thumb out of her mouth, and her round face lit up with a happy smile.

"Kiss," she said.

Bowman kissed her.

"Hug," she said.

Bowman hugged her. As he cuddled her soft round body, he remembered. Today was the day of Pinpin's first test. She was only two years old, too little to mind how well or badly she did, but from now till the day she died she would have a rating. That was what was making him sad.

Tears started to push into Bowman's eyes. He cried too easily—everyone told him so—but what was he to do? He felt everything too much. He didn't mean to, but when he looked at somebody else, anybody else, he found he knew what they were feeling, and all too often it was a fear or a sadness. And then he would understand what it was they were afraid of or sad about, and he would feel it, too, and he would start to cry. It was all very awkward.

This morning what made him sad wasn't what Pinpin was feeling now, but what he knew she would feel one day. Now there were no worries in her sunny little heart. Yet from today, she would begin, at first only dimly, but later with sharp anxiety, to fear the future. For in Aramanth, life was measured out in tests. Every test brought with it the possibility of failure, and every test successfully passed led to the next, with its renewed possibility of failure. There was no escape from it, and no end. Just thinking about it made his heart almost burst with love for his little sister. He hugged her tight as tight, and kissed and kissed her merry cheeks.

"Love Pinpin," he said.

"Love Bo," said Pinpin.

A sharp rending sound came from the bathroom, followed by yet another explosion of oaths.

"Sagahog! Bangaplop!"

And then the familiar wailing lament:

"O, unhappy people!"

This had been the cry of the great prophet Ira Manth, from whom his mother was directly, though distantly, descended. The name had been passed down the family ever since, and his mother, too, was called Ira. When she flew into one of her rages, his father would wink at the children and say, "Here comes the prophetess."

The bathroom door now burst open, and Ira Hath herself appeared, looking flustered. Unable to find the sleeve holes of her dressing gown, she had fought her way into the garment by sheer fury. The sleeves hung empty on either side, and her arms stuck out through burst seams.

"It's Pinpin's test today," said Bo.

"It's what?"

Ira Hath stared for a moment. Then she took Pinpin from Bowman and in her turn held her close in her arms, as if someone was trying to take her away.

"My baby," she said. "My baby."

At breakfast there was no reference to the test until near the end. Then their father put away his book and got up from the table a little earlier than usual and said, as if to no one in particular, "I suppose we'd better get ready."

Kestrel looked up, her eyes bright with determination.

"I'm not coming," she said.

Hanno Hath sighed and rubbed his wrinkly cheeks with one hand.

"I know, darling. I know."

"It's not fair," said Kestrel, as if her father were making her go. And so in a way he was. Hanno Hath was so kind to his children, and understood so exactly what they felt, that they found it almost impossible to go against his wishes.

A familiar smoky smell rose from the stove.

"Oh, sagahog!" exclaimed his wife.

She had burned the toast again.

The morning sun was low in the sky, and the high city walls cast a shadow over all Orange District as the Hath family walked down the street to the Community Hall. Mr. and Mrs. Hath went in front, and Bowman and Kestrel came behind, with Pinpin between them holding a hand each. Other families with two-year-olds were making their way in the same direction, past the neat terraces of orange-painted houses. The Blesh family was ahead of them, and could be heard coaching their little boy as they went along.

"One, two, three, four, who's that at the door? Five, six, seven, eight, who's that at the gate?"

As they came into the main square, Mrs. Blesh turned and saw them. She gave the little wave she always gave, as if she were their special friend, and waited for Mrs. Hath to catch her up.

"Can you keep a secret?" she said in a whisper. "If our little one does well enough today, we'll move up to Scarlet."

Mrs. Hath thought for a moment.

"Very bright, scarlet," she said.

"And did you hear? Our Rufy was second in his class yesterday afternoon."

Mr. Blesh called back, "Second? Second? Why not first?
That's what I want to know."

"Oh, you men!" said Mrs. Blesh. And to Mrs. Hath, in
her special-friend voice, "They can't help it, can they? They
have to win."

As she spoke these words, her slightly poppy-out eyes rested
for a moment on Hanno Hath. Everyone knew that poor
Hanno Hath hadn't been promoted for three years now,
though of course his wife never admitted how disappointed
she must feel. Kestrel caught her pitying look, and it made
her want to stick knives into Mrs. Blesh's body. But more
than that, it made her want to hug her father, and cover his
wrinkly-sad face with kisses. To relieve her feelings, she bom-
barded Mrs. Blesh's broad back with rude thoughts.

Pocksicker! Pompaprune! Sagahog!

At the entrance to the Community Hall, a lady Assistant
Examiner sat checking names against a list. The Bleshes went first.

"Is the little one clean?" asked the Assistant Examiner.
"Has he learned to control his bladder?"

"Oh, yes," said Mrs. Blesh. "He's unusually advanced for
his age."

When it was Pinpin's turn, the Assistant Examiner asked
the same question.

"Is she clean? Has she learned to control her bladder?"

Mr. Hath looked at Mrs. Hath. Bowman looked at Kestrel. Through their minds floated pictures of Pinpin's puddles on the kitchen floor. But this was followed by a kind of convulsion of family pride, which they all felt at the same time.

"Control her bladder, madam?" said Mrs. Hath with a bright smile. "My daughter can widdle in time to the national anthem."

The Assistant Examiner looked surprised, then checked the box marked CLEAN on her list.

"Desk twenty-three," she said.

The Community Hall was buzzing with activity. A great chalkboard at one end listed the names of the examinees, all ninety-seven of them, in alphabetical order. There was Pinpin's name, looking unfamiliar in its full form: Pinto Hath. The Hath family formed a protective huddle round desk twenty-three while Mrs. Hath removed Pinpin's nappy. Now that she was down as CLEAN, it would be counted as cheating to leave her in a nappy. Pinpin herself was delighted. She liked to feel cool air on her bottom.

A bell rang, and the big room fell quiet for the entrance of the Examiners. Ninety-seven desks, at each of which sat a two-year-old; behind each one, on benches, their parents and siblings. The sudden silence awed the little ones, and there wasn't so much as a cry.

The Examiners swept in, their scarlet gowns billowing, and stood on the podium in a single line of terrible magnificence. There were ten of them. At the centre was the tall figure of the Chief Examiner, Maslo Inch, the only one to wear the simple shining white garments of the highest rating.

"Stand for the Oath of Dedication!"

Everyone stood, parents lifting little ones to their feet. Together they chanted the words all knew by heart.

"I vow to strive harder, to reach higher, and in every way to seek to make tomorrow better than today, for love of my Emperor, and for the glory of Aramanth."

Then they all sat down again, and the Chief Examiner made a short speech. Maslo Inch, still only in his mid-forties, had been recently elevated to the highest level, but so tall and powerful was his appearance, and so deep his voice, that he looked and acted as if he had been wearing white all his life. Hanno Hath, who had known Maslo Inch a long time, saw this with quiet amusement.

"My friends," intoned the Chief Examiner, "what a special day this is, the first test day of your beloved child. How proud you must be to know that from today, your little son or daughter will have his or her own personal rating. How proud they will be, as they come to understand that by their own efforts they can contribute to your family rating." Here he raised a hand in friendly warning, and gave them all a grave look. "But never forget that the rating itself means nothing. All that matters is how you improve your rating. Better today than yesterday. Better tomorrow than today. That is the spirit that has made our city great."

The scarlet-gowned Examiners then fanned out across the front row of desks and began working their way down the lines. Maslo Inch, as Chief Examiner, remained on the podium like a tower, overseeing all. Inevitably his scanning gaze fell in time on Hanno Hath. A twinkle of recognition glowed for a moment in the corner of one eye, and then faded again as his gaze moved on. Hanno Hath shrugged to himself. He and Maslo Inch were exact contemporaries. They had been in the same class at school. But that was all long ago now.

The tests were marked as they were completed, and the marks conveyed to the big chalkboard at the front. Quite soon, a ranking began to emerge among the infants. The Blesh child was close to the top, with 23 points out of a possible 30, a rating of 7.6. Because B came earlier than H, the Blesh family was finished before the Haths had begun, and Mrs. Blesh came down the aisle with her triumphant infant in her arms to pass on the benefit of their experience.

"The silly fellow left out number five," she explained. "One, two, three, four, six." She wagged a mock-angry finger at the child. "Four, *five*, six, you silly! You know that! I'm sure Pinto does."

"Actually, Pinpin can count to a million," said Kestrel.

"I think we're telling tiny stories," said Mrs. Blesh, patting Kestrel on the head. "He got cow, and book, and cup," she went on. "He didn't get banana. But 7.6 is a good start. Rufy's first rating was 7.8, I remember, and look at him now. Never below 9. Not that I care for ratings as such, of course."

The Examiner was now ready for Pinpin. He approached the desk, his eyes on his papers.

"Pinto Hath," he said. And then raising his eyes, his face took on an all-embracing smile. Pinpin met this look with instinctive suspicion.

"And what are we to call you, my little fellow?"

"By her name," said Mrs. Hath.

"Well, then, Pinto," said the Examiner, still beaming. "I've got some pretty pictures here. Let's see if you can tell me what they are."

He presented Pinpin with a sheet of coloured images. Pinpin looked, but said nothing. The Examiner pointed with his finger to a dog.

"What's this?"

Not a sound from Pinpin.

"What's this, then?"

Silence.

"Does he have a hearing problem?"

"No," said Mrs. Hath. "She can hear you."

"But he doesn't speak."

"I suppose there's nothing much she wants to say."

Bowman and Kestrel held their breath. The Examiner frowned and looked grave, and made a note on his papers. Then he returned to the pictures.

"Well, now, Pinto. Show me a doggy. Where's a doggy?"

Pinpin gazed back at him, and neither spoke nor pointed.

"A house, then. Show me a little house."

Nothing. And so it went on, until at last the Examiner put his pictures away, looking graver still.

"Let's try some counting, shall we, little chap?"

He started counting, meaning Pinpin to follow him, but all she would do was stare. He made another note.

"The last part of the test," he said to Mrs. Hath, "is designed to assess the child's level of communication skills. Listening, understanding, and responding. We find the child is usually more at his ease when held in the arms."

"You want her in your arms?"

"If you have no objection."

"Are you sure?"

"I have done this before, Mrs. Hath. The little fellow will be quite safe with me."

Ira Hath looked down at the ground, and her nose twitched just a little. Bowman saw this, and sent an instant thought to Kestrel.

Mama's going to crack.

But all she did was lift Pinpin from her seat and give her into the Examiner's waiting arms. Bowman and Kestrel watched with keen interest. Their father sat with his eyes closed, knowing it was all going as wrong as it possibly could, and there was nothing he could do about it.

"Well, Pinto, you're a fine fellow, aren't you?" The Examiner tickled Pinpin under the chin and pressed her nose. "What's this, then? Is this your nosey?"

Pinpin remained silent. The Examiner pulled out the large gold medal that hung round his neck on a chain, and dangled it in front of Pinpin's eyes. It shone in the morning light.

"Pretty, pretty. Do you want to hold it?"

Pinpin said nothing. The Examiner looked up at Mrs. Hath in exasperation.

"I'm not sure you realise," he said. "As matters stand at this moment, I shall have to give your child a zero rating."

"Is it as bad as that?" said Mrs. Hath, her eyes glittering.

"I can get nothing out of him, you see."

"Nothing at all?"

"Is there some rhyme or word game he likes to play?"

"Let me think." Mrs. Hath proceeded, rather ostentatiously, to mime the act of thinking, lips pursed, finger stroking brow.

Bowman sent a thought to Kestrel.

She's cracking.

"Yes," said Mrs. Hath. "There is a game she likes to play. Try saying to her, 'Wiss wiss wiss.'"

"Wiss wiss wiss?"

"She'll like that."

Bowman and Kestrel sent the same thought at the same time.

She's cracked!

"Wiss wiss wiss," said the Examiner to Pinpin. "Wiss wiss wiss, little fellow."

Pinpin looked at the Examiner in surprise, and wriggled a little in his arms, as if to settle herself more comfortably. Mrs. Hath watched, her nose now twitching uncontrollably. Bowman and Kestrel watched, their hearts thumping.

Any minute now, they thought to each other.

"Wiss wiss wiss," said the Examiner.

"Any minute now," said Mrs. Hath.

Now, Pinpin, now, willed Bowman and Kestrel. *Do it now.*

Mr. Hath opened his eyes and saw the looks on their faces. Suddenly realising what was going on, he rose from the bench and reached out his arms.

"Let me take her—"

Too late.

Hubba hubba, Pinpin! exulted Bo and Kess in the joyous silence of their thoughts. *Hubba hubba hubba, Pinpin!*

A faraway look of contentment on her round face, Pinpin

was emptying her bladder in a long and steady stream down the Examiner's arms. The Examiner felt the spread of the gentle warmth without at first understanding what was happening. Then seeing the look of rapt attention on the faces of Mrs. Hath and her children, he dropped his gaze downward. The stain was seeping into his scarlet cloak. In utter silence, he held Pinpin out for Mr. Hath to take, and turned and walked gravely back up the aisle.

Mrs. Hath took Pinpin from her husband and smothered her with kisses. Bowman and Kestrel dropped to the floor and rolled about there, quaking with silent laughter. Hanno Hath watched the Examiner report the incident to Maslo Inch, and he gave a small private sigh. He knew what his wife and children did not, which was that they had needed a good rating this morning. Now, with no points at all, they would probably have to leave their house in Orange District and make do in humbler quarters. Two rooms if they were lucky; more likely one room, with the use of a kitchen and bathroom on a communal landing. Hanno Hath was not a vain man. He cared very little what others thought of him. But he loved his family dearly, and the thought of failing them hurt him deep inside.

Ira Hath cuddled Pinpin tight and refused to think about the future.

"Wiss wiss wiss," murmured Pinpin happily.

CHAPTER TWO

KESTREL MAKES A HORRIBLE FRIEND

ON ARRIVING AT SCHOOL, BOWMAN AND KESTREL FOUND they had forgotten to bring their homework.

"Forgot?" roared Dr. Batch. "You forgot?"

The twins stood side by side at the front of the long classroom, facing their teacher. Dr. Batch smoothed his hands over his substantial stomach, and ran the tip of his tongue over his substantial lips, and proceeded to make an example of them. Dr. Batch liked making an example of his pupils. He considered it part of his job as a teacher.

"Let's begin at the beginning. Why did you forget?"

"Our little sister had her first test this morning," said Bowman. "We left the house early, and we just forgot."

"You just forgot? Well, well, well."

Dr. Batch liked lame excuses.

"Hands up," he said to the class, "hands up who else attended an infant test this morning."

A dozen hands went up among the serried ranks of desks, including the hand of Rufy Blesh.

"And hands up who else forgot their homework."

All the hands went down again. Dr. Batch turned to Bowman, his eyes popping out with friendly attention.

"It seems you are the only ones."

"Yes, sir."

Throughout this proceeding, Kestrel remained silent. But Bowman could hear the seething of her angry thoughts, and knew she was in one of her wild moods. Dr. Batch, unaware of this, began to waddle up and down in front of them, conducting a ritual exchange with the class.

"Class! What happens if you don't work?"

Back came the familiar response from fifty-one young mouths.

"No work, no progress."

"And what happens if you make no progress?"

"No progress, no points."

"And what happens if you get no points?"

"No points ends up last."

"Last." Dr. Batch relished the word. "Last! La-a-ast!"

The whole class shivered. Last! Like Mumpo, the stupidest

boy in the school. Some eyes turned furtively to look at him, as he sat glowering and shivering right at the back, in the seat of shame. Mad Mumpo, whose upper lip was always shiny with nose-dribble, because he had no mother to tell him to wipe it. Smelly Mumpo, who stank so badly that no one would ever go near him, because he had no father to tell him to wash.

Dr. Batch waddled over to the class ratings board, on which every pupil's name was written in class order. Every day, at the end of the day, the new points were calculated, and the new class order written up.

"I shall deduct five points each," said Dr. Batch. And there and then, he recalculated the class order. Bowman and Kestrel dropped two places, to twenty-fifth and twenty-sixth respectively, while the class watched.

"Slipping, slipping, slipping," said Dr. Batch as he made the changes. "What do we do when we find ourselves slipping down?"

The class chanted the response.

"We strive harder, and reach higher, to make tomorrow better than today."

"Harder. Higher. Better." He turned back to Bowman and Kestrel. "You will not, I trust, forget your homework again. Take up your places."

As they walked back down the rows of desks, Bowman

could feel Kestrel seething with hatred, for Dr. Batch, and the big ratings board, and the school, and all Aramanth.

It doesn't matter, he thought to her. *We'll catch up.*

I don't want to, she replied. *I don't care.*

Bowman came to a stop at the desk where they were now to sit, two places behind their old desks. But Kestrel went on, all the way to the back, where Mumpo sat. Beside Mumpo there was an empty place, because he was always bottom of the class. Here Kestrel sat down.

Dr. Batch stared in astonishment. So did Mumpo.

"Hallo-o," he said, breathing his stinky breath all over her.

Kestrel turned away, covering her face.

"Do you like me?" said Mumpo, leaning closer.

"Get away from me," said Kestrel. "You stink."

Dr. Batch called sharply from the other end of the room.

"Kestrel Hath! Go to your correct place at once!"

"No," said Kestrel.

The whole class froze.

"No?" said Dr. Batch. "Did you say no?"

"Yes," said Kestrel.

"Do you wish me to deduct five more points for disobedience?"

"You can if you want," said Kestrel. "I don't care."

"You don't care?" Dr. Batch went a bright red. "Then I shall teach you to care. You'll do as you're told, or—"

"Or what?" said Kestrel.

Dr. Batch stared back, lost for words.

"I'm already at the bottom of the class," said Kestrel. "What more can you do to me?"

For a moment longer, Dr. Batch struggled with himself in silence, searching for the best way to respond. During this moment, in which the whole class held its breath, Mumpo shuffled closer still to Kestrel, and Kestrel twisted farther away from him, screwing up her face in disgust. Dr. Batch saw this, and the look of bewilderment on his face was replaced by a vindictive smile. He set off at a slow pace down the room.

"Class," he said, his voice smoothly under control once more. "Class, turn and look at Kestrel Hath."

All eyes turned.

"Kestrel has found a new friend. As you see, Kestrel's new friend is our very own Mumpo. Kestrel and Mumpo, side by side. What do you think of your new friend, Mumpo?"

Mumpo nodded and smiled. "I like Kess," he said.

"He likes you, Kestrel," said Dr. Batch. "Why don't you sit closer? You could put your arm round him. You could hug him. He's your new friend. Who knows, maybe in later years you'll marry each other, and you can be Mrs. Mumpo, and have lots of little Mumpo babies. Would you like that? Three or four little Mumpo babies to wash and wipe?"

The class tittered at that. Dr. Batch was pleased. He felt he had regained the upper hand. Kestrel sat stiff as a rod and burned with shame and anger, and said nothing.

"But perhaps I'm making a mistake. Perhaps Kestrel is making a mistake. Perhaps she simply sat down in the wrong seat, by mistake."

He was close to Kestrel now, standing gazing at her in silence. Kestrel knew that he was offering her a deal: her obedience in exchange for her pride.

"Perhaps Kestrel is going to get up, and go back to her correct place."

Kestrel trembled, but she didn't move. Dr. Batch waited a moment longer, then hissed at her:

"Well, well. Kestrel and Mumpo. What a sweet couple."

All that morning, he kept up the attack. In the grammar lesson, he wrote on the board:

NAME THE TENSES
KESTREL LOVES MUMPO
KESTREL IS LOVED BY MUMPO
KESTREL WILL LOVE MUMPO
KESTREL HAS LOVED MUMPO
KESTREL SHALL HAVE LOVED MUMPO

In the arithmetic lesson, he wrote on the board:

IF KESTREL GIVES MUMPO 392 KISSES AND
98 HUGS, AND HALF THE HUGS ARE ACCOMPA-
NIED BY KISSES, AND ONE-EIGHTH OF THE
KISSES ARE SLOBBERY, HOW MANY SLOBBERY
KISSES WITH HUGS COULD KESTREL GIVE
MUMPO?

And so it went on, and the class snickered away, as Dr. Batch intended. Bowman looked back at Kestrel many times, but she just sat there, doing her work, not saying a word.

When time came for the lunch break, he joined her as she walked quietly out of the room. To his annoyance, he found the dribbling Mumpo was coming with Kestrel, sticking close to her side.

"Get lost, Mumpo," said Kestrel.

But Mumpo wouldn't get lost. He simply trotted along beside Kestrel, his eyes never leaving her face. From time to time, unprompted, he would murmur, "I like Kess," and then wipe his nose-dribble onto his shirt sleeve.

Kestrel was heading for the way out.

"Where are you going, Kess?"

"Out," said Kestrel. "I hate school."

"Yes, but Kess—" Bowman didn't know what to say. Of course she hated school. Everyone hated school. But you had to go.

"What about the family rating?"

"I don't know," said Kestrel. And walking faster now, she began to cry. Mumpo saw this and was devastated. He skipped around her, reaching out his grubby hands to paw her, and uttered small cries designed to give her comfort.

"Don't cry, Kess. I'll be your friend, Kess. Don't cry."

Kestrel brushed him away angrily.

"Get lost, Mumpo. You stink."

"Yes, I know," said Mumpo humbly.

"Kess," said Bowman, "come back to school, sit in your proper place, and Batch will leave you alone."

"I'm never going back," said Kestrel.

"But you must."

"I'm going to tell Pa. He'll understand."

"And I will," said Mumpo.

"Go away, Mumpo!" shouted Kestrel, right in his face. "Go away or I'll bash you!"

She raised a threatening fist. Mumpo dropped whimpering to his knees.

"Hurt me if you want. I don't mind."

Kestrel's fist remained suspended in midair. She stared at Mumpo. Bowman, too, was watching Mumpo. Suddenly he was caught unaware by the feeling of what it was like to be Mumpo. A dull, cold terror rolled over him, and a penetrating loneliness. He almost cried out loud, so intense was the hunger for kindness.

"She doesn't mean it," he said. "She won't hit you."

"She can if she wants."

Mumpo's face gazed adoringly up at her, his eyes now as shiny as his upper lip.

"Tell him you won't hit him, Kess."

"I won't hit you," said Kestrel, dropping her fist. "You're too stinky to touch."

She turned and walked fast down the street, Bowman at her side. Mumpo followed a few paces behind. So that he wouldn't hear, Kestrel talked to Bowman in her head.

I can't go on like this, I can't.

What else can we do?

I don't know, she said. *Something. Something soon, or I'll explode.*

CHAPTER THREE

BAD WORDS
SAID LOUD

AS SHE LEFT ORANGE DISTRICT WITH BOWMAN AND MUMPO
following her, Kestrel had no plan in her head other than
to get away from the hated school. But in fact she was making her way down one of the city's four main streets to the
central arena, where the wind singer stood.

The city of Aramanth was built in the shape of a circle, a
drum even, since it was enclosed by high walls, raised long
ago to protect the people from the warrior tribes of the
plains. No one had dared attack mighty Aramanth for many
generations now, but the great walls remained, and few people ventured out of the city. What was there in the world
beyond that anybody could possibly want? Only the rock-
strewn seashore to the south, where the great grey ocean

thundered and rolled; and the barren desert wastes to the north, stretching all the way to the distant mountains. No food out there; no comfort, no safety. Whereas within the walls there was all that was necessary for life—more, for a good life. Every citizen of Aramanth knew how fortunate they were to live in this rare haven of peace, plenty, and equal opportunity for all.

The city was arranged in its districts in concentric rings. The outermost ring, in the shadow of the walls, was formed by the great cube-shaped apartment blocks of Grey District. Next came the low-rise apartments that made up Maroon District, and the crescents of small terraced houses of Orange District, where the Hath family lived. Nearest the central sector of the city lay the broad ring of Scarlet District, a region of roomy detached houses, each with its own garden, laid out in a pleasing maze of twisting lanes, so that each house felt special and different, though of course all were painted red. And finally and most gloriously, at the heart of the city, there was White District. Here was the Imperial Palace, where the Emperor, Creoth the Sixth, the father of Aramanth, looked out over his citizen-children. Here were the great houses of the city leaders, built in marble or polished limestone, beautiful and austere. Here was the huge pillared Hall of Achievement, where the family ratings were displayed, and facing it, across the plaza where the statue of Emperor Creoth the First stood, the many-windowed College of Examiners, home of the Board of Examiners, the supreme governing body of Aramanth.

Next to the plaza, beneath the towering walls of the Imperial Palace, at the meeting point of the four main streets, lay the city arena. This great circular amphitheatre had originally been designed to bring together the entire population of Aramanth for the debates and elections that had been necessary before the introduction of the ratings system. Today there were far too many citizens to cram into the arena's nine descending marble tiers, but it had its uses, for concerts and recitals. And of course this was the venue for the annual High Examination, when the heads of all the households were tested and their family ratings adjusted for the following year.

In the centre of the arena, in the circle paved with white marble that formed the stage, there stood the curious wooden tower known as the wind singer. Everything about the wind singer was wrong. It was not white. It was not symmetrical. It lacked the simplicity and calm that characterised the whole of White District. It creaked this way and that with every passing breeze, and when the wind blew stronger, it let out a dismal moaning sound. Every year a proposal would come up at the meeting of the Board of Examiners to dismantle it and replace it with a more dignified emblem of the city, but every year the proposal was vetoed—by the Emperor himself, it was whispered. And it was true to say that the people regarded the wind singer with affection, because it was so very old, and had always been there, and because there was a legend that one day it would sing again.

Kestrel Hath had loved the wind singer all her life. She loved it because it was unpredictable, and served no purpose, and seemed, by its sad cry, not to like the orderly world of Aramanth. Sometimes, when the frustrations of her existence grew too hard to bear, she would run down the nine tiers of the arena and sit on the white flagstones at the bottom and talk to the wind singer, for an hour or more. Of course, it didn't understand her, and the creaky groany noises it made back weren't words, but she found that rather restful. She didn't particularly want to be understood. She just wanted to vent her feelings of fury and powerlessness, and not feel entirely alone.

On this day, the worst so far, Kestrel headed instinctively for the arena. Her father would not be home from the library yet, and her mother would be at the clinic, where Pinpin had to have her two-year-old physical assessment. Where else was there to go? Later she was accused of plotting her disgraceful actions in advance, but Kestrel was not a schemer. She acted on impulse, rarely knowing herself what she would do next. It would be more true to say that

Bowman, following her, sensed that she would get herself into trouble. As for Mumpo, he followed her just because he loved her.

The main street to the centre led past the courtyard of the Weavers' Company, where, because it was lunchtime, all the weavers were out in the yard doing their exercises.

"Touch the ground! Touch the sky!" called out their trainer. "You can do it! If you try!"

All the weavers bent and stretched, bent and stretched, in time with each other.

A little farther on they came upon a street-cleaner sitting by his barrow eating his midday meal.

"I don't suppose you've got any litter you'd care to drop," he asked them.

The children searched their pockets. Bowman found a piece of charred toast that he'd put there so as not to hurt his mother's feelings.

"Just drop it in the street," said the street-cleaner, his eyes brightening.

"I'll put it in your barrow," said Bowman.

"That's right, do my job for me," said the street-cleaner bitterly. "Don't you worry about how I'm to meet my target, let alone exceed it, if nobody ever drops any litter in the street. Don't ask yourself how I'm supposed to get along, you're from Orange, you're all right. It doesn't occur to you that I want to better myself, same as everyone else. You try living in Grey District. My wife has set her heart on one of those apartments in Maroon, with the little balconies."

Bowman dropped his piece of toast onto the street.

"Well, there you are," said the street-cleaner. "I may just look at it for a while before I sweep it up."

Kestrel was already far ahead, with Mumpo trailing after her. Bowman ran to catch them up.

"When are we going to have lunch?" said Mumpo.

"Shut up," said Kestrel.

As they crossed the plaza the bell in the high palace tower struck two. *Mnang! Mnang!* Now their classmates would all be trooping back to their desks, and Dr. Batch would be marking the three truants down as absent without leave. That meant more lost points.

They passed through the double row of marble columns that ringed the highest tier of the arena, and made their way down the steps to the bottom.

Mumpo came to a sudden stop on the fifth tier and sat down on the white marble step.

"I'm hungry," he announced.

Kestrel paid no attention. She went on down to the bottom, and Bowman followed her. Mumpo wanted to follow her, but now that he had become aware of his hunger, he could think of nothing else. He sat on the step and hugged his knees and yearned for food with all his heart.

Kestrel came to a stop at last, at the foot of the wind singer. Her rage at Pinpin's test, and Dr. Batch's taunts, and the whole suffocating order of Aramanth, had formed within her into a wild desire to upset, to confuse, to shock—she hardly knew who or what or how—just to fracture the smooth and seamless running of the world, if only for a moment. She had come to the wind singer because it was her friend and ally, but it was only when she stood at its foot that she knew what she was going to do.

She started to climb.

Come down, Bowman called in alarm. *They'll punish you. You'll fall. You'll hurt yourself.*

I don't care.

She hauled herself up onto the platform, and then she started climbing the tower. This wasn't easy, because it swung in the wind, and the footholds were slippery among the pipes. But she was wiry and agile, and held on tight as she ascended.

A sharp cry sounded from the top tier of the arena.

"Hey! You! Get down at once!"

A scarlet-robed official had seen her, and came hurrying down the steps. Finding Mumpo sitting hunched on the fifth tier, he stopped to question him.

"What do you think you're doing? Why aren't you in school?"

"I'm hungry," said Mumpo.

"Hungry? You've just had lunch."

"No, I haven't."

"All children eat school lunch at one o'clock. If you didn't eat your lunch, then you have only yourself to blame."

"Yes, I know," said the unhappy Mumpo. "But I'm still hungry."

By now Kestrel had reached the wind singer's neck and was making an interesting discovery. There was a slot cut into the broad metal pipe, and an arrow etched above it pointing to the slot, and a design above the arrow. It looked like the letter S, with the tail of the S curling round and right over its top.

The scarlet-robed official arrived at the base of the wind singer.

"You, boy," he said sharply to Bowman. "What's she doing? Who is she?"

"She's my sister," said Bowman.

"And who are you?"

"I'm her brother."

The fierce official made him nervous, and when nervous, Bowman became very logical. Momentarily baffled, the official looked up and called to Kestrel, "Get down, girl! Get down at once! What do you think you're doing up there?"

"Pongo!" Kestrel called back, climbing ever higher up the structure.

"What?" said the official. "What did she say?"

"Pongo," said Bowman.

"She said pongo to me?"

"I'm not sure," said Bowman. "She might have been saying it to me."

"But it was I who spoke to her. I ordered her to come down, and she replied, Pongo."

"Perhaps she thinks it's your name."

"It's not my name. No one is called Pongo."

"I didn't know that. I expect she doesn't know that."

The official, confused by Bowman's tremulous but reasonable manner, turned his face back up to Kestrel, who was now almost at the very top, and called out, "Did you say pongo to me?"

"Pongo pooa-pooa pompaprune!" Kestrel called back.

The official turned to Bowman, his face rigid with righteousness.

"There! You heard her! It's a disgrace!" He called back up to Kestrel, "If you don't come down, I'll report you!"

"You'll report her even if she does come down," said Bowman.

"I certainly shall," said the official, "but I shall report her more if she doesn't." He shouted up at Kestrel, "I shall recommend that points be deducted from your family rating!"

"Bangaplop!" called Kestrel. She was on a level with one of the wide leather scoops as she called out this rude word, and the sound travelled down the pipes of the wind singer and emerged from the horns, a second or so later, in a fuzzy distorted form.

"Bang-ang-anga-plop-op-p!"

Kestrel then put her head right into the leather scoop and shouted.

"Sagahog!"

Her voice came booming out of the horns:

"Sag-ag-ag-a-hog-g-g!"

The official heard this, aghast. "She's disturbing the afternoon work session," he said. "They'll hear her in the College."

"Pompa-pompa-pompaprune!" called Kestrel.

"POMP-P-PA POMP-P-PA POMP-P-PA-PRU-U-UNE!" boomed the wind singer across the arena.

Out of the College of Examiners, in a flurry of white robes, poured the high officials of the city to see what was intruding on their afternoon.

"I ha-a-ate schoo-oo-ool!" cried Kestrel's amplified voice. "I ha-a-ate ra-a-atings!"

The examiners heard this in shock.

"She's having a fit," they said. "She's lost her wits."

"Get her down! Send for the marshals!"

"I won't strive ha-a-arder!" cried Kestrel. "I won't rea-ea-each hi-i-igher! I won't make tomorr-orr-ow better than today-ay-ay!"

More and more people were gathering now, drawn by the noise. A long crocodile of children from Maroon District, who had been on a visit to the Hall of Achievement, appeared between the double row of columns to listen to Kestrel's voice.

"I don't love my Emperor-or-or!" Kestrel was now crying. "There's no glor-or-ory in Aramanth-anth-anth!"

The children gasped. Their teacher was too shocked to speak. A band of grey-coated marshals came running down the steps, their batons in their hands.

"Get her down!" cried the scarlet-robed official.

The marshals formed a ring round the wind singer, and their captain called up to Kestrel, "You're surrounded! You can't get away!"

"I don't want to get away," Kestrel replied, and putting her head back into the leather scoop, she called out, "Pongo-o-o to exam-am-ams!"

The Maroon children started to titter.

"Oh, the evil child!" exclaimed their teacher, and herded

her class back to the Hall of Achievement. "Come along, children. Don't listen to her. She's a wild thing."

"Come down!" roared the captain of the marshals. "Come down or you'll be sorry!"

"I'm sorry now," Kestrel called back. "I'm sorry for me, and I'm sorry for you, and I'm sorry for this whole sorry city!"

She put her head into the scoop and called out over the wide arena, "Won't strive har-ar-arder! Won't reach hi-i-igher! Won't make tomorrow-ow-ow better than today-ay-ay!"

Bowman made no more attempts to control his sister. He knew her too well. When she got into one of her rages, there was no reasoning with her until her passions were exhausted. The schoolteacher was right: Kestrel had become a wild thing. The wildness coursed through her, glorious and liberating as she swung from side to side on the top of the wind singer and shouted all the terrible, unthinkable thoughts that had been buried within her for so long. She had gone so far now, she had broken so many rules and said such wicked things, that she knew she would suffer the most severe punishment; and since what was done could not be undone, she was free to be as bad as she wanted to be.

"Pongo to the Emperor!" she cried. "Where is he, anyway? I've never seen him! There isn't any Emperor!"

The marshals started to climb the wind singer to bring her

down by force. Bowman, afraid they would hurt her, slipped away to fetch their father from the sub-library in Orange District where he worked. As he left the arena on one side, the Chief Examiner himself entered from the other and stood gazing down on the chaotic scene in grim silence.

"Pomp-pa pomp-pa-pru-u-une to the Emperor-or-or!" rang out Kestrel's amplified voice.

Maslo Inch drew a long breath and strode steadily down the steps. By the fifth tier he felt a small hand clutch at the hem of his clean white robe.

"Please, sir," said a small voice. "Do you have any food?"

The Chief Examiner looked down and saw Mumpo, his nose dribbling, his face grimy, his moist, stupid eyes gazing up at him, and he snatched his robe away in sudden fury.

"Don't you touch me, you poxy little brat!" he hissed.

Mumpo was used to being brushed off or laughed at, but the pure hatred he heard in the Chief Examiner's voice astounded him.

"I only wanted—"

Maslo Inch did not wait to hear. He strode on down to the stage of the arena.

His arrival caused panic among the officials and marshals.

"We've ordered her down—we're doing all we can—she must be drunk—have you heard her? —she won't listen to us—"

"Be quiet," said the Chief Examiner. "Someone remove the filthy child back there, and wash him." He made a gesture over his shoulder towards Mumpo.

One of the marshals hurried up the steps and took Mumpo by the wrist. Mumpo went slowly, looking back many times at Kestrel high in the wind singer. He didn't complain, because he was used to being dragged here and there by people in authority. The marshal took him to the fountain by the statue of Creoth the First and held his head under the stream of cold water. Mumpo screamed and struggled violently.

"You better watch out," the marshal said, cross at being splashed. "We don't want your sort in Aramanth."

He released his hold and washed his hands in the fountain bowl.

"I don't want to be in Aramanth," said Mumpo, shivering. "But I don't know where else to go."

In the arena, Maslo Inch watched the efforts of the marshals clambering over the wind singer, trying to catch hold of the lighter and more agile child.

"Come down," he ordered the marshals.

"They'll get her in the end, sir," said the captain of the marshals.

"I said, Come down."

"Yes, sir."

The marshals descended, panting and red in the face.

Maslo Inch looked with his steady and contemptuous gaze at the assembled crowd.

"Has nobody here got any work to do this afternoon?"

"We couldn't let her say those wicked things—"

"You are her audience. Go away, and she will become silent. Captain, clear the arena."

So the officials and the marshals trickled away, looking back over their shoulders as they went to see what the Chief Examiner would do next.

Kestrel did not become silent. She made a kind of song out of all the bad words she knew, and sang it through the wind singer.

"Pocksicker pocksicker pompaprune!

"Banga-banga-banga plop!

"Sagahog sagahog pompaprune!

"Udderbug pongo plop!"

Maslo Inch gazed up at her for a few moments, as if to familiarise himself with her face. He said nothing more. The girl had mocked and insulted everything that Aramanth most respected. She would be punished, of course; but the case called for more than punishment. She must be broken. Maslo Inch was not a man to shrink from hard decisions. Young as she was, it must be done, and it must be done once and for all. He gave a single brisk nod of his head, and turned and strode calmly away.

CHAPTER FOUR

PRACTISING FOR MAROON

BY THE TIME BOWMAN RETURNED WITH HIS FATHER, the arena was empty and the wind singer was silent. The marshals guarding the perimeter refused to let them enter. Hanno Hath told them he was the wild child's father and had come to take her home. The marshals sent for their captain, and their captain sent for instructions to the College of Examiners. Back came a simple order.

"Send her home. She'll be dealt with later."

As father and son made their way down the arena steps, Bowman asked in a low voice, "What will they do to her?"

"I don't know," said Hanno.

"They said we'd lose points from our family rating."

"Yes, I expect they'll do that."

"She said pompaprune to the Emperor. She said the Emperor doesn't exist."

"Did she, now?" said her father, smiling to himself.

"Does the Emperor exist, Pa?"

"Who knows? I've never seen him, and I've never met anyone who's seen him. Perhaps he's just one of those useful ideas."

"Will you be cross with Kess?"

"No, of course not. But it would have been better if she hadn't done it."

They reached the wind singer, and Hanno Hath called up to the top, where they could see Kestrel curled up among the leather scoops.

"Kestrel! Come down now, darling."

Kestrel looked over the edge and saw her father below.

"Are you angry with me?" she said in a small voice.

"No," he replied gently. "I love you."

So Kestrel climbed down, and as she reached the ground her courage suddenly forsook her, and she started to tremble and cry. Hanno Hath took her in his arms, and sat down on the bottom step of the arena, and held her close. He hugged her and let her sob out all her tears of anger and humiliation.

"I know, I know," he said over and over again.

Bowman sat beside them, waiting for his sister to calm

down, and shivered, and wanted to cuddle close to his father, too. He moved nearer and leaned his head against a wool-rough arm. Pa can't help us, he thought. He wants to, but he can't. It was the first time he had ever thought this thought, clear and simple like that. He said it to Kestrel in his head.

Pa can't help us.

Kestrel thought back, *I know. But he does love us.*

Then they both felt it at the same time, how much they loved their father, and they both started kissing him at once, all over his ears and eyes and scratchy cheeks.

"That's better," he said. "That's my bright birds."

They walked home quietly, the three of them arm in arm, and nobody troubled them. Ira Hath was waiting for them, with Pinpin in her arms, and they told her briefly what had happened.

"Oh, I wish I'd heard you!" she exclaimed.

Neither of Kestrel's parents blamed her, or said she'd done wrong. But they all knew there would be a price to pay.

"It'll be bad for us, won't it?" said Kestrel, watching her father's eyes as she spoke.

"Well, yes, I expect they'll want to make an example of us somehow," said Hanno, sighing.

"Will we have to go to Maroon District?"

"Yes, I think so. Unless I astonish the world with my brilliance at the next High Examination."

"You are brilliant, Pa."

"Thank you, darling. Unfortunately, whatever brilliance I have remains undetected in exams."

He pulled a funny face. They all knew how he hated exams.

There was no visit from the marshals that evening, so they had supper together, and Pinpin was given her bath, just as if nothing had happened. Then before Pinpin's bedtime, as the setting sun turned the sky a soft, dusty pink, they made their family wish huddle, as they always did. Hanno Hath knelt down on the floor and reached up his arms. Bowman nestled under one, and Kestrel under the other. Pinpin stood with her face pressed to his chest, and her short arms round his body. Ira Hath knelt behind Pinpin and wrapped her arms over Bowman on one side and Kestrel on the other, making a tight ring. Then they all leaned their heads inwards until they were touching, and took turns to say their night wish. Often they wished for comical things, especially their mother, who had once wished five nights running for the Blesh family to get ulcerated boils. But tonight the mood was serious.

"I wish there were no more exams ever," said Kestrel.

"I wish nothing bad happens to Kess," said Bowman.

"I wish my darling children to be safe and happy forever," said their mother. She always wished like that when she was worried.

"I wish the wind singer would sing again," said their father.

Bowman nudged Pinpin, and she said, "Wish wish." Then they all kissed each other, bumping noses as they always did, because there wasn't an agreed-upon order. Then Pinpin was put to bed.

"Do you think it'll ever happen, Pa?" said Bowman. "Will the wind singer ever sing again?"

"It's only an old story," said Hanno Hath. "Nobody believes it anymore."

"I do," said Kestrel.

"You can't," objected her brother. "You don't know any more about it than anyone else."

"I believe it because nobody else believes it," she retorted.

Her father smiled at that.

"That's more or less how I feel," he said.

He had told them the old story many times before, but Kestrel wanted to hear it again. So to calm her down, he told them once more about the time long ago when the wind singer sang. Its song was so sweet that everyone who heard it was happy. The happiness of the people of Aramanth angered the spirit-lord called the Morah—

"But the Morah's not real," put in Bowman.

"No, nobody believes in the Morah anymore," said his father.

"I do," said Kestrel.

The Morah was angry, went the old story, and sent a terrible army, the army of the Zars, to destroy Aramanth. Then the people were afraid, and took the voice out of the wind singer, and gave it to the Morah. The Morah accepted the offering, and the Zars turned back without destroying Aramanth, and the wind singer never sang again.

Kestrel became very excited as she heard this.

"It's true!" she cried. "There's a place in the wind singer's neck for the voice to go. I've seen it!"

"Yes," said Hanno. "So have I."

"So the story must be true."

"Who knows?" said Hanno quietly. "Who knows?"

Kestrel's words reminded them all of her defiance that afternoon, and they fell silent.

"Maybe they'll just forget about it," said Ira Hath hopefully.

"No," said Hanno. "They won't forget."

"We'll have to go down to Maroon District," said Bowman. "I don't see what's so bad about that."

"The apartments are quite small. We'd all have to sleep together in the one room."

"I'd like that," said Bowman. "I've always wanted us to sleep in one room."

Kestrel thanked him with her eyes, and his mother kissed him and said, "You're a dear boy. But your father snores, you know."

"Do I?" said Hanno, surprised.

"I'm quite used to it," said his wife, "but the children may be kept awake for a while."

"Why don't we try it?" said Bowman. "Why don't we practise for Maroon District tonight?"

They took the mattresses from the twins' beds and carried them into their parents' room. There stood the big bed, with its bedspread in stripes of many colours: pink and yellow, blue and green, colours rarely seen in Aramanth. Ira Hath had made it herself, as a small act of rebellion, and the children loved it.

By pushing the big bed against the far wall they could fit both mattresses side by side on the floor, but there was no room left to walk, and certainly no space for Pinpin's cot. So they decided Pinpin would sleep between Bowman and Kestrel, on the crack of their mattresses.

When they were all ready for bed, the twins lay down, and their father lifted the sleeping Pinpin out of her cot in the hall, and laid her between them. She half woke, and finding her brother on one side and her sister on the other, her small round face broke into a sleepy smile. She wriggled in her space, turned first one way and then the other, murmured, "Love Bo, love Kess," and went back to sleep.

Their parents then went to bed. For a little while they all lay there, squeezed together in the dark, and listened to one another's snuffles. Then Ira Hath said, in her prophetess voice, "O unhappy people! Tomorrow comes the sorrow!"

They laughed softly, as they always did at their mother's prophetess voice, but they knew what she said was true. Shivering, they wriggled deeper into the bedclothes. It felt so friendly and safe and family-ish to be sleeping together in the same room that they wondered why they had never done it before, and when, if ever, they would be able to do it again.

CHAPTER FIVE

A WARNING FROM THE CHIEF EXAMINER

THE SUMMONS CAME EARLY, WHILE THEY WERE STILL AT breakfast. The doorbell rang, and there outside was a messenger from the College of Examiners. The Chief Examiner wished to see Hanno Hath at once, together with his daughter Kestrel.

Hanno rose to his feet.

"Come on, Kess. Let's get it over with."

Kestrel stayed at the table, her expression showing stubborn resistance.

"We don't have to go."

"If we don't, they'll send marshals to fetch us."

Kestrel stood up slowly, staring with extreme hostility at the messenger.

"Do what you like to me," she said. "I don't care."

"Me?" said the messenger, aggrieved. "What's it got to do with me? All I do is carry messages. You think anyone ever explains them to me?"

"You don't have to do it."

"Oh, don't I? We live in Grey District, we do. You try sharing a toilet with six families. You try living with a sick wife and two thumping great lads in one room. Oh no, I'll do my job all right, and more, and one fine day, they'll move us up to Maroon, and that'll do me nicely, thank you very much."

Maslo Inch was waiting in his spacious office, sitting at his broad desk. He rose to his full imposing height as Hanno and Kestrel entered, and to their surprise, greeted them with a smile in his high grand way. Coming out from behind the fortress desk, he shook their hands and invited them to sit down with him in the circle of high grand chairs.

"Your father and I used to play together when we were your age," he told Kestrel. "We sat together in class, too, for a while. Remember, Hanno?"

"Yes," said Hanno. "I remember."

He remembered how Maslo Inch had been so much bigger than the rest of them, and had made them kneel before him. But he said nothing about that. He just wanted to get the interview over with as soon as possible. Maslo Inch's white clothes were so very white that it was hard to look at him for long—that, and his smile.

"I'm going to tell you something that may surprise you," the Chief Examiner said to Kestrel. "Your father used to be cleverer than I was at school."

"That doesn't surprise me," said Kestrel.

"Doesn't it?" said Maslo Inch evenly. "Then why am I Chief Examiner of Aramanth, while your father is a sub-district librarian?"

"Because he doesn't like exams," said Kestrel. "He likes books."

Hanno Hath saw a shadow of irritation pass across the Chief Examiner's face.

"We know this is about what happened yesterday," he said quietly. "Say what you have to say."

"Ah, yes. Yesterday." The smile turned to hold Hanno in its steady shine. "Your daughter gave us quite a perfor- mance. We'll come to that in due course."

Hanno Hath looked back at the smooth face of the Chief Examiner, and saw there in those gleaming eyes a deep well of hatred. Why? he thought. This powerful man has noth- ing to fear from me. Why does he hate me so?

Maslo Inch rose to his feet.

"Follow me, please. Both of you."

He set off without a backward glance, and Hanno Hath and

Kestrel followed behind, hand in hand. The Chief Examiner led them down a long empty corridor, lined on both sides with columns of gold-painted names. This was such a commonplace sight in Aramanth that neither father nor daughter looked twice at them. Anyone who achieved anything noteworthy was named on some wall somewhere, and this practice had been going on for so long that virtually no public wall was spared.

The corridor linked the College of Examiners to the Imperial Palace, and emerged into a courtyard at the heart of the palace, where a grey-clothed warden was sweeping the pathways. Maslo Inch began what was clearly a rehearsed speech.

"Kestrel," he said, "I want you to listen to what I say to you today, and look at what I show you today, and remember it for the rest of your life."

Kestrel said nothing. She watched the warden's broom: *swish, swish, swish.*

"I've been making enquiries about you," said the Chief Examiner. "I'm told that at school yesterday morning you placed yourself at the bottom of the class."

"What if I did?" She was watching the warden. His eyes looked down as he worked, and his face looked vacant.

What is he thinking? Bo would know.

"And that you said to your class teacher, What more can you do to me?"

"What if I did?"

Why does he go on sweeping? There's nothing to sweep.

"You then went on to indulge in a childish tantrum in a public place."

"What if I did?"

"You know of course that your own rating affects your family rating."

"What if it does?"

Swish, swish, swish, goes the broom.

"That is what we are about to find out."

He came to a stop before a door in a stone wall. The door was heavy, and closed with a big iron latch. He put his hand on the latch and turned to Kestrel once more.

"What more can you do to me? An interesting question, but the wrong one. You should ask, What more can I do to myself, and to those I love?"

He heaved on the iron latch and pushed the heavy door open. Inside, a dank stone tunnel sloped downwards into the gloom.

"I am taking you to see the salt caves. This is a privilege, of a kind. Very few of our citizens see the salt caves, for a reason that will soon become evident."

They followed him down the tunnel, their footsteps echoing from the arched roof. The sides of the tunnel, Kestrel now saw, were cut out of a white rock that glistened in the dim light: salt. She knew from her history that Aramanth had been built on salt. The Manth people, a wandering tribe in search of a homeland, had found traces of the mineral and had settled there to mine it. The traces became seams, the seams became caverns, as they tunnelled into a huge subterranean treasure-house. Salt had made the Manth people rich, and with their wealth they had built their city.

"Have you ever asked yourself what became of the salt caves?" said Maslo Inch, as they descended the long curving tunnel. "When all the salt had been extracted, there was left only a great space. A great nothingness. A void. What use, do you think, is a void?"

Now they could hear the sound of slow-moving water, a low, deep gurgle. And on the dank air they could smell an acrid gassy smell.

"For a hundred years we took from the ground what we wanted most. And for another hundred years, we have poured back into the ground what we want least."

The sloping tunnel suddenly opened into a wide underground chamber, an indistinct and shadowy space loud with the sounds of moving water, as if a thousand streams here disgorged into a subterranean sea. The smell was unmistakable now: pungent and nauseating.

Maslo Inch led them to a long railing. Beyond the railing, some way below, lay a vast, slow-swirling lake of dark mud, which here and there bubbled up in ponderous burps, like a gigantic simmering cauldron. The walls of the chamber above this lake glistened and shone, as if with sweat. They were pierced at intervals by great iron pipes, and out of these pipes issued grey water, sometimes at a trickle, sometimes at a gush.

"Drains," said the Chief Examiner. "Sewers. Not beautiful, but necessary."

Instinctively, both Kestrel and her father raised their hands to cover their noses against the stench.

"You think, young lady, that if you do as you please, and make no effort at school, you and your family will go down from Orange to Maroon. You think you don't mind that. Perhaps you will go down again, from Maroon to Grey. You think you don't mind that, either. Grey District isn't pretty, or comfortable, but it's the bottom, and at least they'll leave you alone there. That's what you think, isn't it? The worst that can happen is we'll go all the way down to Grey."

"No," said Kestrel, though this was exactly what she thought.

"No? You think it could be worse?"

Kestrel said nothing.

"You're quite right. It could be far, far worse. After all, Grey District, poor as it is, is still part of Aramanth. But there is a world below Aramanth."

Kestrel stared out over the murky surface of the lake. It

stretched far into the distance, farther than she could see. And far, far away she seemed to glimpse a glow, a pool of light, like the light that sometimes breaks through clouds onto distant hills. She fixed her gaze on this distant glow, and the stinking lake appeared to her to be almost beautiful.

"You're looking at the Underlake, a lake of decomposing matter that's bigger than all Aramanth. There are islands in the lake, islands of mud. Do you see?"

They followed his pointing finger and could just make out, far away across the slithering grey-brown surface of the lake, a group of low mounds. As they watched, they caught a movement near the mounds, and staring, half incredulous, saw what looked like a distant figure pass over the mud and sink abruptly out of sight. Now, their eyes attuned to the gloom, they began to spot other figures, all as uniformly dark as the mud over which they crept, slipping silently in and out of the shadows.

"Do people live down here?" asked Hanno.

"They do. Many thousands. Men, women, children. Primitive, degraded people, little better than animals."

He invited them to step closer to the railing. Directly ahead, through a gate in the rails, there projected a narrow jetty. Tethered to its timbers some twenty feet below were several long, flat-bottomed barges, half filled with refuse of every kind.

"They live on what we throw away. They live in rubbish, and they live on rubbish." He turned to Kestrel. "You asked, What more can you do to me? Here's your answer. Why do we strive harder? Why do we reach higher? Because we don't want to live like this."

Kestrel shrugged. "I don't care," she said.

The Chief Examiner watched her closely.

"You don't care?" he said slowly.

"No."

"I don't believe you."

"Then don't."

"Prove you don't care."

He opened the gate in the railing and held it wide, inviting her to pass through. Kestrel looked out along the slick boards.

"Go on. Walk right to the end. If you really don't care."

Kestrel took one step onto the narrow jetty, and stopped. In truth, she was frightened of the Underlake, but she was bursting inside with angry pride, and would have done anything to wipe that smooth smile from the Chief Examiner's face. So she took another step.

"That's enough, Kess," said her father. And to the Chief Examiner, "You've made your point, Maslo. Leave her to me."

"We've left your children to you for too long, Hanno." He spoke evenly as always, but now there was an undertone of sharp displeasure. "Children follow the example given by their parents. There's something broken inside you, my friend. There's no fight in you anymore. No will to succeed."

Kestrel heard this and went cold inside with fury. At once, she started to walk briskly down the jetty. She looked straight ahead, fixing her gaze on the place where the far-off light streamed down onto the dark surface of the lake, and put one foot in front of the other, and walked.

"Kess! Come back!" called her father.

He started after her, but Maslo Inch seized his arm with one hand and held him in a grip of iron.

"Let her go," he said. "She has to learn."

With his other hand, he operated a long lever by the jetty gate, and there came a hissing gurgling sound as the posts supporting the far end of the jetty began to sink into the lake. The jetty sloped downwards, becoming a ramp tilting ever more steeply down into the mud. Kestrel gave a cry of alarm and turned and tried to run back up the boards, but they were coated with slime, and she couldn't get a grip. She started to slither backwards.

"Papa!" she cried, "help me!"

Hanno lunged towards her, pulling furiously in the Chief Examiner's hold, but he could not free himself.

"Let me go! What are you doing to her? Are you insane?"

Maslo Inch's eyes were locked onto Kestrel as she tried in vain to stop her downward slide.

"Slipping, slipping, slipping," he cried. "Well, Kestrel, do you care now?"

"Papa! Help me!"

"Get her out! She'll drown!"

"Do you care now? Will you try harder now? Tell me! I want to hear!"

"Papa!" Kestrel screamed as she slithered off the end of the sloping jetty and into the lake. Her feet hit the brown water, and with an awful sucking sound they disappeared into liquid mud.

"I'm sinking!"

"Tell me you care!" called out Maslo Inch, his hand gripping Hanno's arm so tight his fingers had gone white. "I want to hear!"

"You're mad!" said Hanno. "You've gone mad!"

In desperation, he swung his free arm and struck the Chief Examiner hard across the face.

Maslo Inch turned on him, and suddenly he lost all his self-control. He shook Hanno like a doll.

"Don't you dare touch me!" he screamed. "You worm! You dribble! You maggot! You failure! You fail your exams, you fail your family, you fail your country!"

At the same time, Kestrel realised she wasn't sinking

anymore. Somewhere beneath the surface there was hard ground, and she had sunk only to her knees. So she took hold of the sides of the narrow jetty with both hands and began to claw her way back up. She didn't call out anymore. She just fixed her eyes on the Chief Examiner and willed herself up the slope.

Maslo Inch was too absorbed in screaming at her father to notice.

"What use are you? You're a nothing! You do nothing, you make no effort, you expect others to do it all for you, all you do is read your useless books! You're a parasite! You're a germ! You infect everyone around you with your sick, lazy failure! You disgust me!"

Kestrel reached the top of the jetty, took a deep breath, and with a yell of bloodcurdling fury, threw herself on the Chief Examiner's back.

"Pocksicker!"

She locked her arms round his neck and her legs round his waist and squeezed with all her might, to make him let go of her father.

"Sagahog! Pooa-pooa-pooa-banga-pompaprune! Pocksicking udderbug!"

The Chief Examiner, taken by surprise, released Hanno Hath's arm and turned about to pull Kestrel off him. But whichever way he swung, she was always behind him, her wiry little arms throttling him, her muddy feet kicking at his ribs.

The tussle was short but intense. During it, much of the mud on Kestrel's legs was wiped onto the Chief Examiner's clothing. When at last he got a grip on her and tore her off, she let go, and he threw her farther than he intended. At once she sprang to her feet and ran.

He made no attempt to chase her. He was too shocked at the sight of his muddy clothes.

"My whites!" he said. "The little witch!"

Kestrel was gone, streaking away as fast as she could, up the tunnel towards the distant door.

Maslo Inch brushed himself down and pulled back the lever that raised the jetty to its former position. Then he turned to Hanno Hath.

"Well, old friend," he said, icily calm. "What do you have to say to that?"

"You shouldn't have done that to her."

"Is that all?"

Hanno Hath was silent. He would not apologise for his daughter's behaviour, but nor was it wise to say what he really felt, which was that he was intensely proud of her. So he kept a neutral expression on his face, and looked with inner satisfaction at the mud stains on the Chief Examiner's once-pure robes.

"I now see," said Maslo Inch quietly, "that we have a far more serious problem with the girl than I realised."

CHAPTER SIX

SPECIAL TEACHING

KESTREL RAN OUT OF THE TUNNEL AND STRAIGHT INTO the grey-clothed warden. He must have heard her coming, since he had dropped his broom and was waiting for her, arms spread wide. As soon as he had her tight, he picked her up and dangled her in the air, where she kicked as hard as she could and screamed at the top of her voice. But he was a big man, bigger than he'd looked bent over his broom, and he was strong, and her screams didn't seem to trouble him in the least.

Maslo Inch came out into the courtyard, followed by her father, just as two more wardens came running, drawn by the noise she was making.

"Papa!" she screamed. "Papa-a-a!"

"Put her down," said Hanno Hath.

"Be silent!" cried the Chief Examiner, with such terrible authority that even Kestrel stopped screaming.

"Get this man out of here," he said more quietly, and the two wardens started to hustle Hanno Hath away. "Take the girl to Special Teaching."

"No!" cried Hanno Hath. "I beg you, no!"

"Papa!" screamed Kestrel, kicking and struggling. "Papa-a-a!"

But she was already being carried off in the opposite direction. The Chief Examiner watched them both go with a grim and unmoving look on his face.

"'What more can you do to me, 'eh?" he said softly to himself. And he strode away to change into clean white robes.

The separate building set aside for Special Teaching was inside the old palace compound, on one side of a small deserted square. It was a solid stone structure, much like any other in this grandest of the city's districts, with a high handsome door at the top of three steps. This door was opened from the inside as the warden approached with Kestrel in his arms. It was closed after them by a doorman dressed in grey.

"Referred by the Chief Examiner," said the warden.

The doorman nodded and opened an inner door. Kestrel was pushed through into a long narrow room and left there without a word. The door closed with a click behind her.

She was alone.

She realised for the first time that she was shaking violently, out of a combination of fear, rage, and exhaustion. She took several deep breaths to steady herself and looked round the room. It was empty and windowless.

She turned her attention to the door, hoping to find a way of opening it. The door had no handle. She felt all over it, and around its edges, but it was close-fitting, and there seemed to be no way to open it from the inside. So she turned back to examining the room.

All along one wall hung a plain grey floor-length curtain. She drew the curtain back and found there was a window behind it, looking through to a much larger inner room. Cautiously, she drew the curtain all the way back and stared at the strange scene beyond. It was a classroom. Sitting at the rows of desks, with their backs to her, were a large number of children, perhaps as many as a hundred. They were all bent studiously over their books, working away in silence, or so she supposed, for no sound of any kind came through the glass. There was a teacher's desk at the far end, and a blackboard, but no teacher.

The children at the back of the class were quite close to the window. Perhaps they would help her. She tapped on the glass softly, just in case a teacher was nearby. The children didn't move. She tapped more loudly, and then as loudly as she could, but they seemed to hear nothing. It began to strike her that there was something strange about them. They kept their heads so low to their books that she couldn't see their faces, but their hands were unusually wrinkly. And their hair was grey, or white, or—she saw it now—some of them were bald. Now that she looked properly, she asked herself why she had thought they were children at all. And yet, they were the size of children, and the shape of children. And surely—

The door opened behind her. Kestrel turned round, her heart hammering. A scarlet-robed examiner entered, a middle-aged lady, and closed the door behind her. She held a file open in her hands, and she looked from the papers in it to Kestrel and back again. She had a friendly face.

"Kestrel Hath?" she said.

"Yes," said Kestrel. "Ma'am."

She spoke quietly, clasping her hands before her and lowering her gaze to the floor. She had decided, on the spur of the moment, to be a good girl.

The examiner looked at her in some perplexity.

"What have you done, child?"

"I was frightened," said Kestrel in a tiny voice. "I think I must have panicked."

"The Chief Examiner has referred you for Special Teaching." As she spoke, she glanced through the window at the silent class working in the room beyond, and shook her head. "It does seem a little extreme."

Kestrel said nothing, but tried very hard to look sad and good.

"Special Teaching, you know," said the lady examiner, "is for the most disruptive children. The ones who are entirely out of control. And it is so very, well, permanent."

Kestrel went up to the lady examiner, and took her hand and held it trustingly, gazing up at her with big innocent eyes.

"Do you have a little girl of your own, ma'am?" she asked.

"Yes, child. Yes, I do."

"Then I know you'll do what's best for me, ma'am. Just as you would for your own little girl."

The lady examiner looked down at Kestrel, and gave a little sigh, and patted her hand.

"Well, well," she said. "I think we should go and see the Chief Examiner, don't you? Maybe there's been a mistake."

She turned to the handleless door and called, "Open, please!"

The door was opened by a warden on the far side, and the lady examiner and Kestrel, hand in hand, went out into the square.

Now that she wasn't being carried, Kestrel could see that one side of the square was formed by the back wall of the Great Tower, which was the building at the centre of the Imperial Palace. This tower, the highest building in Aramanth, could be seen even from Orange District. This close, it seemed immensely tall, reaching up and up even higher than the city's encircling walls.

As they crossed the square, a small door at the foot of the tower opened, and two white-robed men came sweeping out. Seeing the lady examiner holding Kestrel's hand, the older of the two frowned and called out to them.

"What is a child from Orange District doing here?"

The lady examiner explained. The man in white studied the file.

"So the Chief Examiner ordered Special Teaching for the girl," he said sharply. "And you have taken it upon yourself to question his judgement."

"I think there may have been a mistake."

"Do you know anything about this case?"

"Well, no," said the lady examiner, going rather pink. "It's more a kind of feeling, really."

"A kind of feeling?" The man's voice was cutting

with contempt. "You propose to make a decision that affects the rest of this child's life on a kind of feeling?"

The rest of this child's life! A chill ran through Kestrel. She looked round for a way of escape. Behind her stood the Special Teaching building from which they had come. Ahead, the men in white.

"I meant only to speak to the Chief Examiner, to make sure I understood his wishes."

"His wishes are written here. They are perfectly clear, are they not?"

"Yes."

Kestrel saw that the door into the tower had not closed all the way.

"Do you suggest that when he made this order and signed it, he didn't know what he was doing?"

"No."

"Then why do you not carry it out?"

"Yes, of course. I'm sorry."

Kestrel knew then that she had lost her one source of protection. The lady examiner turned distressed eyes on her, and said once again, this time to Kestrel, "I'm sorry."

"That's all right," said Kestrel, and gave the lady's hand a little squeeze. "Thank you for trying."

Then she released the hand, and she ran.

She was through the tower door and pushing it shut

behind her before they realised what was happening. There was a bolt on the inside, which she drew shut. Only then, heart beating fast, did she look to see where she was.

She was in a small lobby, with two doors and a narrow curving flight of stairs. Both doors were locked. She heard voices shouting outside, and the outer door rattling as they tried to open it. Then she heard louder bangs as they tried to break the bolt. Then she heard a voice call out, "You stay here. I'll go round the other way."

She had no choice, so she set off up the stairs.

Up and up she climbed, and the stairwell grew darker and darker. She thought she could hear doors opening and closing below, so she kept climbing as fast as she could. Up and up, round and round, and now there was light above. She came to a small barred window, set deep in the stonework of the tower. Through the window she could see the roofs of the palace and a brief glimpse of the square where the statue of Emperor Creoth stood.

Still the stairs rose above her, so breathing hard now, her legs aching, she climbed on and on, and the light from the little window dwindled away below her. Strange, distorted sounds came floating up from below, the clatter of running feet, the boom of voices. Up and up she climbed, slower now, wondering where the staircase led, and whether, when at last she reached the top, there would be another locked door.

A second window appeared. Exhausted, trembling, she allowed herself to rest a moment here and looked out over the city. She could make out people passing in the streets, and the elegant shops and houses of Scarlet District. Then she heard a sound that was very like boots climbing the winding stairs below her, and fear gave her strength to get up and go on. Up and up, forcing her legs to push, half giddy with exhaustion, she followed the tightly winding staircase that seemed to have no end. *Clop, clop, clop*, went the noise of the boots below, carried up to her by the stone walls. Not far now, she said to herself, in time with her steps. Not far now, not far now. Though in truth she had no way of knowing how much farther she must climb.

And then, just when she knew she could go no farther, she came out on to a tiny landing, and there before her was a door. Her hand shook as she reached out to try the handle. Please, she said inside her head. Please don't be locked. She turned the handle and felt the latch open. She pushed, but the door didn't move. At once her fear, held at bay by this last hope, broke through and overwhelmed her. Bursting into bitter tears, she crumpled up in a ball at the foot of the door. There she hugged her knees and sobbed her heart out.

Clop, clop, clop. The boots were coming up the stairs,

getting nearer all the time. Kestrel rocked and sobbed, and wished she were dead.

Then she heard a new sound. Shuffling footsteps, close by. The slither of a bolt.

The door opened.

"Come in," said an impatient voice. "Come in quickly."

Kestrel looked up and saw a blotchy red face staring down at her: watery, protruding eyes, and a grizzly grey beard.

"You've certainly taken your time," he said. "Come in, now you're here."

CHAPTER SEVEN

THE EMPEROR WEEPS

THE BEARDED MAN CLOSED THE DOOR AND BOLTED IT after Kestrel, and then made a sign to her to stay quiet. On the far side they could hear quite clearly now the sound of the climbing boots. Then whoever it was reached the landing at the top and came to a stop.

"Well, boggle me!" said a surprised voice. "She's not here!"

They saw the door handle turn, as he tried to open it. Then the sound of his voice shouting down the stairs.

"She's not here, you stupid pocksickers! I've climbed all these hogging stairs and she's not hogging here!"

With that, he set off back down the long winding staircase, muttering as he went. The bearded man gave a soft chortle of pleasure.

"Pocksicker!" he said. "I haven't heard that for years. How reassuring to know that the old oaths are still in use."

Taking Kestrel's hand, he led her into the light of one of the windows, so that he could see her better. She in her turn stared at him. His robes were blue, which astonished her. No one wore blue in Aramanth.

"Well," he said. "You're not what I expected, I must say. But you'll have to do."

He then went to a table in the middle of the room, where there stood a glass bowl full of chocolate buttons, and ate three, one after the other. While he did this, Kestrel was gazing in wonder out of the window. The room must have been near the top of the tower, if not at the top itself, for it was higher than the city walls. In one direction, she could see over the land to the ocean; in the other, the desert plains lay before her, reaching all the way to the misty line of the northern mountains.

"But it's so big!" she said.

"Oh, it's big all right. Bigger than you can see from here, even."

Kestrel looked down at the city below, laid out in its districts, the scarlet and the white, her own orange streets, the maroon and the grey, all circled by the massive city walls. For the first time, it struck her that this was an odd arrangement.

"Why do we have to have walls?"

"Why indeed?" said the bearded man. "Why do we have to have districts in different colours? Why do we have to have examinations, and ratings? Why do we have to strive harder, and reach higher, and make tomorrow better than today?"

Kestrel stared at him. He was speaking thoughts she supposed only she had ever had.

"For love of my Emperor," she said in the words of the Oath of Dedication. "And for the glory of Aramanth."

The bearded man gave a soft chuckle.

"Ha!" he said. "I'm your Emperor."

And he ate three more chocolate buttons.

"You!"

"Yes, I know, it must seem implausible. But I am Creoth the Sixth, Emperor of Aramanth. And you are the person I've been waiting for all these years."

"Me?"

"Well, I didn't know it would be you. To be honest, I had assumed it would be a strapping young man. Someone brave and strong, you know, given what has to be done. But it turns out to be you."

"Oh, no," said Kestrel. "I wasn't looking for you. I didn't even know you existed. I was running away."

"Don't be foolish. It must be you. No one else has ever found me. They keep me shut away here so no one will ever find me."

"You're not shut away. You opened the door yourself."

"That's another matter entirely. The point is, here you are."

He was clearly put out at being contradicted, so Kestrel said nothing more, and he went on eating chocolate buttons. He seemed to be unaware that he was eating them, and altogether unaware that it would have been polite to offer her some. She wasn't sure if she believed that he was the Emperor, but as she looked about her, she saw that the room was furnished in a very grand manner indeed. On one side was an ornate bed with curtains round it, like a tent. On the other was a beautifully carved writing desk, flanked by bookcases filled with handsome volumes. There was the round table, where the glass bowl stood, and some deep leather armchairs, and a great high-sided bath, and soft rugs on the floor, and embroidered drapes at the windows. The windows that ran all round the room were deeply recessed, and between each set was a door. Eight windows, eight doors. One was the door she had entered by. Two others stood open, and she could see that they led into cupboards. That left five. Surely one out of five would lead her out of the tower again.

The bearded man now moved away from the bowl of chocolate buttons and went to his writing desk. Here he started opening the little drawers, one by one, clearly searching for something.

"Please, sir," said Kestrel. "Can I go home now?"

"Go home? What are you talking about? Of course you can't go home. You have to go to the Halls of the Morah, and fetch it back."

"Fetch what back?"

"I have the directions here somewhere. Yes, here it is."

He drew out a paper scroll, dusty and yellow with age, and unrolled it. "It should have been me, of course."

He sighed as he looked at it. "There, now. All perfectly clear, I think."

Kestrel looked at the scroll he held out before her. The paper was cracked and faded, but it was recognisably a map. She could make out the line of the ocean, and a little drawing that was clearly meant to be Aramanth itself. There was a marked trail that led from Aramanth across plains to a line of pictured mountains. Here and there on the map, and most of all where the trail ended, there were scribbled markings, clusters of symbols that seemed to be words written in letters that were unfamiliar to her.

She looked up, bewildered.

"Don't gape at me, girl," said the Emperor. "If you don't understand, just ask."

"I don't understand anything."

"Nonsense! It's all perfectly simple. Here we are, you see."

He pointed to Aramanth on the map.

"This is the way you must go. You see?"

His finger traced the track north from Aramanth. "You have to follow the road, or you'll miss the bridge. It's the only way, do you see?"

His finger was pointing to a jagged line that crossed the map from side to side. It had a name, in spidery lettering, but like the rest of the writing, it meant nothing to her.

"But why must I do this?"

"Beard of my ancestors!" he exclaimed. "Have they sent me an infant with no brain? To fetch back the voice, so the wind singer sings again."

"The voice of the wind singer!"

A shiver went through Kestrel.

It's real, she said inside herself. It's real.

The Emperor turned the map over, and there on the other side was more writing, in the strange letters, beside a faded drawing of a shape that Kestrel recognised. It was the curled-over letter S she had seen etched into the wind singer.

"Here it is."

Kestrel stared at the drawing and was filled with a confused mixture of excitement and fear.

"What will happen when the wind singer sings again?"

"We'll be free of the Morah, of course."

"Free of the Morah?"

"Free—of—the—Morah," he repeated slowly and loudly.

"But the Morah's just a story."

"Just a story! Beard of my ancestors! Just a story! The city worse than a prison, the people scratching their lives away in envy and hatred, and you say it's just a story! The Morah rules Aramanth, child! Everybody knows that."

"No," said Kestrel, "they don't. Nobody knows it. They all think the Morah is a story from long ago."

"Do they?" The Emperor peered at her suspiciously. "Well then, that just goes to show how clever the Morah is, doesn't it?"

"Yes, I suppose it does," said Kestrel.

"So you believe me now?"

"I don't know. All I know is I hate school, and I hate tests, and I hate examiners, and I hate Aramanth."

"Of course you do. That's all the work of the Morah. They call Aramanth the perfect society. Ha! Have they done away with fear and hatred? Of course not. The Morah sees to that."

The strange thing was, as Kestrel listened to him, it all made a kind of sense. She looked again at the drawing on the back of the map.

"Where did you get this?"

"From my father. He had it from his father, who had it from his, and so on back to Creoth the First. He was the one who took the voice out of the wind singer."

"To save the city from the Zars."

"Oh, so you do know something, after all."

"Why did the Morah want the voice?"

"To stop the wind singer from singing, of course. The wind singer was there to protect Aramanth from the Morah."

"Then why did the first Emperor give the voice away?"

"Why? Ah, why indeed!" He sighed and shook his head. "But who are we to blame him? He had seen the army of the Zars, and we have not. Fear, child. That is the answer to your question. He knew the wind singer had power, but could it stop the Zars? Dared he take the risk? No, it's not for us to blame him for what he did so long ago. As you see" —he pointed one finger at the strange lettering that ran round the frame of the map— "he lived to regret what he had done."

Kestrel stared at the incomprehensible writing.

"So does the wind singer have the power to stop the Morah?"

"Who knows? My grandfather, who was a wise man, said that there must be power in the voice, or why did the Morah want it so much? And as you see, it says on the back of the map, The song of the wind singer will set you free."

"Free of the Morah?"

"Of course, free of the Morah. What else would it be, free of flying fish? And don't gape at me, child!" The Emperor was becoming impatient again. "I thought we'd been over this already."

"So why hasn't anyone gone to get it back before now?"

"Why? Do you think it's easy? Mind you," he interrupted himself hastily, "I'm not necessarily saying it's all that difficult. And it must be done, of course. But you see, for a long time, it seemed like it was all for the best. The Zars had gone away, and the changes came so slowly that nobody really noticed what was happening. It wasn't till my grandfather's time that it was clear it had all been a terrible mistake. And he was very old by then. So he gave the map to my father. But my father became ill. My father gave me the map before he died, but I was only a very small child. So now you've come, and I'm giving the map to you. What could be simpler than that?'

He went back to his desk and started closing all the little drawers he had opened: *click, click, click.*

"You're not little now," said Kestrel.

"Of course I'm not little now."

"So why can't you go?"

"Because I can't, that's all. It has to be you."

"I'm sorry," said Kestrel. "There's been some kind of mistake. I'm nobody special."

The Emperor looked at her accusingly.

"If you're nobody special, how come you're the only person who's ever found their way here?"

"I was running away."

"Who from?"

"The examiners."

"Ha! There you are! That's a very unusual thing to be doing in Aramanth. Nobody else runs away from examiners. So you must be someone special."

"I just hate examiners and I hate school and I hate tests." She was close to tears.

"Well, now," said the Emperor. "That shows you're precisely the right person. Once you've got the voice, and put it back in the wind singer, there'll be no more tests."

"No more tests?"

"So you have to go, you see."

"You should go, if you're the Emperor."

He gazed at her sadly.

"I would," he said. "Truly, I would. Only, there's a difficulty."

He went from door to door, opening them all. Three doors led on to landings, from which stairs could be seen descending.

"I sometimes think of going," he said. "For example, I might like the look of that door. So I might set off."

He took a few steps towards the doorway, and then stopped.

"Just one more chocolate button before I go."

He returned to the bowl in the middle of the room.

"Take a handful," said Kestrel. "Then you won't need to come back."

"It sounds so easy," said the Emperor with a sigh. But he

did as she said, and scooped up a handful of chocolate buttons. Then, eating as he went, he headed back to the door.
On the threshold, he stopped once again.

"What about when these run out?" He started to count
the chocolate buttons in his hand. "One, two, three—"

"Take the bowl," said Kestrel.

So he went back to the table and picked up the glass bowl.
But just before the doorway, he stopped again.

"It looks like a lot," he said, "but eventually they'll run
out."

"They'll run out anyway."

"Ah, that's just it, you see. The bowl is filled up again
every day. But if I've taken the bowl away, how can they fill it
up?"

He returned to the table and put the glass bowl back.

"Probably best to leave it here."

Kestrel stared at him.

"Why do you like chocolate buttons so much?"

"Well, I don't know that I like them particularly. They just
seem necessary."

"Necessary?"

"Do we have to talk about this? It's very hard to explain.
I must have them there, even if I don't eat them. To tell the
truth, sometimes days go by and I don't have any at all."

"You've been eating them without stopping."

"That's because I'm feeling nervous. I don't get many visitors. In fact, I don't get any at all."

"How long have you been like this?"

"Oh, all my life."

"All your life? You've lived all your life in this room?"

"Yes."

"But that's stupid!"

"I know."

He raised one hand, and suddenly smacked himself in the face.

"I am stupid. I'm good for nothing."

He smacked himself again, harder.

"I'm a disgrace to my ancestors."

He started to beat himself all over, on his face and chest and stomach.

"I do nothing but eat and sleep, I'm fat and tired, and so, so dull! I never go anywhere, I never see anyone! No conversation, no fun! I'd be better off dead, but I don't even have the strength of mind to die!"

He sobbed as he beat himself.

"I'm sorry," said Kestrel. "I don't know what I can do."

"Oh, it doesn't matter," said the Emperor, weeping copiously. "It always ends like this. I get overtired very easily, you see. I'd better have a rest."

And without further ado, he climbed fully clothed into

his grand canopied bed, pulled the covers over himself, and went to sleep.

Kestrel waited, expecting something more. After a few moments, he began to snore. So she tiptoed softly to one of the doors that opened onto a staircase, and trod cautiously down the stairs, still carrying the rolled-up map.

CHAPTER EIGHT

THE HATH FAMILY SHAMED

WHEN KESTREL REACHED THE TOWER DOOR THROUGH which she had entered, she stopped and peeped through the keyhole into the courtyard beyond. There she saw two marshals striding up and down, in a cross but aimless fashion. She pushed the map out of sight in one pocket, drew a deep breath, opened the door, and shouted.

"Help! The Emperor! Help!"

"What!" cried the nearest marshal. "Where?"

"Up in his room! The Emperor! Help him quickly!"

She sounded so distressed that the marshals didn't stop to ask any more, but set off up the spiral staircase as fast as they could go. Kestrel at once ran helter-skelter across the courtyard, down the long corridor, out of the door at the end, and found herself in the main plaza, by the statue of Creoth the First.

She made her way back to Orange District by alleys and back ways, taking care not to be seen by anyone in authority. But as she turned into her home street, she saw at once that there was no hope of slipping into her house unnoticed. A small crowd was gathered in front of the house, and most of the neighbours were leaning out of their windows to watch. On the doorstep, on either side of the closed door, stood two district marshals, fingering their medallions of office and looking grave. Everyone seemed to be waiting for something to happen.

As Kestrel drew near, her footsteps dragging ever more slowly, Rufy Blesh saw her and came running to her side.

"Kestrel," he cried excitedly. "You're in big trouble. So's your father."

"What's happened?"

"He's being taken away on a Residential Study Course." He lowered his voice. "Really it's a kind of prison, my father says, whatever they call it. My mother says it's awfully shaming, and thank goodness we're going up to Scarlet, because after this we won't be able to talk to you anymore."

"Then why are you talking to me?"

"Well, he hasn't actually been taken away yet," said Rufy.

Kestrel went as close to the house as she dared, and then

slipped down the side. She ran swiftly along the alley where the rubbish bins stood, and came to the back of her home. She could see her mother through the kitchen window, moving back and forth, carrying Pinpin in her arms, but no sign of Bowman. She sent him a silent call.

Bo! I'm here!

She felt him at once, and his wave of relief that she was safe.

Kess! You're all right!

He appeared at their bedroom window, looking out. She showed herself.

Don't let them see you, Kess. They've come to take you away. They're taking Pa away.

I'm coming in, said Kestrel. *I have to talk to Pa.*

Bowman left the window and went downstairs to the front room, where his father was standing in the middle of the floor, packing an open suitcase. The twins' class teacher, Dr. Batch, sat on the sofa beside a senior member of the Board of Examiners, Dr. Minish. Both men wore expressions of grim seriousness. Dr. Batch took out a watch and looked at it.

"We're already half an hour behind schedule," he announced. "We have no way of knowing when the girl will return. I suggest we proceed."

"You are to notify the district marshals as soon as she comes home," said Dr. Minish.

"But I won't be here," said Hanno Hath mildly.

"Come along, sir, come along."

It irritated Dr. Batch to see how the fellow stood looking so distractedly at the muddle of clothing and books on the floor.

"Don't forget your wash things, Pa," said Bowman.

"My wash things?"

Hanno Hath looked at his son. Bowman himself had brought down his toothbrush and his razor half an hour ago.

"In the bathroom," said Bowman.

"In the bathroom?" He understood. "Ah, yes."

Dr. Minish followed this exchange with exasperation.

"Well, get on with it, man."

"Yes, very well."

Hanno Hath went away up the stairs to the bathroom. Ira Hath came into the front room, carrying Pinpin, who could feel the anxiety in the house and was crying in a low, whining way.

"Would you like a drink while you're waiting?" Mrs. Hath asked the two teachers.

"Perhaps a glass of lemonade, if you have it," said Dr. Minish.

"Do you like lemonade, Dr. Batch?"

"Yes, ma'am. Lemonade would do very well."

Mrs. Hath went back into the kitchen.

Up in the bathroom, Hanno Hath found his daughter waiting for him. He took her silently in his arms and kissed her, deeply relieved.

"My darling, darling Kess. I had feared the worst."

Speaking very low, she told him about the Special Teaching, and he groaned aloud. "Don't ever let them take you there, ever, ever."

"Why? What happens there?"

But he would only shake his head and repeat, "Don't let them take you there."

Then she told him about the man who had said he was the Emperor.

"The Emperor! You've seen the Emperor?"

"He said I was to get the wind singer's voice. He gave me this."

She showed him the map. He unrolled it and stared at it in astonishment, his hand trembling as he held the stiff old scroll.

"Kess, this is extraordinary. . . ."

"He told me the Morah's real, and we're all in his power."

Her father nodded, deep in thought. "This is written in old Manth. This map was made by Singer People."

"What are Singer People?"

"I don't exactly know, except that they lived long ago, and they built the wind singer. Oh, Kess, oh, Kess, my darling, my dear one. How am I to get away? And what will they do to you?"

Kestrel was by now infected by her father's intense excitement. She held tightly to his arm, as if to stop him from going anywhere without her.

"So it's real?"

"Yes, it's real, I know it. I can read old Manth. Look, here it says THE GREAT WAY. Here, CRACK-IN-THE-LAND. Here, THE HALLS OF MORAH. Here, INTO THE FIRE."

He turned the map over and looked at the writing there, and the curious S shape drawn beside it.

"This is the mark of the Singer People."

"The emperor said it was the voice of the wind singer."

"Then it must be made in the shape of their mark."

He studied the faded writing carefully, piecing together the words, speaking slowly.

"The song of the wind singer . . . will set you free. Then seek . . . the homeland."

He looked up at Kestrel, his eyes shining.

"Oh, Kess. If only I could get away . . ."

He began to pace up and down the tiny bathroom, his mind racing with wild plans, each of which, after a moment of hope, ended in a frustrated shake of his head.

"No . . . They'd take Ira, and the children. . . ."

He shivered.

"It's best if I cooperate. My punishment isn't so bad. I'm to go on a study course, until the High Examination."

"Study course! Prison, you mean."

"Well, well," said her father gently. "It'll do me no harm. And perhaps if I work hard, I'll do better in the High Examination, and then I'll ask for you to be given a second chance."

"I don't want a second chance. I hate them."

"But I couldn't bear it if you—"

He cut himself off with a shrug. "I'd do anything for you, my darling one. I'd die for you. But it seems the trial I have to endure is knowing I can do nothing."

He fell silent, gazing at the map. They heard Dr. Minish's cross voice calling up from the foot of the stairs.

"Come along, sir! We're waiting!"

"The Emperor said if I brought the voice back, and the wind singer sang, there'd be no more tests."

"Ah, did he say that?"

For a moment the sadness left his eyes.

"But my darling one, you can't go, you're only a child. And anyway, they'll never let you leave the city. They're watching out for you. No, this must wait until I come home again."

In the front room downstairs, the waiting teachers were

growing more impatient and thirstier by the minute. When Mrs. Hath returned from the kitchen, she was carrying Pinpin, now fast asleep in her arms. Dr. Batch, eagerly awaiting his lemonade, stared at her in a pointed way. Dr. Minish frowned and looked at his watch again.

"You said something about lemonade," said Dr. Batch.

"Lemonade?" said Mrs. Hath.

"You offered us a drink," said Dr. Batch, a little more sharply.

"Did I?" She sounded surprised.

"You did, ma'am. You asked if we would like some lemonade."

"Yes. I remember that."

"And we replied in the affirmative."

"Yes. I remember that, too."

"But you don't bring it."

"Bring it, Dr. Batch? I don't understand."

"You asked us if we would like some lemonade," said the teacher slowly, as if to a particularly stupid pupil, "and we said yes. Now it is for you to fetch it."

"Why?"

"Because—because—because we want it."

"But Dr. Batch, there must be some misunderstanding. I have no lemonade."

"No lemonade? Madam, you offered us lemonade. How can you deny it?"

"How could I offer you lemonade, when I have none in the house? No, sir. I asked you if you liked lemonade. That is not the same thing at all."

"Good grief, woman! Why ask a man if he likes something if you don't mean to give it to him?"

"This is very odd, Dr. Batch. Am I to give you everything you say you like? No doubt you like long summer evenings, but I hope you don't expect me to fetch you one."

Dr. Minish stood up.

"Call the marshals," he said. "Enough is enough." Dr. Batch stood up.

"Your daughter will be found, and she will be dealt with. You can be sure of that."

Dr. Minish called up the stairs.

"Are you coming, sir? Or must you be fetched?"

The bathroom door opened and Hanno came out. As Hanno came down the stairs, Dr. Batch opened the street door.

"Mr. Hath is leaving now," he said to the marshals.

The crowd outside pressed closer.

Hanno Hath came into the front room and made his farewells. He kissed baby Pinpin, still sleeping in Mrs. Hath's arms. He kissed his wife, who for all her defiance couldn't keep the tears from her eyes. Then he kissed Bowman, whispering to him as he did so, "Look after Kess for me."

He swung his suitcase into one hand and strode out the door. The marshals fell into step, one on each side, and the two scarlet-gowned teachers waddled along behind. The crowd fell back to gaze in silence at the little procession as it passed. The Hath family stood together on their front step, watching him go. They held their heads high, and waved after him, as if he was going on a holiday. But the onlookers shook their heads and murmured "Poor man" at the shame of it all.

As the procession reached the corner of the street, Hanno Hath stopped for a brief moment, and looked back. He gave a last wave, a wide sweep of his arm above his head, and smiled. Bowman never forgot that wave, or that smile, because as he watched from the steps he caught his father's feelings in a sudden very clear moment. He felt the immensity of his father's love for them all, warm and strong and inexhaustible, and he felt too a silent cry of desolation, which if it had words would be saying, Must I leave you forever?

At the same time, Rufy Blesh's father, who was standing close by, saw that smile and that defiant wave, and Bowman heard him say to his wife, "He can smile as much as he wants—they'll never let him see his family again."

That was when Bowman decided, deep inside himself,

that there was nothing he would not do to bring his father back, that he would destroy all Aramanth if he had to, for what did he care for a lifetime of this neat and orderly world compared with one moment of his father's brave loving smile?

CHAPTER NINE

ESCAPE FROM ARAMANTH

THAT NIGHT, WARDENS TOOK UP POSITIONS IN FRONT
of the house, so that they could catch Kestrel when she came
home, which they believed she would do once it was dark.
Kestrel, of course, was already inside the house, keeping out
of sight of the windows. Once night fell, and the family
could draw the curtains without arousing suspicion, she
moved about more freely.

Ira Hath refused to panic or cry. She repeated so many
times, so steadfastly, "Your father will come back to us," that
the twins began to believe it. She fed Pinpin and bathed her,
just as always. She made the wish huddle with her three children, just as always, though it felt wrong without their
father. But they all wished for him to come home, which

somehow made it feel as if he were there after all. Then she tucked Pinpin up in her cot, just as always. And only after Pinpin was asleep did she sit down with the twins and fold her hands in her lap and say, "Tell me everything."

Kestrel told all that had happened to her, and also what her father had said. Then she took out the map and, before she forgot them, wrote beside each set of squiggly letters the words her father had told her: THE GREAT WAY, CRACK-IN-THE-LAND, THE HALLS OF MORAH, INTO THE FIRE.

On the back she copied out the translation of the writing, also from memory: "The song of the wind singer will set you free. Then seek the homeland."

"Ah, the homeland," said Ira Hath with a sigh. "This place was never meant to be our true home."

"Where is the homeland?"

"Who knows? But we'll know it when we find it."

"How?"

"Because it'll feel like home, of course."

She looked a little longer at the map, and rolled it up again.

"Whatever it is, it had better wait till your father comes back," she said. "Right now, we have to decide what to do about you."

"Can't I hide here, in the house?"

"My darling, I don't think we'll be allowed to stay in this house very much longer."

"I won't let them take me away. I won't."

"No, no. We must hide you. I'll think of something."

The emotions of the long day had exhausted them, Kestrel most of all, so Ira Hath decided to leave further discussion until the morning. But they had not reckoned how speedily they were to be punished.

The sun had barely risen when they were woken by a loud banging on the front door.

"Up! Get up! Time to go!"

Mrs. Hath opened her bedroom window and leaned out to see what was going on. A squad of marshals was outside in the street.

"Pack up your things!" cried one of the marshals. "You're moving out!"

They had been reallocated—not to Maroon, as they had expected, but to Grey District. Their new home was to be a single room in a ten-storey-high block, shared by three hundred families. Their house in Orange was to be handed over by noon at the latest to a new family.

Ira Hath was undaunted.

"All the less cleaning to do," she said, as she roused Pinpin from sleep.

The immediate problem was Kestrel. The marshals were still on the lookout for her, and they had now taken up positions at the back as well as the front of the house. How could the family leave without Kestrel being discovered?

In a little while, two wardens came down the street wheeling an empty cart to move the Hath family's possessions to Grey District. The neighbours were now up, and many of them had come out of their houses to watch the interesting spectacle that would soon unfold.

"There'll be tears. The mother'll come out weeping. They always do when it's a demotion. But the new ones, oh, they'll be smiling."

"What about the baby? Isn't there a baby? She'll have no idea what's happening to her."

"Those twins, though, they're sharp as knives, the two of them."

"Did you hear what the girl did? I knew she'd come to no good."

"Well, she'll be sorry now."

Inside the house they were discussing whether Kestrel could be smuggled out inside the big blanket trunk. Bowman looked out of the window at the marshals, and the wardens, and the neighbours, and shook his head.

"It's too risky."

As he looked, his eyes fell on a small figure at the back of the crowd. It was Mumpo. He was skulking about, his eyes fixed hopefully on the front door, evidently waiting for Kestrel.

"Mumpo's out there," he said.

"Not stinky old Mumpo," said Kestrel.

"I've had an idea."

Bowman went to the cupboard in their bedroom and took out Kestrel's winter cloak, a long orange garment with a hood for the cold weather. He bundled it up tight and pushed it down the front of his tunic.

"I'm going out to talk to Mumpo," he said. "Don't do anything till I come back."

"But Bo—"

He was gone.

"You ready, then?" called one of the grey wardens, as he came out of the front door.

"Not yet," said Bowman, trotting past him on to the street. "My mother's a fussy packer."

He ran all the way down the street to avoid having to talk to the curious neighbours, and only came to a stop when he was out of sight round the corner. As he had expected, Mumpo shortly came into view, puffing and dribbling.

"Bo!" he cried. "What's happening? Where's Kess?"

"Do you want to help her?"

"Yes. I'll help her. Where is she?"

Bowman pulled the orange cloak out from under his tunic and shook it open.

"Here's what you have to do."

Bowman had been back in the house a good hour when at last his mother opened the door and told the wardens they could carry out the trunks. To the wardens' surprise, the trunks had been packed in the top back bedroom, the farthest point in the house from the front door.

"Why couldn't you pack in the hall? These hogging stairs are no joke, you know?"

To add to the confusion, the family who were to move into the house, who were called Warmish, arrived early, trailed by two heavily laden carts. They were naturally eager to come in and look around, but Ira Hath planted herself in the doorway so that they couldn't get past, and smiled at them implacably.

"How much room is there in the kitchen?" asked Mrs. Warmish. "Would you call it a kitchen—breakfast room, or more like a kitchen-dinette?"

"Oh, it's very roomy," said Mrs. Hath. "The kitchen table seats thirty-six, in a pinch."

"Thirty-six? Good heavens! Are you sure?"

"And just you wait till you see the bathroom! We've had eight fully grown adults bathing at once, and every one of them with room to lie and soak."

"Well, my word!" Mrs. Warmish was so bewildered by this information that she didn't know what to say, and fell back on the little she could see beyond Mrs. Hath's broad body.

"So is the flooring polished, or is it varnished?"

"Varnish?" said Mrs. Hath witheringly. "Pure beeswax, I assure you, as in all the best homes."

One by one the trunks were hauled out into the cart. The furniture was all to stay behind, since their new apartment would be so much smaller. When the last trunk had been carried out of the house, Mrs. Hath, still guarding the doorway against the eagerness of the Warmishes, hoisted Pinpin up into her arms, and turned to catch Bowman's eye. He gave her a brief nod, and slipped past her onto the front step. From here, he set off as if to the laden cart, but then suddenly pointed to the back of the crowd, and called, "Kess!"

Everybody turned, and saw the figure of a child, hooded and cloaked, standing at the far end of the street.

"Run, Kess, run!" shouted Bowman.

The child turned and ran.

At once, the marshals and the wardens set off at a gallop after the child, and the crowd of neighbours hurried down the street in the hope of witnessing the moment of capture.

Kestrel slipped out of the front door, and would have got away entirely unnoticed, had Pinpin not seen her and cried in delight, "Kess!" The slowest of the wardens, who had been tying the trunks onto the cart when the chase began, heard this cry and turned to see Kestrel bolting down the side alley, with Bowman close after her.

"She's here! I seen her!" he yelled, and lumbered off down the alley after them.

The children were faster on their feet than the warden and had soon put some distance between them, but the truth was, they did not know where they were going. The plan had been to get Kestrel out of the house. After that, they had trusted to instinct and luck.

They stopped running, to get their breath back. Nearby was a small alcove, where rubbish bins stood waiting to be emptied. They ducked down behind the bins for safety.

"We have to get out of the city," said Kestrel.

"How? We haven't got passes. They don't open the gates without a pass."

"There's a way out through the salt caves. I've seen it. Only I don't know how to get into the salt caves."

"You said the caves are used for sewage, didn't you?" said Bowman.

"Yes."

"Then it must be where all the sewers go."

"Bo, you're brilliant!"

Their eyes searched the street, and there, not far away,

was a manhole cover. At the same time, they heard the distant sounds of their pursuers, shouting to each other as they searched the streets.

"They're getting closer."

"You're sure we can get out of the salt caves?"

"No."

A warden came into view at the far end of the street. They had no choice. They ran for the manhole.

The cover was round, and made of iron, and very heavy. There was a ring set into it that lifted up to pull it open. Just raising the ring wasn't easy—it had rusted into its socket—but at last they got it up enough to fit their fingers round it. The warden had spotted them now, and set up a cry.

"Here they are! Hey, everybody! I've found them!"

Fear gave them strength, and they pulled together, and succeeded at last in getting the manhole cover to move. Inch by inch they dragged it clear of the hole, until there was enough space for them to pass through. There were iron rungs in the brick-lined shaft beneath, and below that, the sound of water.

Kestrel went first, and Bowman followed. Once he was below the level of the cover, he tried to push it back into place above them, but it was impossible.

"Leave it," said Kestrel. "Let's go."

So Bowman followed her down the ladder, and stepped

into the dark water at the bottom. He was too anxious about where he was going to look back, but had he done so, he would have seen a shadow fall over the open manhole above.

"It's all right," said Kestrel. "It's not deep. Follow the water."

They made their way along the dark tunnel, up to their ankles in water, and slowly the light from the open shaft down which they had come faded into darkness. They walked steadily on, for what seemed like a very long time. Bowman said nothing, but he was afraid of the dark. They could hear many strange sounds around them, of water gurgling and dripping, and the echo of their own steps. They passed other channels flowing into their tunnel, and they could sense that the tunnel was becoming bigger the farther they went.

Then for the first time they heard a sound that was watery, but not made by water. It was some way behind them, and it was unmistakable: *splosh, splosh, splosh.* Someone was following them.

They hurried on faster. The water was deeper now, and pulled at their legs. There was a glow of faint light ahead, and a thundery sound. Behind them they could still hear the steady footfall of their pursuer.

All at once the tunnel emerged into a long cave, through the middle of which ran a fast-flowing river. The light that faintly illuminated the glistening cave walls came from a low wide hole at the far end, through which the river plunged out of sight. The water through which they had been wading now drained away to join the river, and they found themselves on a smooth bank of dry rock.

Almost at once, Bowman felt something terrible, very close by.

"We can't stop here," he said. "We must go, quickly."

"Home," said a deep voice. "Go home."

Kestrel jumped, and looked into the darkness.

"Bo? Was that you?"

"No," said Bowman, trembling violently. "There's someone else here."

"Just a friend," said the deep voice. "A friend in need."

"Where are you?" said Kestrel. "I can't see you."

In answer, there came the hiss of a match being struck, and then a bright arc of flame as a burning torch curved through the air to land on the ground a few feet away from them. It lay there, hissing and crackling, throwing out a circle of amber light. Out of the darkness beyond, into the soft fringe of its glow, stepped a small figure with white hair. He walked with the slow steps of a little old man, but as he came closer to the flickering light, they saw that he was a boy of about their own age—only his hair was completely white, and his skin was dry and wrinkly. He stood there gazing steadily at them, and then he spoke.

"You can see me now."

It was the deep voice they had heard before, the voice of an old man. The effect of this worn and husky voice coming from the child's body was peculiarly frightening.

"The old children," said Kestrel. "The ones I saw before."

"We were so looking forward to having you join our class," said the white-haired child. "But all's well that ends well, as they say. Follow me, and I'll lead you back."

"We're not going back," said Kestrel.

"Not going back?" The soothing voice made her defiance sound childish. "Don't you understand? Without my help, you'll never find the way out of here. You will die here."

There was a sound of laughter in the darkness. The white-haired child smiled.

"My friends find that amusing."

And into the pool of light, one by one, stepped other children, some white-haired like himself, some bald, all prematurely aged. At first it seemed there were only a few, but more and more came shuffling out of the shadows, first ten, then twenty, then thirty and more. Bowman stared at them and shivered.

"We're your little helpers," said the white-haired child. And all the old children laughed again, with the deep rumbling laughter of grown-ups. "You help us, and we'll help you. That's fair, isn't it?"

He took a step closer and reached out one hand.

"Come with me."

Behind him all the other old children were moving closer, with little shuffling steps. As they came, they, too, reached out their hands. They didn't seem aggressive so much as curious.

"My friends want to stroke you," said their leader, his voice sounding deep and soft and far away.

Bowman was so frightened that the only thought in his head was how to get away. He stepped back, out of reach of the fluttering arms. But behind him now was the river, flowing rapidly towards its underground hole. The old children shuffled closer, and he felt a hand brush his arm. As it did so, an unfamiliar sensation swept through him: it was as if some of his strength had been sucked out of him, leaving him tired and sleepy.

Kess! he called silently, desperately. *Help me!*

"Get away from him!" cried Kestrel.

She stepped boldly forward and swung one arm at the white-haired child, meaning to knock him to the ground. But as her fist touched his body, the blow weakened, and she felt her arm go limp. She swung at him again, and she felt herself grow weaker still. The air around her seemed to become thick and squashy, and sounds grew far away and blurred.

Bo! she called to him. *Something's happening to me.*

Bowman could see her falling to her knees, and could feel the overwhelming weariness that was taking possession of her body. He knew he should go to help her, but he was frozen, immobilised by terror.

Come away, Kess, he pleaded. *Come away.*

I can't.

He knew it, he could feel it. She was growing faint, as if already the old children were carrying her away.

I can't move, Bo. Help me.

He watched them gather round her, but he was sick with fear, and he did nothing; and knowing he was doing nothing, he wept for shame.

Suddenly there came a crash and a splash, and something came charging out of the tunnel behind them. It roared like a wild animal, and struck out on all sides with windmilling arms.

"Kakka-kakka-kak!" it cried. "Bubba-bubba-bubba-kak!"

The old children jumped back in alarm. The whirlwind passed Bowman, pushing him off the bank and into the fast-moving river. The splash doused the flaming torch. In the sudden darkness, Kestrel felt herself being dragged to the river's edge and toppled into the water. There came a third splash, and there were three of them tumbling round and round in the current, being swept towards the roaring hole.

The cold water revived Kestrel, and she began to kick. Forcing herself to the surface, she gulped air. Then she saw the low roof of rock approaching, and ducked back down under water, and was sucked through the hole. A few moments of raging water, and suddenly she was flying through air and spray, and falling, falling with the streams of water, down and down, fighting for breath, thinking, This is the end, this is the smash, when all at once, with a plop and a long yielding hiss, she found she had landed in soft, deep mud.

CHAPTER TEN

IN THE SALT CAVES

ONCE SHE HAD RECOVERED FROM THE SHOCK of her fall, Kestrel smelled the sick-making air and realised that she had landed in a part of the Underlake. Up above was the great arching roof of salt rock she had seen before, and not far off was one of the several holes in the cave's roof, through which fell such light as there was in this shadowy land. Before her stretched a dark gleaming region of water and stinking mud. Behind, the gushing waterfall down which they had fallen. She searched for the platform with the jetty and the moored barges, but they must have been in some other part of the great salt caves, lost in the gloom.

She heard a low whimper, and turning, saw Bowman, floundering in the mud.

"Are you all right, Bo?"

"Yes," he said, and then started to cry, a little out of relief that they had survived, but mostly from shame.

"Don't cry, Bo," said Kestrel. "We don't have the time."

"Yes, I know. I'm sorry."

Silently he begged her forgiveness.

I should have helped you. I was so afraid.

"This is the Underlake," said Kestrel aloud, to turn his thoughts to practical matters. "There's a way out onto the plains, I'm sure."

She turned to look across the watery mud, and as she did so, a half-familiar form rose up, spluttering and grunting. It got itself upright, and wiped the mud from its face, and beamed at her.

"Mumpo!"

"Hallo, Kess," said Mumpo happily.

"It was you!"

"I saw you go down the hole," he said. "I followed you. I'm your friend."

"Mumpo, you saved me!"

"They were going to hurt you. I won't let anyone hurt you, Kess."

She gazed at him, covered from head to toe in mud, and

marvelled that he could look so pleased with himself. But then, they were all just as muddy, and all stank as much as each other now.

"Mumpo," she said, "you were brave and strong, and I'll always thank you for saving me. But you must go back."

Mumpo's face fell.

"I want to be with you, Kess."

"No, Mumpo." She spoke kindly but firmly, as if to a small child. "It's me they're looking for, not you. You have to go home."

"I can't, Kess," said Mumpo simply. "My legs are stuck."

That was when Kestrel and Bowman realised that they were sinking. Not fast, but steadily.

"It's all right," said Kestrel. "I've been here before. We'll sink only as far as our knees."

She tried to pull her leg out, and found she couldn't.

Kess, said her brother silently. *What if they come after us?*

She looked round in all directions, but there was no sign of the old children.

If they do, Kestrel replied, *they'll get stuck, too.*

So there they stood, their drenched clothing clinging to their shivering bodies, breathing the fetid air, feeling themselves sinking. When they had sunk past their knees, Bowman said, "We're still sinking."

"There has to be a bottom somewhere," said Kestrel.

"Why?"

"We can't just sink all the way."

"Why not?"

For a while, nobody said anything, and they went on sinking. Then Mumpo broke the silence.

"I like you, Kess. You're my friend."

"Oh, shut up, Mumpo. I'm sorry. I know you saved me, but honestly . . ."

Another silence fell. By now they had sunk to their waists.

"Do you like me, Kess?" said Mumpo.

"A bit," said Kestrel.

"We're friends," said Mumpo happily. "We like each other."

His idiotic cheerfulness at last goaded Kestrel into saying aloud what she'd been afraid even to think.

"You stupid pongo! Don't you get it? We're going to be sucked under the mud!"

Mumpo stared at her in utter astonishment.

"Are you sure, Kess?"

"Take a look around. Who's going to pull us out?"

He looked around and saw nobody. His face crumpled with fear, and he started to scream.

"Help! I'm sinking! Help! I'll go under! Help!"

"Oh, shut up. There's nobody to help."

But Mumpo only screamed louder—which was just as well, because Kestrel was wrong. There was somebody to help.

Not so far off, a small round mudman named Willum was stooped over the lake surface hunting for tixa leaves. Tixa grew wild in unexpected places, and the only way to find it was to wander about half looking for it in a slow, dreamy sort of way for several hours. If you looked too hard at the murky grey surface of the lake, you could never see the tixa plants, which were murky-coloured, too. You had to not look, and that way, you caught sight of them out of the corner of your eye. Then if you found some, you picked the leaves and put them in your bag, keeping one to chew as you went on. Chewing tixa leaves made you feel slow and dreamy, and that made you even better at finding them.

When Willum heard the faraway screams, he straightened up and peered through the gloom, and tried for once to look.

"My, oh my," he murmured to himself, smiling. He didn't know he was smiling. He'd been out most of the day, chewing tixa most of the time, and really he should be thinking about going home. The nut-socks strung round his neck were full, and his wife would have expected him back long ago.

But the shrill shrieks didn't stop, so Willum decided to

set off towards them, following the network of trails that all the mudpeople learned as soon as they could walk. These trails ran beneath the surface of the mud, sometimes just below, sometimes down to the knees. There was a way of walking the trails that all the mudpeople had, a slow steady stride, easing one foot in, easing the other out, in a swinging even pace. You couldn't go fast, you just swung along, particularly after a day of tixa hunting.

All this time, the children went on sinking. The mud was up to their necks now, and still their desperately wriggling toes could feel no hard ground. Kestrel was frightened, and would have started to cry had Mumpo not been crying enough for all of them.

"Yaa-aa waa-aaa!" shrieked Mumpo, exactly like a baby. "Yaa-aaa waa-aaa!"

None of them heard Willum approaching behind them until he spoke.

"Oh my sweet earth!" he exclaimed, coming to a stop on the nearest part of the trail.

"Yaa-aaa waa—Glup!"

Mumpo suddenly went quiet: not because help was at hand, but because his mouth had filled with mud. All three children tried to twist their heads round, but they couldn't.

"Help us!" said Bowman, choking on mud.

"I should think so," said Willum.

Like every mudman out on the lake, he carried a rope, wound several times round his plump waist. He unwound it now, and threw it neatly over the surface of the lake so that it lay within reach of the three children.

"Take ahold," he said. "Slow, mind."

As the children worked their hands up out of the mud, and towards the rope, Willum noticed a bunch of tixa growing right by them. It was a big bunch, with broad mature leaves, the very best sort.

"They leaves," he said. "Just you bring they along, too, eh?"

The children's efforts to reach the rope were making them sink faster, and now the mud was half suffocating them. Willum was so excited by the sight of the tixa leaves, he forgot this.

"They leaves," he said again, pointing. "Take ahold of they, eh?"

Bowman had the rope now and pulled hard on it, very nearly jerking Willum off the trail. With his other hand, Bowman reached for his sister, and held her while she, too, took the rope. Kestrel in turn reached for Mumpo, who was the one nearest to the tixa plants.

"Pull!" cried Bowman, feeling them start to sink again. "Pull!"

"I should think so," said Willum, not pulling. "Just you fetch me they leaves."

It was pure chance that Mumpo's hand, scrabbling for the rope, closed over the tixa plant. And as soon as Willum saw that he had it, he proceeded to pull. Leaning forward to get all his weight on the rope, he set off along the trail hauling like a pack mule. His short sturdy legs were immensely strong, like all the mudpeople's, and soon the children felt themselves rising up out of the clinging mud.

With a spluttering gasp, Kestrel freed her face and drew a huge gulping breath. Mumpo spat the mud out of his mouth and started howling again. And Bowman, panting, heart hammering, tried hard not to think what would have happened to them if the mudman hadn't found them.

When they felt the solid land of the trail beneath them, they collapsed and lay there in a mud-coated heap, made weak by the shock of it all. Willum bent over Mumpo and took the tixa leaves from his hand.

"That'll do. Thanky kindly."

He was very pleased. He broke off the tip of one leaf, brushed the mud off, and popped it in his mouth. The rest went into his little bag.

He turned then to studying the children he had pulled out of the lake. Who were they? Not mudpeople, certainly. They were far too thin, and no mudpeople wandered off the trails into the deeps, not without being roped. They must have come from up yonder.

"I know who you'm are," he said to them. "You'm skinnies."

They followed the small round mudman down winding
trails that only he could see, across the dark surface of the
Underlake. Too exhausted to ask questions, they tramped
along behind him in single file, still holding the rope.
Their legs ached from the effort of pulling them in and out
of the mud, but on and on they went, until dusk started to
gather in the great sky-holes above.

Willum sang softly as he went along, and occasionally
chuckled to himself. What a stroke of luck it was, finding the
skinnies! he was thinking. Won't Jum be surprised! And he
laughed aloud just thinking about it.

Willum had wandered far in his day's hunting, and by the
time they were back by his home again, it was almost night.
The shadows were so deep that the children could no longer
see where they were going, and kept to the trail by feeling the
tug of the rope. But now at last, Willum had come to a stop,
and with a sigh of satisfaction announced to them, "No
place like home, eh?"

No place indeed: there were no signs of any house or
shelter of any kind, but for a thin wisp of smoke rising from
a small hole in the ground. The children stood and shivered, fearful and exhausted, and looked around.

"Follow me, little skinnies. Mind the steps."

With these words, he walked straight down into the ground. Kestrel, following behind, found that her feet went through the mud into a sudden hole, where there seemed to be a descending staircase.

"Mouth shut," said Willum. "Eyes shut."

One moment Kestrel felt the mud round her neck, the next moment her mouth and nose and eyes were clogged and smothered, and the next moment she had stepped down into a smoky firelit underground room. Bowman followed, and then Mumpo, both spitting and pushing mud from their eyes. Above them, at the top of the staircase, the mud had resealed itself like a lid.

"Well, Willum," said a cross voice. "A pretty time you've been."

"Ah, but looky, Jum!"

Willum stood aside to display the children. A round mud-coated woman sat on a stool by the fire, stirring a pot and scowling.

"What's this, then?" she said.

"Skinnies, my love."

"Skinnies, is it?"

She lumbered up from her seat and came over to them. She patted them with her muddy hand and stroked their trembling cheeks.

"Poor little mites."

Then she turned to Willum and said sharply, "Teeth!"

Obediently, Willum bared his teeth. They were stained a yellowy-brown.

"Tixy. I knew it."

"Only the smallest leaf, my dearest."

"And harvest tomorrow. For shame, Willum! You should lie down and die."

"Mudnuts, Jum," he said placatingly. Untying the long nut-socks, he fingered out a surprisingly large number of brown lumps.

Jum stumped off back to the fire, refusing to acknowledge the fruit of his labours.

"But my love! My sweet bun! My sugarplum!"

"Don't you sugar me! You and your tixy!"

The children, forgotten for the moment, stared at the room in which they now found themselves. It was a big round burrow, with a dome-shaped roof, at the top of which the smoke of the fire escaped through a hole. The fire was built in the middle of the room on a platform of stone that raised it up to table height, and around it was a kind of wide-barred cage of iron rods. This arrangement allowed pots and kettles to be suspended over the fire on all sides, at various levels. A large kettle hung high up, steaming softly, a stew pot lower down, popping and spitting.

Beside the fire there was a wooden bench, on which sat the members of Willum's immediate family, all as round and mud-covered as each other, so that apart from the differences in size there wasn't much to distinguish them. They were in fact a child, an aunt, and a grandfather. All were staring curiously at the newcomers except for the grandfather, who kept looking at Willum and winking.

The floor of the burrow was covered with a litter of soft rugs, mud-stained and rumpled, thrown one on top of the other like a huge unmade bed.

"Pollum!" said Jum, stirring the stew. "More bowls!"

The mud child jumped up and ran to a wall cupboard.

"Good day, then, Willum?" said the old man, winking.

"Good enough," said Willum, winking back.

"You'll not be wanting your supper, then," said Jum, banging the stew pot. "You'll be in the land of tixy."

Willum went right up close behind her and put both his arms around her and hugged her tight.

"Who loves his Jum?" he said. "Who's come home to his sweet Jum?"

"Who stayed out all day?" grumbled Jum.

"Jum, Jum, my heart does hum!"

"All right, all right!" She put down her ladle and let him kiss her neck. "So what are we going to do with these skinnies of yours?"

The silent aunt now spoke up.

"Fill'um poor skinny little bellies," she declared.

"That's the way," said Willum. And he went and sat down by the old man, and fell to whispering with him.

Pollum put bowls on a table, and Jum filled the bowls with thick, hot stew from the stew pot.

"Sit'ee down, skinnies," she said, her voice more kindly now.

So Bowman and Kestrel and Mumpo sat down at the table and looked at the stew. They were very hungry, but the stew looked so exactly like lumpy mud that they hesitated to eat it.

"Nut stew," said Jum encouragingly. She popped a spoonful into her own mouth, as if to show them the way.

"Please, ma'am," said Bowman. "What sort of nut?"

"Why," said Jum, "mudnut, of course."

Mumpo started to eat. He seemed not to mind it, so Kestrel tried it. It was surprisingly good, like smoky potato. Soon all three were spooning it up. Jum watched with pleasure. Pollum twined herself around her mother's stout legs and whispered to her.

"What are they, Mum?"

"They'm skinnies. They live up yonder. Poor little things."

"Why are they here?"

"They'm escaped. They'm run away."

As they ate, the children's spirits revived, and they began to be curious about where exactly they were.

"Are we in the Underlake?" asked Kestrel.

"I don't know about that," said Jum. "We'm under, that's for sure. We'm all under."

"Is the mud—? I mean, does it come from—?" There didn't seem to be a polite way to ask the question, so she changed tack. "The mud doesn't seem to smell so much down here."

"Smell?" said Jum. "I should hope it does smell. The smell of the sweet, sweet earth."

"Is that all?"

"All? Why, little skinny, that's all and everything."

There came a sudden chuckle from the aunt by the fire.

"Squotch!" she exclaimed. "They'm thinking our mud is squotch!"

"No-o," said Jum. "They'm not daft."

"Ask'ee," said the aunt. "You do ask'ee."

"You'm not thinking our mud is squotch, little skinnies?"

"What's squotch?" said Bowman.

"What's squotch?" Jum was baffled. Pollum started to giggle. "Why, it's—squotch."

Willum now entered the discussion.

"Why, so it is squotch," he said. "And why not?

Everything goes into the sweet earth, and makes for the flavour. One great big stew pot, that's what it is."

He dipped the ladle into the stew pot and drew out a spoonful of thick stew.

"One day I shall lay my body down, and the sweet earth will take it, and make it good again, and give it back. Don't you mind about squotch, little skinnies. We'm all squotch, if you only see it aright. We'm all part of the sweet earth."

He consumed the stew straight from the ladle. Jum watched him, nodding with approval.

"Sometimes you do surprise me, Willum," she said.

Mumpo finished his stew first. As soon as he was done, he lay down on the rug-covered floor, curled himself up into a tight ball, and went to sleep.

"That's the way, little skinny," said Jum, pulling a rug over the top of him.

Bowman and Kestrel wanted to go to sleep, too, but first they wanted to remove the mud that was caked hard all over them.

"Please, ma'am," said Bowman. "Where can I wash?"

"A bath is it you're wanting?"

"Yes, ma'am."

"Pollum! Get the bath ready!"

Pollum went to the fire and unhooked the steaming kettle. She heaved it over to one side of the burrow, where there was a saucer-shaped depression in the earth floor. There she poured the hot water from the kettle in a swirling stream straight onto the ground. It slicked the sides of the hollow and gathered in a shallow, steaming puddle at the bottom.

"Who's go first?" said Jum.

Bowman and Kestrel stared.

"Show'ee, Pollum," called out the aunt. "No baths up yonder. Poor little things."

It wasn't often Pollum was allowed first roll in the bath, when the water was new, so she jumped in without waiting to be told twice. Down onto her back, splayed out like a crab, and then over and over, wriggling and turning, covering herself with a fresh coat of warm slime. She giggled as she writhed about, obviously loving it.

"That's enough, Pollum. Leave some for the skinnies."

Bowman and Kestrel said it was very kind of them, but they were too tired to have a bath after all. So Jum made them up nests on the floor among the piles of rugs, and they curled up as Mumpo had done. Bowman, worn out by the terrors of the day, was soon deeply asleep, but Kestrel's eyes stayed open a little longer, and she lay there watching the mudpeople and listening to what they were saying. Willum had taken something out of his bag and was giving it to the old man, and they were chuckling together softly in the corner. Jum was cooking by the fire, making what seemed to be an enormous amount of stew. Pollum was asking questions.

"Why are they so thin, Mum?"

"Not enough to eat. No mudnuts up yonder, see."

"No mudnuts!"

"They don't have the mud for it."

"No mud!"

"Don't'ee forget, Pollum. You'm a lucky girl."

Kestrel tried to listen, but the voices seemed to be getting softer and fuzzier all the time, and the flame-shadows flickering on the domed ceiling softened into a warm blur. She snuggled deeper into her cosy nest, and thought how much her legs ached, and how good it was to be in bed, and her eyes felt so heavy that she closed them properly, and a moment later she was fast asleep.

CHAPTER ELEVEN

THE MUDNUT HARVEST

WHEN THEY AWOKE, SOFT GREY DAYLIGHT WAS FILTERING into the burrow through the smoke hole above the fire. Everybody had gone except for Pollum, who was sitting quietly by the fire waiting for them to wake. Mumpo was nowhere to be seen.

"Your friend's out on the lake," said Pollum, "helping with the harvest."

She had breakfast waiting for them: a plate of what looked like biscuits, but turned out to be fried sliced mudnuts.

"Don't you ever eat anything but mudnuts?" asked Kestrel. But Pollum seemed not to understand the question.

While they ate, the twins talked over what they should do.

They were lost and frightened. They knew their mother would be sick with worry over them. But Kestrel also knew, beyond a shadow of a doubt, that she could not go back to Aramanth as it was.

"They'll send us to join the old children," she said. "I'd rather die."

"Then you know what we have to do."

"Yes."

She took out the map the Emperor had given her, and they both studied it. Bowman traced the line called the Great Way.

"We have to find this road."

"First we have to find the way out of here."

They asked Pollum if there was a way to go "up yonder" but she said no, she'd never heard of one. Again, the question itself seemed to puzzle her.

"There must be a way," said Kestrel. "After all, the light gets in."

"Well," said Pollum, after some thought. "You can fall down, but you can't fall up."

"The grown-ups'll know. We'll ask them. When are they coming back?"

"Not till late. It's harvest today."

"What kind of harvest?"

"Mudnuts," said Pollum.

She got up and started to clear away the breakfast. Bowman and Kestrel talked in low voices.

"What are we going to do about Mumpo?" said Kestrel.

"He'd better come with us," said Bowman. "He's more use than I am."

"Don't talk like that, Bo. You'll start crying again."

And indeed he was at the point of tears.

"I'm sorry, Kess. I'm just not brave."

"Being brave's not the only thing."

"Pa told me to look after you."

"We'll look after each other," said Kestrel. "You're the one who feels, and I'm the one who does."

Bowman nodded slowly. It felt like that to him, too, but he'd never put it to himself quite so clearly.

By now, Pollum had put all the dishes in a puddle of watery mud to soak. She said to them, "Time to go out on the lake. Harvest time, see. Everyone helps with the harvest."

They decided to go with her, and to look for Willum. Somehow they had to find their way out.

The scene that met their eyes as they climbed out of the burrow was very different from the bleak Underlake of the previous night. There was light gleaming and bouncing everywhere, shafting down through the holes in the great salt-silver cavern roof, creating pools of sunshine so bright they hurt the eyes. From these brilliant pools, the light spread outwards, as if in ripples, softening as it went, making the sheen of watery mud glisten all the way into the hazy distance. And moving back and forth over this sheet of light there were hundreds of busy little people. They were working in lines and in columns, and on great flat rafts. They were gathered round immense open bonfires and round large winch-like contraptions. And wherever they were gathered, they sang. The songs wove in and out of each other like sea shanties; and like sea shanties, they were work songs. For the mudpeople were working, and working hard.

"It doesn't smell stinky anymore," said Kestrel in surprise.

"It does," said Bowman. "We've just got used to it."

They looked round for any sign of the old children, but there was none. They looked, too, for someone they recognised, but all the mudpeople seemed the same to them: all very round, and all very muddy. Following Pollum, they made their way, a little fearfully, along a ridge towards the nearest of the great bonfires. As they went, they watched the people at work, and began to understand what it was they were doing.

The mudnuts grew in shallow fields below the surface of the lake, down in the soft mud. The harvesters were picking them by walking slowly across these fields, and stooping down, and plunging their arms into the mud. Long lines of mudpeople were snaking across the lake in a methodical fashion, all taking a step forward at the same time, all bending and plunging in an arm together. The nuts they pulled up, each one the size of an apple, they dropped into shallow wooden buckets that they drew behind them. As they moved and picked, they sang their song, and so the whole line was kept in time.

It was a remarkable sight to see those swaying strands of people all over the lake, all linked in one great ebb and flow of motion, their chanting voices climbing to the high cavern roof and bouncing back again in deep muffly echoes. Around the tall bonfires the people were singing, too, though in a more ragged and disorganised way, picking up the thread of one song here, another there. The task of the people by the fire was far less active; indeed, several of them appeared to be doing nothing at all, though they did it with a great deal of laughter. Some were roasting mudnuts, rolling them into the embers and raking them out again with long sticks; and some were scouring mudnuts, chipping the mud off the skins; and a considerable number were coming and going with buckets.

Pollum picked up three empty buckets, gave one each to Bowman and Kestrel, and said, "Follow me. I'll show you what to do."

She took it for granted they would help with the harvest, and because there was no sign of Willum, and everyone else was so hard at work, it seemed ungrateful to refuse. So they followed Pollum into the mudfield and did as she told them.

The children of the mudpeople had the job of emptying the wooden buckets as they became full. The mudnut pickers worked away in their lines, and as the buckets filled up they would cry, "Bucket up!" and a child would dash forward with an empty bucket and haul the full one away. The mudnuts were piled up in great mounds around the bonfires, which were built on the ridges alongside the fields, so the children didn't have all that far to go. Even so, as Bowman and Kestrel soon discovered, it was exhausting work. The full buckets were heavy, and had to be carried through squelchy mud that came halfway up their shins. By the time they reached the fire, their arms and legs were aching, and they were sweating into their layer of mud. But in a while they found that there was a rhythm to it, and the singing of the lines of harvesters somehow lifted up their tired hearts. There was usually a moment of rest before the cry went out, "Bucket up!" and the heaving struggle began again. As they approached the fire they felt its fierce exhilarating heat, and heard the laughter of the mudmen raking the nuts out of the embers. Then came the sweet moment when the bucket tipped and the load fell out, and suddenly their bodies felt light as air. The journey back over the lake was like flying, it was so effortless, like dancing among the sunbeams and the shadows that speckled the lake's surface.

After they had been working for what felt like all of a long day, and the sunlight had long faded in the sky-holes, the twins saw that the harvesters were straightening up and rubbing their sore backs, and turning to head for the bonfires.

"Dinner," said Pollum.

The people gathered in large crowds round the fires, where there were big basinfuls of fresh-roasted mudnuts waiting for them, and tubs of water. They drank first, straight from the long-handled scoops, scoop after scoop to quench the thirst of a day's labour. Then they sat down in little chattering clusters, and the basins were handed round, and they chewed away at the mudnuts as if they were apples.

The twins made no attempt to look for their friends. They were so hungry that they simply took themselves a big fat mudnut each and started to eat. They ate in silence for a few moments, and then their eyes met. They both knew they had never tasted anything so good in all their lives. Sweetly nutty, and yet somehow creamy at the same time; crisp towards the rind, tender in the middle; the skin singed by the embers to give it a smoky tang that crunched tastily in the mouth—

"Nothing like it, eh?"

This was Willum, wandering up to them, grinning from ear to ear.

"Fresh out of the mud, hot out of the fire. Life don't come sweeter than a harvest mudnut."

He winked at them, and then burst into laughter for no apparent reason.

"Please, sir," said Kestrel, seeing that he was about to wander away again. "Could you help us?"

"Help you, little skinny? Help you how?"

He stood there, rolling gently from side to side and chuckling.

"We want to know the way out of the salt caves, and on to the plains."

Willum blinked and frowned and then started to smile again.

"Out of the salt caves? Onto the plains? No, no, no, you don't want any of that!"

And off he wobbled, laughing softly to himself.

The twins looked round and saw that several other mud-people were acting like Willum, moving in a slow, random sort of way and laughing. Here and there they were gathered in swaying groups, roaring with laughter.

"I think it's those leaves they chew," said Bowman.

"So it is," said a familiar voice with a sigh. "All the menfolk'll be in tixyland tonight."

It was Jum, taking round a full basin of roasted mudnuts.

"The womenfolk have too much sense, see. And too much to do."

"Please, ma'am," said Kestrel. "Do you know the way out of here?"

"The way out? Well, now. That depends on where you want to go."

"To the north. To the mountains."

"The mountains?" Jum wrinkled up her brow. "What would you be'm wanting with the mountains?"

"We're going to the Halls of the Morah."

A sudden silence fell all around her. People began to get up and shuffle away, glancing nervously back at the twins as they went.

"We don't talk of such things here," said Jum. "Nor even give them a name."

"Why not?"

Jum shook her round head.

"There's none of that here, and we don't want any, neither. There's enough of that up yonder."

She turned her eyes up to the cave roof.

"In Aramanth?"

"Up yonder," said Jum, "live the people of the one we don't name. But you know that, little skinny. That's why you'm running away."

"No—" said Kestrel. But her brother cut her off.

"Yes," he said. "We know that."

Kestrel stared at him.

"Do we?"

"Yes," said her brother, though he hardly knew how to explain what it was he had just realised. Indistinctly, he was sensing that the world he knew so well, the only world he had ever known until now, was a sort of prison, and that its people, his people, were trapped within its high walls.

"Up yonder is the world of the one we don't name," said Jum again. "One way or t'other, they'm all belong to the one. Only here in the sweet earth, they do let us alone."

"But when the wind singer sings again," said Bowman, "we won't belong to—to the one you don't name—not anymore."

"Ah, the wind singer, is it?"

"Do you know about it?"

"They'm be stories. Old stories. I should like to hear that wind singer, I should. We do take pleasure in song."

"Then please help us find our way."

"Well," she said after a moment's thought. "You'm best talk with the Old Queen. She'll know what to tell you."

She pointed with a stubby finger to a mound that rose up out of the lake, some way off. On the top of the mound was a low timber stockade.

"You'll find her in the palace, over yonder."

"Will they let us in to talk to her?"

Jum looked surprised.

"Why wouldn't they?" she said. "Yes, you talk with the Old Queen."

So the twins thanked her and set off along the ridge towards the palace. All around them the mudmen were in high spirits, laughing and singing, even dancing in a roly-poly fashion. The tixa leaves evidently filled them with affection for all mankind, for as the twins passed they were forever receiving waves and smiles, and even hugs.

In a little while they passed a region of mudfields where the mud was too deep for harvesting on foot, and the mud-nuts were reached by rafts. These long wooden frames were designed to lie on the lake's surface, over which they were slowly pulled by ropes wound around great winches. During the harvest, the pickers lay prone all round the edges of the raft, reaching their arms into the mud below. Now that work had stopped for the day, the rafts had come to rest, and the winches were unmanned. This was the opportunity for the bolder young men to compete in the sport of mud-diving.

Bowman and Kestrel paused to watch them, amazed at the sight. At the corners of one of the rafts, tall slender poles had been fixed, rising up about twenty feet into the air. The mud-divers tied ropes round their waists and shinned up these poles like monkeys. They hung on at the top, swaying back and forth, throwing out first one hand, then the other, in a display of daring. Then, with a loud cry, they leapt from the pole into the mud, the rope snaking out behind them. The mud was so liquid here that they disappeared at once below the surface. For a few heart-stopping moments, nothing at all happened. Then the rope began to twitch and jerk, and there was a surge in the mud, and up would pop the mud-diver, to wild cheers. The ones who were cheered the loudest were those who stayed under the longest.

Kestrel was watching the mud-divers with admiration, when she saw a familiar figure shinning up one of the poles.

"That's Mumpo!"

And so it was. He looked thin and fragile alongside the others, but he was the most daring of them all. He swung himself about on top of the pole, and swooped and sprang back again, as if he hadn't a care in the world. And when he dived, he flung himself farther than any of them, and stayed beneath the mud longer than any of them, and surfaced to the grandest cheer of all.

The twins were astounded.

"How did he learn to do that?"

"Mumpo!" cried Kestrel. "Mumpo! We're over here!"

"Kess! Kess!"

As soon as he spotted them, he made another dive, just to

show off. Then he unhitched his rope, and came bounding along the trail to join them.

"Did you see me?" he cried. "Did you see me?"

He was tremendously pleased with himself, all grinning and bouncy like a puppy. Bowman saw the yellowish stains on his teeth.

"He's been eating those leaves."

"I love you, Kess," said Mumpo, embracing her. "I'm so happy. Are you happy? I want you to be as happy as me." And he gambolled around her, laughing and waving his mud-encrusted arms.

Bowman saw the look on Kestrel's face, and before she could speak he said quietly, "Let him be, Kess."

"He's gone mad."

"We can't leave him here."

He took hold of Mumpo's outstretched arm as he came swirling by.

"Come on, Mumpo. Let's go and see the Old Queen."

"I'm so happy! Happy, happy, happy!" chortled Mumpo.

"Honestly," complained Kestrel, "I think I liked him better when he was crying."

But Bowman was reflecting on the image of Mumpo diving from the top of the high pole. His body had been so surprisingly graceful. It gave him a different sense of Mumpo altogether. He was like a wild goose: ungainly on the ground, but beautiful in flight. Bowman liked this thought, because there was no pity in it. It struck him now that the pity he felt for Mumpo was a form of indifference. Why had he not been more curious about him? After all, Mumpo was in his way a mystery. Where did he come from? Why did he have no family? Everybody in Aramanth had a family.

"Mumpo—" he began.

"Happy, happy, happy," sang Mumpo.

This was not the time to ask questions. So they walked on, and Mumpo didn't stop laughing and singing all the way to the palace.

CHAPTER TWELVE

A QUEEN REMEMBERS

As they got near the palace, they realised there was a very odd noise coming from within. A babbling squeaking gurgling sort of noise. There also seemed to be an immense amount of pattering footsteps, and voices calling out, "Stop that!" and "Get down!" Whatever was going on was screened from their view by the timber stockade, in which there was a single door.

As they approached the door, even Mumpo became interested, and stopped his own carolling to listen. This came as a relief to Kestrel.

"Now, try and behave yourself, Mumpo. We're going to see the Queen. She's the most important person here, so we have to be very respectful."

She then knocked on the door. After a few moments, realising that no one inside could possibly hear her knock with such a cacophony going on, she opened it.

Inside there was a wide open space, completely full of muddy babies. There were tiny ones lying on mats, and crawling ones scurrying about like small dogs, and toddling ones toppling into each other, and walking ones, and ones that ran about yelling at the tops of their little voices. They were all completely naked, though of course also completely coated in mud. And they seemed to be having the time of their lives. They were forever colliding and trampling on one another in the most chaotic way, but somehow none of them came to any harm, or even made much complaint. They just bounced up again, and got on with their infant concerns.

In the midst of this writhing mass of babies there sat a number of very fat old ladies. Unlike the children, they remained motionless, like mountain islands in a seething sea. The babies clambered over and around them exactly as if they were land masses, and here and there the old ladies reached out a protective arm, or called out a warning. But mostly, they did nothing at all.

Faced with such confusion, the twins weren't sure what to do. They saw that there was a wide opening in the middle of the stockaded space, with steps leading down to what was presumably an underground room or rooms, and they guessed that the Queen was to be found down there. But clearly the thing to do was to ask.

Kestrel approached the nearest old lady.

"Please, ma'am," she said. "We've come to see the Queen."

"Of course you have," the old lady replied.

"Could you tell us where to go, please?"

"I shouldn't go anywhere, if I were you," the old lady said.

"Then may we be taken to the Queen, please?"

"Why, I'm the Queen," she replied. "Leastways, I'm one of them."

"Oh," said Kestrel, going very red. "Are there very many queens?"

"A good many, yes. All these ladies here, and plenty more besides."

Seeing Kestrel's confusion, she shook her head and said, "Don't you worry yourself about that, young skinny. You just tell me what it is you want."

"We want to talk to the Old Queen."

"Ah! The Old Queen, is it?"

At this point, three toddlers who had been mountaineering over her back all fell off at once and set up a lamentation. The Queen put them on their feet again, and patted them, and said, "It'll be bedtime soon enough. I'll take you to see the Old Queen after they've gone to bed. It'll be quieter then."

At that moment, a bell rang, and all the old ladies lumbered to their feet and started shooing the babies down the broad steps. Bowman, Kestrel, and Mumpo followed behind, more or less unnoticed. The effect of the tixa leaves was wearing off, and Mumpo had gone quiet.

At the bottom of the steps there was a burrowlike room of the same kind they'd seen before, only this one was enormous. It was so wide that when it had been dug out, pillars of hard earth had been left in place to support the roof. The effect of these rows of pillars was to make the room seem to go on forever, as alcove succeeded alcove far into the shadowy distance.

The tribe of babies was put to bed in the simplest possible way. As in Willum's burrow, the floor was deep in soft cloths, and the babies laid themselves down, crowded together in piles, all tangled up with each other, and mumbled and squeaked. The fat old ladies waddled among them, patting and stroking and rearranging, pinning on nappies where necessary, pulling rugs over the tops of them in places, but mostly leaving them to lie as they chose. Then they sat down around the edges and sang them a lullaby in their creaky old voices, and the song filled the great burrow, lapping softly around the great nest, and the babies snuffled and yawned and slipped quickly into sleep.

Mumpo complained that his head felt funny. Then he looked at the sleeping babies, and gave an enormous yawn, and said he might sit down for a moment. Before they could stop him, he had curled up on the rugs among the babies, and he, too, was fast asleep.

Within a surprisingly short time, silence reigned—if silence it can be called when the air is rippled by hundreds of tiny breaths. Then the old lady who had first spoken to the twins turned to them and beckoned them, and they made their way to the farther end of the colonnaded room.

As they went, she told them that her name was Queen Num, and they mustn't think that the babies usually spent the night at the palace. On ordinary days the Queens looked after the babies during the day only, but tonight it was harvest night, and the people stayed up late feasting. Kestrel said it was strange to have Queens looking after babies, and Queen Num laughed and said, "Why, what else are Queens good for? We'm too old to work in the fields, you know."

At the far end of the great underground hall they found a little group of even older ladies, sitting in a circle of armchairs round a fire, staring vacantly into space. One of these was so very old that she really did seem to be almost dead. It was to this one that Queen Num led the children.

"Are you awake, dear?" she said, speaking very clearly. And to the children, "This is the Old Queen. She doesn't hear very well."

There was a moment of silence, then a cross little voice emerged from the withered face.

"Of course I'm awake. I haven't slept in years. I wish I could."

"I know, dear. Very trying for you."

"What would you know about it?"

"There's some young skinnies come to see you, dear. They want to ask you some questions."

"Not riddles, is it?" said the peevish voice. She hadn't shown any sign of seeing the children, though they stood directly before her. "Riddles bore me."

"I don't think it's riddles," said Queen Num. "I think it's memories."

"Oh, memories." The Old Queen sounded disgusted. "Too many of them." Suddenly her birdlike eyes fixed on Kestrel, who was the nearest. "I'm a thousand years old. You believe that?"

"Well, not really," said Kestrel.

"Quite right. It's a lie." And she burst into a cackle of slow dry laughter. Then the laughter faded away, and her face set once more into disagreeable lines. "You can go now," she said.

"Please, dear, won't you talk to them just a little?" said Queen Num. "They have come a long way."

"More fools them. They should have stayed at home."

She shut her eyes, screwing them up tight. Queen Num turned to the twins with a helpless shrug.

"I'm sorry. When she gets like this, there's nothing we can do."

"Could I talk to her?" said Bowman.

"I don't think she'll answer you."

"It doesn't matter."

Bowman settled himself down on the ground beside her and closed his own eyes, and turned his mind towards the Old Queen. After a few moments, he began to feel the slow buzz of her thoughts, like winter flies. He felt her angry mutterings, and faraway regrets, and beneath it all, a dull, bone-aching weariness. And then, waiting patiently, reaching deeper and deeper, he came upon a region of fear that was dark and silent as night. And there—suddenly he felt it—was a hole, an emptiness, a nothingness, that opened into terror.

Without realising he was doing it, he cried out loud.

"Aah! Horrible!"

"What is it?" said Kestrel anxiously.

"She's going to die." Bowman was whispering, his voice shaking. "It's so close now, and so horrible! I never knew dying was like that."

At this, the Old Queen spoke, more to herself than to Bowman.

"Too tired to live," she said, her creaky voice breaking in what could have been amusement. "Too afraid to die."

And as she spoke, tears began to stream down her withered cheeks. She opened her eyes and gazed on Bowman.

"Ah, skinny, little skinny," she said, "how did you creep into my heart?"

Bowman wept, too, not out of sadness, but because for the moment the two of them were joined. The Old Queen raised her thin trembling arms, and knowing what she wanted, Bowman climbed onto her chair and let her fold him in a fragile embrace. She pressed her wet cheeks to his face, and their tears mingled.

"You'm a little thief," she murmured. "You'm a little heart thief."

Kestrel watched, proud and full of wonder. Even though she was Bowman's twin and sometimes felt as close to him as if they shared the same body, she didn't understand this trick he had of going into people's feelings. But she loved him for it.

"There, there," said the Old Queen, soothing herself and Bowman together. "No use crying over it."

Queen Num looked on, awestruck.

"My dear," she said. "Oh, my dear."

"Nothing to be done," said the Old Queen, stroking Bowman's mud-encrusted hair. "Nothing to be done."

"Please," said Bowman. "Will you help us?"

"What use is an old lady like me, little skinny?"

"Tell us about—" He hesitated, and caught Kestrel's silent warning. "About the one you don't name."

"Ah, so that's it."

She stroked him some more in silence. Then she began to speak, in a faraway, remembering kind of voice.

"They say the nameless one is sleeping, and must never be woken, because . . . There was a reason, but I forget. All long, long ago. Ah! Wait! I remember now. . . ."

Her eyes widened in memory of a long-forgotten fear.

"They march, and they kill, and they march on. No pity. No escape. Oh, my dears, let me die before the Zars come again."

She stared into the shadowy space before her, sitting up stiff with terror, as if she could see them coming even now.

"The Zars! Oh, my little skinnies!" said the Old Queen, trembling. "All these long years, and I had forgotten till now. My grandmother told me such tales of terror. It was her grandmother saw the last march of the Zars—oh, pity, pity! Better we all die than the Zars march again."

She began to breathe with difficulty, showing signs of distress. Queen Num stepped forward.

"That's enough, my dear. You rest now."

"We know how to make the wind singer sing again," said Kestrel.

"Ah . . ." The Old Queen seemed to become calmer when she heard this. "The wind singer . . . If I could hear the song of the wind singer, I'd not be afraid. . . ."

Kestrel took out the map and unrolled it for the Old Queen to see.

"This is where we have to go," she said. "Only we don't understand it."

The Old Queen took the map and peered at it with watery eyes. Several times as she studied it, she sighed, as if for the lost days of long ago.

"Where did you get this, little one?"

"From the Emperor."

"Emperor! Tchah! Emperor of what, I'd like to know."

"Do you understand it?"

"Understand it? Yes, oh yes . . ."

She raised one trembling wrinkled finger, and traced the path on the yellowed paper.

"This is what they called the Great Way. . . . Ah, it was fine once! There were giants to guide you. I saw them, when I was a little girl. . . ."

The bony finger moved on.

"Just the one bridge over the ravine. Over the—the—what was it called? Oh, perish it, I hate growing old!"

"Crack-in-the-land," said Kestrel.

"That's it! How did you know that?"

"My father can read old Manth."

"Can he? There's not many left can do that. He must be even older than me. Crack-in-the-land, there, you see. You must follow the Great Way, because it leads to the only bridge. . . ."

Her voice faded.

"You're getting tired, my dear," said Queen Num. "You should rest."

"Time enough to rest, soon enough," came the murmured reply.

"And what happens after that?" asked Bowman.

"After that, there's the mountain. . . . There's fire. . . . There's the one we don't name. . . . There's going into the fire, but there's no coming out. . . ."

"Why not? What would it do to us?"

"What does it do to all the world, little skinnies? It steals your loving heart."

"We have no choice," said Kestrel in a low voice. "We have to make the wind singer sing again, or the unkindness will never end."

The Old Queen opened her eyes and squinted at her.

"The unkindness will never end. . . . You're right there. Well, well, maybe this is how it's to be. . . . You'd best put the skinnies on the path to the uplands, Num. Help them in any way you can. Send our love after them. Do you hear me?"

"Yes, dear."

The Old Queen's voice sank to an exhausted murmur.

"If it must come, it must come," she said. And they were the last words she spoke before falling into a shallow, dream-tossed sleep.

Queen Num indicated to the visitors that they should leave and took them to another part of the palace, where there was a late supper laid out.

"Nothing to be done till morning," she said in her sensible way.

She showed them an empty space where they could lie down after they had eaten. She herself was proposing to pass the night in a chair, watching over the sleeping babies.

"I never sleep on harvest nights," she said. "I just sit and watch till morning. It does my heart good, watching the sleeping babies."

The twins knelt down on the rug-strewn floor, and there, before settling down for the night, they made a small wish huddle. It all felt sad and wrong without the broad arms of their parents, and without their little sister's hot breath on their faces, but it was better than nothing, and it reminded them of home.

Kestrel laid her brow against her brother's brow and

made her wish first, speaking very quietly in the sleepy, soft-breathing room.

"I wish we might find the wind singer's voice and come quickly home."

Bowman then made his wish.

"I wish Ma and Pa and Pinpin are safe and not sad that we're away and know that somehow we'll come back again."

Then they curled up in each other's arms to go to sleep.

"Kess," whispered Bowman. "Are you afraid?"

"Yes," whispered Kestrel back. "But whatever happens, we'll be together."

"I won't mind if you're with me."

And so at last they slept.

CHAPTER THIRTEEN

THE HATH FAMILY PUNISHED

IRA HATH HAD NOT SLEPT SINCE THE TWINS HAD VANISHED. That night, alone with Pinpin in their one room in Grey District, she had put her to bed as usual, and had then sat up late into the night, expecting to hear a soft tap at the door. They were hiding somewhere in the city, she knew, and would surely make their way to her under cover of darkness. But they did not come.

The next morning she had a visit from two stern-faced marshals, who asked her many questions about the twins and warned her that she must report them as soon as they came home. This visit gave her new hope. Clearly they had not been caught. She now realised they would not have dared to approach their new apartment, in case it too was being watched. So she decided to go out into the district and show herself, in the hope that they might see her from their hiding place, and send her a message.

As soon as she stepped out onto the street with Pinpin by her side, she found every passerby stared at her in an angry sneering sort of way. None of them approached her, or spoke to her. They just stared, and sneered.

There was a bakery nearby, and she went into it to buy some corn cakes for their breakfast. The baker's wife also stared, in the same insolent manner, and said as she handed over the cakes, "I don't suppose they eat corn cakes in Orange."

"Why do you say that?" said Ira, surprised.

"Oh, they'll have fancy cakes in Orange," said the baker's wife, tossing her fringe out of her eyes. "Quite a comedown for you, I'm sure."

Out in the street she found that a little crowd of grey-clothed neighbours had gathered, all hissing and clucking together like chickens. One of them, the mother from a family that lived on the same passage, suddenly dashed forward and said sharply, "No use putting on airs round here. Grey's good enough for us, so it's good enough for you."

Only then did Ira Hath realise that in all the bustle and stress of the removal, she had forgotten to change her clothing. Both she and Pinpin were still wearing orange.

Another neighbour called out, "We've reported you! You'll be in trouble now, and serve you right."

"I forgot," said Ira.

"Oh, she forgot! Thought she was still in Orange!"

"She's no better than us. Not with children running wild in the streets like rats."

"Look at her poor little mite! It's wrong, that's what it is."

Pinpin began to cry. Ira Hath looked from face to face and saw on them all the same expression of hatred.

"I don't think I'm better than you," she said. "I'm on my own for now, and it's not easy."

This was in its way a plea for sympathy, but she spoke in such a calm voice that it only enraged her neighbours more.

"Whose fault is that?" said Mrs. Mooth, the one from down the passage. "Your husband should work harder, shouldn't he? You don't get anything for nothing in this world."

O unhappy people, thought Ira Hath within herself. But she said no more. She hoisted the crying Pinpin into her arms and made her way back up three flights of stairs, and along the gloomy passage to Number 318, Block 29, Grey District, the single room that was now their home.

She had not spoken back to her neighbours, but as she closed the door behind her and put Pinpin down, her heart was blazing with anger. She missed her husband desperately, she was frantic with worry about the twins, and she hated the people of Grey District with a terrible burning hatred.

She sat down on the bed, which filled half the room, and stared out of the small window at Block 28 across the road. The buildings were made of grey concrete. The walls of her room were unpainted grey cement. The single curtain was grey. The door was grey. The only colour in the room came from the orange clothes she wore, and the striped bedspread she had brought with her from Orange District, on which she was now sitting.

"O my dear ones," she said aloud. "Please come home. . . ."

At about this time, Hanno Hath was sitting at his desk alongside the forty-two other candidates, as they were termed, in the main seminar room of the Residential Study Centre, listening to Principal Pillish telling them that he was only there to help them.

"You have all performed poorly in the High Examination in the past," he intoned, in the kind of voice always used by people who have said the same thing in the same words many times before. "You have all let yourselves down and let your families down, and you are all very sorry. Now you are here to put it all right again, and I am here to help you. But most of all, you are here to help yourselves, because the only way to better your unhappy condition is by hard work."

He clapped his hands sharply together to emphasise this most important point, and repeated, "Hard work!"

He took up four brown-backed books.

"The High Examination is not especially difficult. Its questions are wide-ranging. It does not favour only those with natural aptitude. It favours those who work hard."

He held up the brown books one by one.

"Calculation. Grammar. General Science. General Art. Everything you need to know for the High Examination is in these four study books. Read. Remember. Repeat. That is all you have to do. Read. Remember. Repeat."

Hanno Hath heard none of this. His mind was entirely occupied with fears for his family. During the midmorning break, he walked round the high-walled yard, trying to calm himself and think clearly. He had heard nothing since he left home. That seemed to suggest that Kestrel had not been caught, but was still in hiding somewhere in the city. If so, it was surely only a matter of time, for there was no way she could get out of Aramanth.

The tormenting thoughts went round and round in his brain, following the circular course of his walk, until the sound of low sobbing broke through to him and brought him to a stop. One of the other candidates, a small man with thinning grey hair, was standing with his face to the wall, weeping.

Hanno approached him.

"What is it?"

"Oh, nothing," said the man, and he dabbed at his eyes. "Sometimes I just can't stop myself."

"Is it because of the High Examination?"

The little man nodded. "I do try. But as soon as I sit down at my desk, everything I've ever learned goes clean out of my head."

His name was Miko Mimilith. He was a tailor who lived with his family in Maroon District. He worked hard, he said, and he was good at his job, but the annual High Examination was a terror to him.

"I'll be forty-seven years old this year," he said. "I've sat the High Examination twenty-five times. It's always the same."

"Can you answer any of the questions?"

"I can do the calculations, some of them, if I don't get too flustered. But that's all."

"Then you're lucky." This came from a youngish man with fair hair who had overheard their conversation. "I wish I could do calculations. Now, if they'd only ask me about butterflies, I could tell them a thing or two."

"Or cloud formations," put in a third man.

"I know every butterfly that's ever been seen in Aramanth," said the fair young man earnestly. "And one that's not been seen for thirty years and more."

"Ask me a question about clouds," said the third man, not to be outdone. "Give me the wind strength, the wind direction, and the air temperature, and I'll tell you where the rain will fall, and when."

"What I'd like," said little Miko Mimilith, stroking the air with his delicate fingers, "is questions about fabrics. Fine cotton, cool linen, warm wool tweeds. I know them all. You could blindfold me and touch the tip of my little finger to a swatch of cloth, and I could tell you what it is, and most likely where it was woven."

Hanno Hath looked from one to the other, and saw how the dulled listless look had gone from their eyes, and how they held their heads high and butted in on each other in their eagerness to speak.

"Oh, but wouldn't it be grand," said the cloud man with a long sigh, "if we could be tested on what we really know."

"Maybe we should be," said Hanno Hath.

Before he could explain further, the voice of Principal Pillish came booming across the yard.

"Candidate Hath! Report to the Principal's office."

Hanno entered the book-lined room to find Principal

Pillish in conversation with the Chief Examiner himself, Maslo Inch.

"Ah, here he is," said Principal Pillish. "Should I absent myself?"

"No need," said Maslo Inch. He turned his cold smile on to Hanno. "Well, my old friend. I hate to break in on your studies. But no doubt you want to know what has become of your children."

Hanno said nothing to this, but his heart began to beat hard.

"The news is not good. They were seen entering the Underlake yesterday around noon. They have not emerged. I fear there can be very little hope that they are still alive."

He was watching Hanno closely as he spoke, and Hanno kept his expression as blank as he could, but inside, hope had suddenly blossomed.

There was daylight down there, he told himself. *Kess saw it. They're on their way.*

He felt a surge of pride in his beloved children, that they had dared to set out on such a dangerous journey. But this was followed immediately by a chill of dread.

Keep them safe, he said, as if there was someone or something out there to whom he could appeal. They're so young. Watch over them.

"You have only yourself to blame, my friend."

"Yes," said Hanno. "I see that now."

The Chief Examiner had brought him this news in person because he wanted to punish him. Hanno understood that well enough. He let his head droop low, hoping he looked chastened. He didn't want to arouse any suspicions.

"You have one child remaining to you. As yet, she is too young to have been damaged by your poor example. My advice to you is to apply yourself from this moment on. Let this unfortunate business teach you the value of discipline, proper ambition, and plain hard work."

"Hard work," echoed Principal Pillish reverently.

"I will see to it that your wife is informed."

"She'll be very distressed," said Hanno in a low voice. "Might I be allowed to tell her myself?"

The Chief Examiner looked to the Principal.

"I think a short interview might be permitted, under the circumstances," he said.

Ira Hath was wearing sober grey when she was escorted into the visiting room of the Residential Study Centre. Hanno was waiting for her, also wearing grey. Principal Pillish watched the encounter, as it was his duty to do, through a closed window. He was gratified to see that there was much sobbing and embracing by the bereaved couple. What he did not hear were the words they said to each other, which struck a very different note. Now that they had reason to believe the twins had escaped, they were filled with new courage. Bowman and Kestrel were risking everything to break the grim power that was crushing their lives. They could do no less.

"I'm going to fight back," said Hanno.

"So am I," said his wife. "And I know how."

CHAPTER FOURTEEN

RETURN OF THE OLD CHILDREN

WHEN BOWMAN AND KESTREL WOKE, THEY FOUND all the mud babies were gone, and Mumpo was up and full of bounce, having eaten a large breakfast. An escort of mudmen arrived to guide them out of the Underlake. Among them was Willum, looking very grey and sorry for himself.

"Hard work, harvest," he mumbled to no one in particular. "Leaves a body well wore out."

"We're going on an adventure," Mumpo announced. "Kess is my friend."

The sun was already beaming down through the roof-holes, so the twins ate quickly, and made their farewells. Queen Num patted them, and looked unexpectedly sad as she handed them the nut-socks she'd filled for their journey.

"There's two socks for each of you, which is all you'll want to carry. You'm be careful, little skinnies. 'Tis a cruel dry world up yonder."

They tied the heavy nut-socks together in pairs and hung them round their necks, as the mudmen did. The dangling mudnuts bumped against their chests and stomachs as they walked, but they soon grew used to this, and found it comforting.

They departed from the palace accompanied by an escort about twenty strong. As they marched along the ever-lightening trail, others joined them, and more and more, until in time there were over a hundred mudpeople swinging along behind.

"We're the three friends, we're the three friends," sang Mumpo, until Kestrel told him to shut up.

The land rose almost imperceptibly, and the mud hardened underfoot, the nearer they approached to the mouth of the great salt cave that contained the Underlake. After a while they began to feel a cool breeze on their faces, and the silver stone of the cavern roof seemed to grow brighter as the light strengthened.

Their first sight of the cave mouth was no more than a strip of burning brightness far ahead. But as they drew closer, walking now on moist but firm sand, they saw that the cave narrowed to a span of barely half a mile, and arched downwards, to form an overhead lip no higher than the topmost branches of a tall tree. Beyond the cave, the brightness was now taking shape, revealing an expanse of sandy plain beneath a deep blue sky.

When the marching column at last reached the point where direct sunlight fell on the hard earth, they came to a halt, keeping themselves well in the realm of shadows. The children understood that from this point onwards they were to proceed alone.

"Thank you," they said. "Thank you for looking after us."

"We'll sing for you," said Willum. "To see you on your way."

As they set off, the mudpeople raised their hands in a gesture of farewell, and then they started to sing. It was a sweet, soft farewell song—no words, just wave upon wave of melody.

"It's their love," said Kestrel, remembering what the Old Queen had said. "They're sending it after us."

As the children made their way out of the mouth of the salt cave and up onto the dusty plains, the song of the mudpeople followed them, warm and loving like the burrows in which they slept. And then it came fainter on the breeze, and fainter, until at last they could hear the song no more, and they knew they were alone.

After the protective shadows of the Underlake, the plains across which they now walked seemed to be without limits. Only to the north, far, far away, could they make out the pale grey line of the mountains. Then as the sun climbed higher, the heat haze rising up from the baked earth melted the horizon into the sky, sealing them in a featureless shimmering world in which they were the only living creatures. For a little while they could see, if they turned their heads, the long dark mouth of the cave out of which they had come, but then that, too, was swallowed up by the dusty air and the distance, and they were without any sense of direction at all.

They tramped northward in what they supposed was a straight line, hoping to come upon some signs of the high road called the Great Way. The wind was picking up, skittering the sand, making the land shiver. Bowman and Kestrel didn't speak, but they could sense each other's anxiety. Mumpo alone was without a care, as he followed behind Kestrel, planting his feet in her footsteps, calling out, "I'm like you, Kess! We're the same!"

The wind grew stronger, lifting more sand into the air, dulling the brightness of the sky. Walking became difficult, because the sand stung their faces, and they had to twist their heads away from the wind. Then through the blurred air ahead of them there loomed a low square structure, like a hut without a roof, and they turned their steps towards it to take shelter.

Close up against it, they saw that it was some kind of wagon, lying on its side. Its axles were broken, and its wheels lay half buried. Sand had piled up against the windward side, but on the lee there was a protected space where they could huddle out of the wind. Here they untied their nut-socks and ate a much-needed lunch of roasted mudnuts.

The smoky taste brought back images of the harvest and the cheery faces of the mudpeople, and made them wish they were back in the comfortable burrows of the Underlake. While the wind remained so strong there was no point in struggling on, so Kestrel took out the map, and she and Bowman studied it.

There were no landmarks in the desert, only the position of the sun in the sky to tell them where north was, and perhaps a distant sight of the mountains; but somehow they must find the Great Way, or what was left of it.

"The Old Queen said it had giants."

"That was long ago. There aren't any giants nowadays."

"We'd better just keep going north. As soon as the storm passes."

Kestrel looked up from the map, and saw Mumpo watching her and grinning.

"What are you so pleased about, Mumpo?"

"Nothing."

Then she saw both his nut-socks lying empty before him.

"I don't believe it! Have you eaten all of them?"

"Most of them," admitted Mumpo.

"You have! There's none left!"

Mumpo picked up the empty nut-socks and gazed at them in surprise.

"None left," he said, as if someone else had taken them.

"You great pongo! That was supposed to last you for days and days."

"Sorry, Kess," said Mumpo. But his stomach was full, and he felt very happy and didn't look sorry at all.

Bowman turned to studying the wagon against which they were sheltering, and the pieces of debris lying around. Apart from the wheels, which were surprisingly large and very slender, there were broken sections of long thick pole, and fragments of cloth and netting, and strands of rope—all very like the wreck of a sailing ship. He got up and walked round the wreck, squinting his eyes against the stinging sand, and saw where the masts had been fixed to the wagon's bed, and realised that it had been a land-sailer of some kind. Back in the shelter of the craft, he dug about in the wind-heaped sand and found a pulley-wheel, and then a leather drive-belt, and he almost cut open his hands unearthing two long iron blades. It was clear that the craft had carried machinery. But what had the machinery been designed to do?

Because for the moment he had no better way to occupy

himself, and because his mind worked that way, Bowman began to reconstruct the craft in his mind out of the pieces he could see lying around. It had two masts, that was clear enough; and it must have ridden very high on its four immense wheels. The prow looked as if it had once narrowed to a ramlike prong. On either side there had been arms, stout timber beams reaching outwards; and hanging from them, still visible in a fragmentary form, there were nets. The land-sailer must have been designed to sweep across the plains, arms outstretched, nets trailing, entangling and carrying away—what?

As if looking for an answer, he gazed out into the storm. And as he looked, he thought he saw something that hadn't been there before. He strained his eyes to make out the moving shape far off in the swirling haze of sand. Now he saw two shapes. Now there were three. Dim figures, slowly approaching. His heart began to beat fast.

"Kess," he said. "Someone coming."

Kestrel put away the map and looked out into the wind. They were quite easy to see now, a line of dark forms against the dull sky. She looked round and saw others to the side of them. And behind.

"It's them," said Bowman. "I know it."

"Who?" said Mumpo.

"The old children."

Mumpo at once started to jig about from foot to foot, waving his arms.

"Then I'll give them another bashing!" he cried.

"Don't let them touch you, Mumpo!" Kestrel's warning rang sharp over the sound of the wind. "Something happens when they touch you. Keep out of their reach."

The dim figures kept coming closer, shuffle shuffle shuffle, through the sandstorm, all round the wrecked land-sailer against which the children huddled. A voice now came to them out of the wind, deep and soothing, like before.

"Remember us? We're your little helpers."

And from all around came the low rumble of their laughter.

"You can't get away from us, you know that. So why don't you come home with us now?"

Mumpo danced about, punching the air.

"I'm Kess's friend," he cried. "You come any nearer and I'll bash you!"

Bowman looked around for some sort of weapon with which to fend them off. He pulled at a half-buried section of broken mast, but it wouldn't move. The old children were close enough now for their faces to be visible, those eery wrinkled faces that were ancient and childlike at the same time. Their shrivelled hands started now to reach out towards them, ready for the touch.

"Or shall we stroke you to sleep?" said the deep voice. "Stroke, stroke, stroke, and you wake up old, like us."

The rest of them laughed at that, and their low cackling laughter was swept up by the wind and carried round and round in the roaring air.

We'll have to run for it, said Kestrel silently to Bowman. *Can you see a gap in the circle?*

No. They're all round us.

There's no other way. I'm sure we can run faster than them.

All the time, the old children were coming closer, shuffle shuffle shuffle, tightening the ring around them.

"Bubba-bubba-kak!" shouted Mumpo, punching the air. "You want a squashed nose?"

If Mumpo hits one of them, we could run through the gap.

But what about Mumpo?

Even as Bowman sent this thought, Mumpo bounced forward and biffed one of the old children on the nose. At once he fell back, wailing miserably.

"Kess! Kess!"

Kestrel caught him as he collapsed, whimpering, in her arms.

"I've gone wrong, Kess. Help me."

The old children giggled, and their leader said, "Time to come home now. You've missed too many lessons already. Think of your ratings."

"No!" shouted Kestrel. "I'd rather die right here!"

"Oh, you won't die," said the deep soothing voice, moving closer. "You'll just grow old."

There was no way out. Terrified, Bowman closed his eyes and waited for the dry, bony hands to touch him. He heard their footsteps as they shuffled ever closer. Then, over the moaning of the wind, he heard a new sound, the sound of a horn, rising and falling like a siren, approaching at great speed.

Suddenly the sound was on top of them, accompanied by a tremendous crashing and snapping and creaking, and out of the storm, driven by the wild wind, there swept a high-wheeled land-sailer, its outstretched arms trailing a skirt of flying nets. Kestrel saw it and knew what she must do. In the instant before it passed, she seized Bowman's wrist in one hand, and Mumpo's in the other, and threw all three of them into its path. Almost at once, the nets struck them and swept them away. Entangled in the heavy mesh, they were hurled along in the storm, racing before the wind at heart-stopping speed, over the sand-blind plain.

As soon as she had regained her breath, Kestrel started to climb the net to the supporting arm. Clinging on here, in the rushing air, she was able to look about her. She could see Mumpo below, caught like a wild animal, both legs through the netting, hanging upside down and

screaming. Bowman had righted himself, and was now following her lead and pulling himself up the net. It wasn't
easy, because the land-sailer was travelling so fast that
every rut and stone in the ground over which it passed
made it buck and lurch, and all the time the stinging sand
was whistling by. The horn on the mast-top wailed like a
banshee, and at the outer ends of the projecting timber
arms, huge scythelike blades rotated at speed, making a
fearful hissing, screeching sound.

Kestrel looked into the well of the craft and saw that it was
unmanned. She looked for a tiller or steering mechanism,
hoping to steer them out of the wind, but she could see
none. The land-sailer was completely out of control: any
large rocks or trees in its headlong path, and it would crash
at full speed, smashing them along with itself. Somehow she
had to slow the craft down.

"You all right?" she called to Bowman.

"Yes. I think so."

"Get Mumpo into the ship. I'm going to cut the sails."

He turned at once and climbed down to Mumpo. Chivvied
by Bowman, Mumpo managed to right himself and follow
him up the net. Once inside the craft, the two of them held
tight to the masts as the land-sailer thundered on its way.

Kestrel found the anchorage for the mainsail and started
to unwind the rope. A sudden savage lurch threw her clear

of the craft, but she was holding tight to the rope, and swung crashing back against the timber side. Hand over hand, she pulled herself up again, and braced herself against the timbers once more, and loosed the mainsail. She meant the whole sail to fly free, to cut their frantic speed, but only one side came undone. The sail veered sharply, forcing the craft onto two wheels. For a few crazy moments, the land-sailer hurtled along with two wheels in the air, the blade on the lower side thrashing the sand. Then the blade locked, and the craft cartwheeled into the air, spun over itself and over again, tumbling and somersaulting, impelled by the sheer force with which it had been travelling. As it rolled, the great blades snapped and the masts broke and the wheels smashed, but the heavily built chassis to which the children clung remained intact. When at last the battered craft came tumbling to a rest, the children found that although their bodies hurt all over, and they were struggling for breath, they were still alive, and none of their bones were broken.

They lay in silence, feeling their wildly beating hearts gradually settle into a more even rhythm. The storm still raged, but the horn was silent, and the machinery of the land-sailer had come to a stop. All that remained was the clap-clap-clap of grounded sails snapping in the wind. Once again they were sheltered in the lee of a crashed craft.

There was nothing to do but lie there and wait for the wind-storm to pass.

Worn out by the terror of the old children and the violence of their escape, all three of them fell into a fitful sleep, in which their bodies felt as if they were still careering wildly across the plains in the runaway land-sailer. Dream and memory mingled with the howling wind, and in sleep they were tumbled over and over, and they awoke crying out loud and holding on to each other for dear life.

As the confusion of daytime sleep passed, they realised that a great silence had fallen all around them. The storm was over. The wind had dropped to a breeze. The air had cleared, and above them, when they crept out from under the crashed land-sailer, the sky was a brilliant blue. Now for the first time since they had left the salt caves, they were able to see for a long way in every direction.

They were in the middle of a featureless sandy plain made up of low undulations as far as the eye could see. To the north, the line of mountains rose up on the horizon. Apart from that, there was nothing by which the traveller could orient himself. The mountains were nearer, but still many days' walk away. They had enough food left to last them for perhaps one more day, if they were careful. What after that?

"We go on," said Kestrel. "Something will happen."

The sun was descending in the sky; no point in continuing

their journey today. So she took out her supply of mudnuts.

Mumpo at once announced that he was hungry, as she had known he would.

"We all had the same amount, Mumpo."

"But mine's all gone."

"I'm sorry about that," said Kestrel. "But you're not having any of mine."

"But I'm hungry."

"You should have thought of that before."

She was determined to make him learn the lesson, and so she ate her mudnuts in proud silence. Mumpo sat and watched her, like a sad, faithful dog.

"It's no use looking like that, Mumpo. You've had yours and now I'm having mine."

"But I'm hungry."

"Too late now, isn't it?"

He started to weep, in a quiet dribbly sort of way. After a few moments, Bowman pulled out one of his mudnuts and gave it to him.

"Thank you, Bo," said Mumpo, cheering up at once.

Kestrel watched him eating it and felt annoyed. Her brother's kindness made her feel cross with herself.

"You really are useless, Mumpo," she said.

"Yes, Kess."

"We've got a long way to go, you know."

"No, I don't," he said simply. "I don't know where we're going."

It was true: they had never taken the time to tell him. Bowman suddenly felt ashamed.

"Show him the map, Kess."

Kestrel unrolled the map and explained their journey as best as she could. Mumpo listened quietly, watching Kestrel's eyes. When she was finished, he said, "Are you afraid, Kess?"

"Yes."

"I'll help you. I'm not afraid."

"Why aren't you afraid, Mumpo?" asked Bowman.

"What is there to be afraid of? Here we are, the three friends. The storm's gone away. We've had our supper. Everything's all right."

"But don't you worry about what might happen to us later?"

"How can I? I don't know what's going to happen until it happens."

Bowman looked at Mumpo curiously. Maybe he wasn't so stupid after all. Maybe—

He froze. Kestrel sensed his fear at once.

"What is it, Bo?"

"Can't you hear it?"

She listened, and she heard: a far-off thunder. They all turned their eyes to the near horizon.

"Something's coming. Something big."

CHAPTER FIFTEEN

PRISONERS OF OMBARAKA

OUT OF THE DUNES, A FLAG HAD APPEARED AND WAS moving towards the children. A red-and-white flag high on a flagpole, flapping in the breeze. Whatever supported the flagpole was out of sight, on the other side of a rise in the land, but they knew it was heading towards them, because the flagpole was rising higher all the time.

Soon they saw that it wasn't a flagpole at all, but a mast, because now a sail was coming into view. They crept into the hull of the crashed land-sailer, so as not to be seen by whoever was approaching, and from this hiding place they went on watching.

The one sail became many, ranged in a long line of masts, smaller sails at the top, larger sails beneath. Now they

could see the superstructure of the craft, an elaborate housing
lined with windows and crossed with walkways. There were
people on the walkways, running about, though too far away
to identify. Still the craft was rising, as it climbed slowly out of
the hollow, and now they could hear its noise clearly: a huge
low rumble. More sails were appearing, on lower masts, below
the level of the walkways. And then a second level of superstructure loomed over the sand, far wider than the first, a
higgledy-piggledy collection of shacks and shelters linked by
rope bridges and wooden passages. Crowds of people were
milling about here, and now that they were nearer they could
be heard shouting instructions to each other. They wore long
flowing robes, and moved about with agility, swinging themselves from level to level, their robes ballooning about them.

The low sun caught the flank of the giant craft as it creaked
and clambered up the rise, its myriad sails puffing in the
breeze. Now as the children watched in fearful wonder, a third
level of wooden buildings loomed up into view. This level was
far more elaborately constructed, a classical sequence of houses
with beautifully carved windows and handsome porticoes,
gathered around three pillared open-sided halls. The great
masts rose up through these buildings, and up through the
two farther levels above, all the way to the highest sails and the
flags at the very top. And still the vast structure was growing in
size, as it crested the rise towards the crashed land-sailer. Its

noise was deafening now, a groaning and a rattling and a creaking that seemed to fill the whole world. Already it towered high above, filling the sky. Now the wheels on which it moved became visible, each one higher than a house. And between the wheels there was yet another level, of storerooms and manu-factories and farmyards and smithies, all joined by winding gangplanks and internal roads. This was no land-ship—this was a town on wheels, a whole rolling wind-driven world.

For all its colossal size, the mountainous craft was being steered with great accuracy directly towards the crashed land-sailer. The children could do nothing but crouch inside and hope they would not be crushed by the passing of the juggernaut. But it did not pass. As its shadow fell over them, they heard a new series of cries ring out from level to level, and the hundred sails were reefed in, and the monster shuddered and rolled to a halt, its nearest wheels within a few yards of where the children lay.

More commands were issued. A long timber crane arm came swinging out from a level high above, and from its end there descended a pair of massive iron jaws. The men work-ing the beam and tackle were skilled at their job. Before the children realised what was going on, the jaws had closed about the land-sailer, and with a great jerk, they felt them-selves being hoisted up into the sky.

As they rose up and up, they saw people on the mother

craft pointing towards them and gesticulating. The crane arm now swung inwards, and the smashed land-sailer was lowered with shuddering jerks down a well in the upper decks, to a lower deck. Already the order to move on had been given, the sails had been unfurled, and the whole huge edifice was juddering on its way. As the land-sailer hit the deck, the children saw a ring of ferocious-looking men waiting on every side, their arms folded before them. They all looked alike: they were tall and bearded, they wore sand-coloured robes cinched by leather belts, and their long hair was tied in hundreds of narrow braids, each one of which had plaited into it a brightly coloured thread.

"Out!" commanded one of the men.

The children climbed out. At once they were seized and held.

"Chaka spies!" said the commander, and spat contemptuously onto the deck. "Saboteurs!"

"Please, sir—" began Kestrel.

"Silence!" screamed the commander. "Chaka scum! You don't speak until I tell you to speak!"

He turned to the land-sailer. Some of his men were inspecting it to assess the damage.

"Is the corvette destroyed?"

"Yes, sir."

"Lock them up! They'll hang for this!"

He strode away, followed by a gaggle of his subordinates. Bowman, Kestrel, and Mumpo were pushed towards a cage on the side of the deck. Their guards came into the cage with them and called out, "Down! All the way!" The cage was then lowered, running between vertical timber rails, to the lowest level. As they descended, the guards glared at the children with hatred and open disgust.

The cage bumped to a stop, and the children were marched down a dark passage to a barred door. A rough push sent them tumbling into what was all too clearly a prison cell. The door closed behind them, and they could hear the sounds of a big key being turned in the lock.

The cell was empty, not even a bench to sit on. It had one window, which looked out to an exercise yard. As the children stood up, and looked around them, and took stock of their new situation, they heard the sound of marching feet. Through the window they saw a troop of bearded robed men lining up in the yard. The men's leader barked out an order, and they all drew long swords and held them out before them.

"Kill the Chaka spies!" he cried.

"Kill the Chaka spies!" cried all his men.

There followed a sequence of violent cries and gestures, which seemed to be a war dance. The leader called out on a rising note, "Baraka!" and the men struck the air with their swords and howled back at the tops of their voices, "Raka ka!

ka! ka!" and "Kill the Chaka spies!" This was repeated many
times, louder and more violently each time, until the men
were stamping and red-faced with passionate fury, ready to
fight anything and everything.

Kestrel and Bowman watched this with mounting dismay,
but Mumpo followed the war dance with admiration. Most
of all, he was struck by their hair.

"Do you see how they do it?" he said, fingering his own
lank locks. "They wind red and blue string into each plait.
And green and yellow. And every colour."

"Shut up, Mumpo."

The lock rattled, and the door opened to admit a man
who looked just like all the others, except that he was older
and somewhat stouter. He was breathing heavily and carried
a tray of food.

"Can't say I see the point," he said, putting the tray down
on the floor. "Seeing as you're to be hanged. But it's as the
Morah wills."

"The Morah!" exclaimed Kestrel. "You know about the
Morah?"

"And why wouldn't I?" said the guard. "The Morah
watches over all of us. Even me."

"To protect you?"

"Protect me!" He laughed at the idea. "Oh, yes, the
Morah protects me, all right. With storms and diseases, and

good milk cows dying for no reason. That's how the Morah protects me. Just you wait and see. Here you are, all bright and bonny, but tomorrow you'll be hanged. Oh, yes, the Morah watches over every one of us, all right."

The food was corn bread, cheese, and milk. Mumpo sat down and started eating at once. After a moment's hesitation, the twins followed suit, eating more slowly. Their guard stayed by the door, watching them suspiciously.

"You're small for spies," he observed.

"We're not spies," said Kestrel.

"You're Chaka scum, aren't you?"

"No, we're not."

"Are you telling me you're Barakas?"

"No—"

"Then if you're not Barakas, you're Chakas," said the guard simply. "That's what Chakas are."

Kestrel didn't know what to say to this.

"And we kill Chakas," added the guard.

"I like your hair," said Mumpo, who had now finished his food.

"Do you?"

The guard was taken by surprise, but it was evident he was pleased. He reached up and tugged carelessly at his braids.

"I'm trying greens and blues this week."

"Is it difficult to do?"

"I wouldn't say it's difficult. But getting the braids evenly spaced as well as tight—that takes a bit of practice."

"I bet you're good at it."

"I do have quite a deft hand," said the guard. "You're a bright young fellow, I must say. For a Chaka scum."

The twins followed this with astonishment. All the hostility had left the guard's voice.

"The blue's the same as your eyes," said Mumpo.

"Well, that was the idea," the guard admitted. "Most people like a touch of red, but I prefer the natural tones."

"I don't suppose you could do mine," said Mumpo wistfully. "I'd love to look like you."

The guard contemplated him thoughtfully.

"Well, I could," he said at last. "I mean, seeing as you're going to hang anyway, I don't see that it would make much difference. What colours would you like?"

"What colours have you got?"

"All of them. Any colour you please."

"Then I'd like all of them," said Mumpo.

"That's not very subtle, you know," said the guard. "But then, it is your first time."

The guard left them, locking the door behind him.

"Honestly, Mumpo!" said Kestrel. "How can you be thinking about your hair at a time like this?"

"What else is there to think about?" said Mumpo.

The guard reappeared, carrying a comb and a bag full of hanks of coloured string. He sat down cross-legged on the floor and set about braiding Mumpo's hair. As he worked away, he became almost friendly to them. His name was Salimba, and his normal job was being a cowman. He told them that Ombaraka, the huge rolling town in which they lived, carried a herd of more than a thousand cows, as well as a herd of goats and a flock of long-horned sheep. Kestrel took advantage of the guard's friendliness to discover more essential information. Who, for a start, were the Chakas?

Salimba took this question to be a trick.

"Ah, you don't catch me like that. Now, here's a fine rich purple. Your hair could do with a wash, you know."

"Yes, I know," said Mumpo.

"Are the Chakas the enemies of the Barakas?" pursued Kestrel.

"How can you ask me that? Enemies? You Chakas have butchered us without mercy for generations! You think we've forgotten the Massacre of the Crescent Moon? Or the murder of Raka the Fourth? Never! No Baraka will rest until every Chaka scum is dead!"

Salimba became so agitated that his hand slipped, and the braiding went wrong. Cursing, he undid the braid and started again.

Kestrel asked the same question, but in a more politic way.

"So Baraka will win in the end?"

"Of course," said Salimba. Every Baraka male over the age of sixteen, he explained, was drafted into the army and underwent daily military training. He gave a nod towards the yard outside, where the troop had just ended their round of exercises. They all had other jobs, he said, as sailmen or carpenters or fodder gatherers, but their first duty was always the defence of Ombaraka. When the battle horns sounded, every man would drop his work, gird on his sword, and report to his assigned station. They came eagerly, because more than anything else in the world, a true Baraka lived for the day when Omchaka would be destroyed. And that day would surely come, he said, as the Morah wills.

The braiding of Mumpo's hair took more than an hour, but when it was done it was a thing of glory. He still looked filthy, but from the eyebrows up, he was dazzling. His hair had been so matted with mud that when braided, it stuck out in stiff spikes. Salimba said that wasn't customary, but it did have a certain panache, and it was clear from the way he looked at Mumpo that he was rather proud of the result.

There was no mirror in the prison cell, and Mumpo was impatient to see his new look.

"What's it like? Do you like it, Kess? Do you?"

Kestrel truly didn't know what to say. It was mesmerising. He looked like a rainbow porcupine.

"You look completely different," she said.

"Is that good?"

"It's just—different."

Then Salimba remembered that the tray had a shiny underside. He held it up for Mumpo to get a blurry reflection of his new hair. Mumpo gazed at himself and sighed with pleasure.

"Thank you," he said. "I knew you'd be good at it."

The tramp of many footsteps in the passage outside brought guard and prisoners down to earth. There came a loud hammering on the door. Salimba hastily assumed a stern expression and unlocked the door.

"Prisoners, stand!" he yelled.

The children stood.

In came an elderly Baraka man with a long grey braided beard and long grey braided hair. Behind him, stiffly at attention, arms folded across their chests, stood a troop of a dozen soldiers. The grey-haired man looked in surprise at Mumpo, but chose not to comment on his colourful hair.

"I am Kemba, counsellor to Raka the Ninth, Warlord of the Barakas, Suzerain of Ombaraka, Commander-in-Chief of the Wind Warriors, and Ruler of the Plains," he announced. "Guard, leave us!"

"Yes, counsellor."

Salimba retreated, drawing the door closed behind him. Kemba went to the window and looked out, fingering his belt of coloured beads. Then he sighed, and turned round to face the children.

"Your presence here is profoundly inconvenient," he said. "But I suppose you must be hanged."

"We're not Chakas," said Kestrel.

"Of course you're Chakas. If you're not Barakas, you're Chakas. And we are at war with all Chakas, to the death."

"We're from Aramanth."

"Nonsense! Don't be absurd. You're Chakas, and you must hang."

"You can't hang us!" exclaimed Kestrel hotly.

"As it happens, you're quite right," said the counsellor, more to himself than to her. "We can't hang you, because of the treaty. But on the other hand, we can't possibly let you live. Oh, dear!" He sighed a long exasperated sigh. "This really is most profoundly inconvenient. Still, I shall think of something. I always do."

He clapped his hands to summon the troop outside.

"Door!"

And to the children, almost as an afterthought, "I have to take you before Raka. It's purely a formality. But all sentences of death have to be passed by Raka himself."

The door opened.

"Form escort!" commanded Kemba. "The prisoners will proceed at once to the court."

Closely guarded all the way, the children were marched across the base deck of the huge rolling edifice that was Ombaraka, to a central lift shaft. Here the lift cage was far bigger than the one in which they had been taken down, and easily held the entire troop escorting them. Up it creaked, carrying them past ladders and walkways, to the court deck. From the lift, their route took them across a handsome avenue and into one of the broad pillared halls. As they went, passersby stopped and stared and hissed with hatred, but when they saw Mumpo, they just gaped. Kestrel could hear their escort discussing Mumpo's braids in low voices. "Far too loud," one was saying. "All that orange! So vulgar."

"I wonder how he makes it stick out straight like that," said another. "Not that I'd want that for myself."

They marched right down the echoing open hall to the doors at the far end. The doors opened as they approached. Inside was a long room, dominated by a central table, the entire surface of which was a giant map. Round this table stood several important-looking men, scowling; among them were the commander who had witnessed the children emerging from the crashed land-sailer, and Tanaka, chief of the armed forces, a man with a red face etched all over with deep angry lines. When he saw Mumpo's new braids, he, too, gaped with surprise.

"What did I tell you?" he cried. "Now one of them's in Baraka disguise!"

The smallest of the men round the table came strutting forward, staring at the children with extreme hostility. Raka the Ninth, Warlord of the Barakas, Suzerain of Ombaraka, Commander-in-Chief of the Wind Warriors and Ruler of the Plains, had the misfortune to be short. He made up for his lack of stature by cultivating the most ferocious manner imaginable. His braids were the only ones in all Ombaraka to be threaded with tiny steel blades, which flashed in the light every time he moved his head. His robe was crisscrossed with belts and bandoliers, into which were stuck knives and swords of every size. He moved with a stocky aggression, as if bristling at the world, and his voice positively barked.

"Chaka spies!"

"No, sir—"

"You dare to contradict me? I am Raka!"

His rage was so violent that Kestrel didn't say another word.

"Commander!"

"Yes, my lord." Tanaka stepped forward.

"They destroyed a battle corvette?"

"Yes, my lord."

"The Chakas will pay for this!" He ground his teeth and stamped the deck. "Is Omchaka within range?"

"No, my lord." This came from one of the others, by the map table. He made a rapid calculation. "A day at the most, my lord."

"Set course for interception!" cried Raka. "They have provoked me. They have only themselves to blame."

"You mean to give battle, my lord?" asked Kemba quietly.

"Yes, counsellor! They must learn that if they strike at me, I strike back tenfold!"

"Quite so, my lord."

Already the new orders were ringing out, and even the children could feel from the grinding and shuddering of the timbers around them that Ombaraka was changing course.

"Commander! Prepare the attack fleet for dawn!"

"Yes, my lord!"

"And the Chaka spies, my lord?"

"Hang them, of course."

"I wonder if that is wise."

This was Kemba's pensive voice.

"Wise? Wise?" shrieked the little warlord. "What are you talking about? Of course it's wise! What else is there to do with spies?"

Kemba stepped closer and whispered in his master's ear.

"Interrogate them. Learn the secrets of the Chaka fleet."

"And then hang them?"

"Quite so, my lord."

The little warlord nodded, and strode about the room, deep in meditation. Everyone remained still and silent. Then he came to a stop and announced his decision in a ringing voice.

"The spies will be interrogated first, and then hanged."

Once more, Kemba murmured low in his ear.

"You must tell them they won't be hanged if they cooperate, my lord. Otherwise they won't tell us anything."

"And then hang them?"

"Quite so, my lord."

Raka nodded, and said again, in ringing tones, "The spies will not be hanged, if they cooperate."

Tanaka choked with angry surprise.

"Not hanged, my lord?"

"This is an intelligence matter, commander," said Raka testily. "You wouldn't understand."

"I understand that the counsellor shrinks from doing his duty," said Tanaka with grim pride.

Raka chose to ignore this.

"Take them away, counsellor," he said, making shooing gestures with his hands. "Interrogate them." He moved back to the map table. "You and I, commander, have a battle to prepare."

The children were marched back to their prison cell. Once there, the guards were dismissed, but Kemba himself remained.

"I have bought us a little time," he said. "And I need a little time, to think of a way out of our dilemma. I do not propose to waste any of that little time asking you for the secrets of the Chaka battle fleet."

"We don't know the secrets of the Chaka battle fleet."

"It's really not important. The dilemma is this. We can't hang you without breaking the treaty. But we can't let you live without dishonouring our ancestors and all Ombaraka. To a man, we are pledged to avenge our dead with Chaka blood. This hasn't caused a difficulty up till now, because we've never actually held any Chaka prisoners. And believe you me, I wish we didn't now."

He proceeded to explain. It seemed that some time ago, to stem the bloodshed of the perpetual war between the Barakas and the Chakas, a treaty had come into being between the two warrior peoples. This treaty stated, very simply, that from that time forward no Chaka blood would be spilled by Baraka warriors, unless Baraka blood was spilled first, and vice versa."

"So the war ended?"

"Not at all," said Kemba. "That was and is unthinkable. The war can never end. The very existence of Ombaraka depends on war. We live on a moving island to protect ourselves from attack. We are a warrior people, all the ranks in our society are military ranks, and most important of all, our leader, Raka of Baraka, is a warlord. No, the war goes on. It is the killing that has stopped. No Baraka or Chaka warrior has died in battle for a generation now."

"How can you have a battle where nobody gets killed?"

"With machines."

Kemba pointed out of the window. On the far side of the exercise yard, the masts of land-sailers could just be seen.

"Our battle fleet attacks their battle fleet. Sometimes we come out the winners, sometimes they do. But no men are at risk on either side. The corvettes and the destroyers and the battle cruisers go into battle all by themselves."

"So it's all just a game."

"No, no. It's war, and we fight with all the passions of war. It's not easy to explain to outsiders. Raka truly believes that one day his army will destroy Omchaka, and he will be the sole ruler of the plains. We all believe it; even I, in a way. You see, if we stopped believing it, we'd have to live quite differently, and then we wouldn't be Barakas anymore."

"But even so, you don't really need to hang us, do you? You're not as cruel and heartless as that."

"Oh yes, we are," said the counsellor absently, his mind revolving the problem. "I don't care a button for you. But I do care about the treaty. If the Chakas learn that we've hanged some Chaka spies, they'll have to avenge you, and then all the killing will start again."

"There you are, then. You can't hang us."

"But all Ombaraka now knows you're here. Everyone's expecting a hanging. You've no idea how excited they are. We're all brought up to kill Chakas, and now here at last, after all these years, we have three Chaka spies, caught in the act of sabotage. Of course you have to be hanged."

He was gazing out of the window once more, speaking more to himself than to them.

"I negotiated the treaty, you know. It was my finest hour."

He sighed a long melancholy sigh.

"You could let us escape."

"No, no. That would bring shame on us all."

"You could pretend to hang us."

"How would that help? If the pretence succeeded, the Chakas would say we'd broken the treaty, and the killing would start again. And if the pretence failed, the people of

Ombaraka would tear you to pieces with their bare hands, and probably me as well. Please try to think clearly, and make sensible suggestions, or remain silent, and let me think for myself."

So silence fell, but for the constant creaking and rumbling of the entire structure as Ombaraka rolled on across the plains.

After a few minutes, the counsellor clapped a palm to his brow.

"Of course! What a fool I've been! There's the answer, staring me in the face!"

Bowman and Kestrel hurried to the window, to see what it was he was gazing at. There was nobody out there in the yard. Nothing seemed to have changed.

"What?"

"The battle fleet! Let the punishment fit the crime!"

He turned to them, his aged face positively glowing with excitement.

"I knew I'd think of something! Oh, what a brain I have! Just listen to this."

There was to be a battle the next day, he explained. The Baraka battle fleet would be launched, and the Chaka battle fleet would be sent out to meet them. The armed land-sailers would collide at enormous speeds in midplains, and would destroy one another with their spinning blades. What better death could there be for the Chaka saboteurs? Send them out in one of the battle corvettes, to be smashed to pulp by the Chaka battle fleet!

"Do you see the beauty of it? You would die, which would satisfy us, but you would be killed by the Chakas themselves, so the treaty would not be broken! Isn't that perfect?"

He strode about the cell, throwing out his arms like a man doing deep-breathing exercises.

"The symmetry of it! The purity, the elegance!"

"But we end up dead?"

"Exactly! And all Ombaraka can watch! Yes, truly, I believe this is one of the best ideas I've ever come up with in all my life!"

He swung around and headed for the door, no longer interested in the children.

"Guard! Open up! Let me out!"

"Please," cried Kestrel, "couldn't we—"

"Silence, Chaka scum!" said the counsellor, not unkindly, and strode out of the cell.

CHAPTER SIXTEEN

THE WIND BATTLE

KEMBA'S PLAN EVIDENTLY MET WITH THE APPROVAL of Raka of Baraka, because when Salimba next came into the prison cell, he told the children that the people of Ombaraka could talk of nothing else.

"We've never had a battle with a real killing before," said Salimba, his eyes glowing. "At least, not that anyone can remember. Oh, I'll be out there to see, you can count on that."

"How can you be so sure we'll be killed?" said Kestrel. "The corvette may be blown off across the plains without hitting anything."

"Oh, no, they'll make sure of that," said Salimba. "They'll wait until the whole Chaka battle fleet is out, and they'll send you right into the middle. Those Chaka cruisers are mounted with the old heavy slashers. They'll rip you into pieces, all right."

"Don't you care?" said Bowman, his eyes glistening.

Salimba looked at him and then looked away, a little awkwardly.

"Well, it won't be good for you," he said. "I do see that. But"—he looked back, brightening—"it'll be grand for us!"

Once he was gone, the twins puzzled over what to do.

"It's a strange thing," said Bowman, "but in spite of all this talk of hanging and killing, I have the feeling that they're quite gentle people, really."

"Whee-eee!" said Mumpo.

"Mumpo?"

"Yes, Kess?"

"Do you realise what's happening?"

"You're my friend, and I love you."

His eyes looked a little odd, but she pressed on.

"We're going to be put in one of those land-sailers tomorrow morning, and attacked by a lot of other ones like it."

"That's good, Kess."

"No, it's not good. They have swinging knives that will chop us into pieces."

"Big pieces or little pieces?" He started to giggle. "Or very teeny-weeny pieces?"

Kestrel looked at him more closely.

"Mumpo! Show me your teeth!"

Mumpo bared his teeth. They were yellow.

"You're chewing tixa, aren't you?"

"I'm so happy, Kess."

"Where is it? Show me."

He reached into his pocket and showed her a bunch of tixa leaves.

"You are useless, Mumpo."

"Yes, Kess, I know. But I do love you."

"Oh, shut up."

Bowman was staring at the grey-green tixa leaves.

"Maybe we can do it."

"Do what?"

"When we were sheltering in the crashed wind-sailer, I worked out how its parts all went together. I think I understand it. If Mumpo was up on the mast, like when he was mud-diving, I think we could do it."

The next morning, as the dawn light began to spread across the eastern sky, the lookouts high up in the watchtowers of Ombaraka sent the signal the navigators had been waiting for: Omchaka in sight! A second great craft, a mirror image of Ombaraka itself, was lumbering towards them over the plain, its sails and masts, its decks and towers, bristling against the pink and golden sky. A strong wind was blowing from the southwest, and the two rolling cities were each tacking at an angle to the wind, to come within range of each other by the time the sun was up.

Raka himself now took up his position on the command deck. Down below, the winches and gantries that held the attack fleet were being readied for action, and all over Ombaraka men were preparing for the coming battle. The wind masters were in place on the outer galleries, their instruments held high; and in the command room, their stream of reports was being processed into ever more accurate predictions on the strength and direction of the wind. In battle, there were two crucial elements: wind direction, and timing of launch. The later the battle fleet was launched, the closer they were to their targets, and therefore the higher the degree of accuracy. However, if the launching was left too late, there was the danger that the fleet wouldn't have time to reach attack speed before the enemy craft struck them.

All this time the two great mother craft, Ombaraka and Omchaka, were lumbering into battle stations, each seeking the advantageous upwind position. Inevitably, as happened every time, they ended up crosswind to each other, where neither had the advantage. This was not a matter of great concern, since both battle fleets were designed, for this very reason, to run best in a crosswind.

As the sun climbed over the horizon, sending dazzling rays across the surface of the plains, Raka gave the order for the battle horns to be sounded. The first horn boomed out high on the lead watchtower, and from there was picked up by the watchmen all over Ombaraka. One after the other, their long deep-throated notes overlapping each other, the horns echoed from deck to deck.

The children heard them in their prison cell and knew what they meant. Soon there came running footsteps outside, and the door burst open. An escort of heavily armed men seized them and dragged them out into the passage. Roughly, without speaking a word, they hustled them across the yard and down a ramp to the launch deck. Here, stretching as far as the eye could see in either direction, ranged the Baraka battle fleet: line upon line of wind-craft, each vessel suspended from gantries projecting from the high sides of the mother craft. Men were crawling all over the ships, aligning the propeller-like blades, hanging the nets, checking the belts and pulleys, and adjusting the sails. Each vessel in the fleet had its team of handlers, for whom this was a climactic moment. The machine they had so lovingly crafted, and were now preparing for battle with such precision, would soon be launched, never to return. It would carry with it their hopes of glory, and if they were fortunate, would bring down a Chaka craft before inevitably falling itself to the blows of the enemy or of the elements.

The children were marched down the line of battle cruisers and ordered to stop before the first of the lighter craft, called corvettes. The soldiers of Baraka were everywhere, and whenever their eyes fell on the children they spat and called out insults. "Chaka scum! I'll be watching as your brains are spattered in the wind!"

By each gantry there were men with long hooked poles, which they used to pull the battle craft in to the side. Three such poles were holding the lead corvette close to the launch deck now, so that the children could be placed on board. The attack blades gleamed silver-sharp in the light of the rising sun, motionless until the corvette itself was in motion.

Counsellor Kemba now appeared to oversee the fate of the Chaka spies. He nodded to the children in a friendly manner, and then issued an order to their escort.

"Tie the Chaka spies to the masts!"

"Please, sir," said Kestrel. "Didn't you say everybody would be watching?"

"What if I did?"

"Well, if you tie us up, it'll be over too quickly, won't it?"

"What are you suggesting?"

"I was thinking that if we were to run about in the corvette, it would be much more fun to watch."

Kemba considered this suggestion, a little taken aback.

"But you might jump out altogether," he pointed out.

"You could tether us loosely," said Kestrel. "And you could give us something to fight back with. Then we could put on a real show for you."

"No, no," said Kemba. "No swords. Not for Chaka spies."

"How about one of those poles?" said Bowman, pointing to the hooked poles that held the corvette to the deck.

"What do you want one of those for?"

"Maybe we can push the Chaka fleet away."

"Push the Chaka fleet away? With a pole?"

The old counsellor smiled at that, and the men around him laughed out loud. They knew the overwhelming speed with which the battle cruisers bore down upon each other.

"Very well," said Kemba. "Give them a pole. We'll watch them push the Chaka cruisers away."

Amid much mocking laughter, the children were carried on board the corvette and each tethered by a long loop of rope to the centre mast. The ropes were slender but extremely strong, and the knots were well and tightly made. A hooked pole was tossed in after them, and another laugh ran round the launch deck. The pole clattered into the well of the craft, and Bowman let it lie there. Kestrel murmured something to Mumpo. Mumpo nodded, and grinned, and picked up the pole.

All along the western flank of Ombaraka, the battle fleet now waited, tensed with readiness for the order to launch. From where the children stood, swaying in the lead corvette, they could count fourteen of the big battle cruisers ahead of them, and behind them, nine more corvettes. Much farther away, they could see the looming bulk of Omchaka, silhouetted against the brightening sky, and they could hear the faraway sounds of the Chaka battle horns.

The two great mother craft moved steadily in the rising wind, narrowing the gap between them. The sails had not yet been set on the battle fleet, though the sailmen stood poised at the ready. Kestrel turned and looked upwards, up the towering decks and galleries above her, and saw hundreds of people, men, women, and children, squeezed into every vantage point, staring silently across the plains. And higher above still, in the watchtowers, the watchmen trained their telescopes on the gantries of Omchaka, poised to cry out when the Chaka battle fleet began its launch.

It was a tense time for all, this waiting, with the enemy rolling nearer all the time—for all, that is, except Mumpo. Mumpo was swinging the long hooked pole round his head and laughing to himself. He seemed not to realise that the

Baraka people hated him, and when they shook their fists at him and made gestures showing how he would be killed in the battle, he waved cheerily back and went on laughing. Bowman and Kestrel, by contrast, remained quiet, wanting to draw as little attention to themselves as possible. They were studying the sail mechanism, and the activities of the member of the launch crew whose task it was to set the craft on course.

Then at last there came the distant cry, followed by a nearer one, and then one nearer still.

"Prepare to engage!"

At once, a ripple of alertness ran through the teams on the launch deck as they braced themselves to follow the expected commands. Ahead, a mile away across the plain, they could see movement on the launch decks of Omchaka. Then, distant but full, like the deep roar of a waterfall, there rose up the war cry of the Chakas.

Cha-cha-chaka! Cha-cha-chaka!

At the same time, the sails on the Chaka battle cruisers unfurled, and the lead cruiser was lowered to the ground, sails straining in the wind. All eyes on Ombaraka watched as the Chaka craft was loosed, and its blades began to churn the air. All eyes followed it as it picked up speed and began its charge.

"Launch one!"

The crisp order threw the launch deck into instant action. Smoothly the launch team by the lead battle cruiser ran through their practised routine: sails loosed, blades released, final wind-direction check, enemy locked in the sights, course set. A curt nod from the sightsman, and the launch leader gave the final command.

"Go!"

The holding clamps snapped open. The brisk wind pulled the heavy craft out from the launch deck, and it rolled away on its high wheels. The huge blades started to turn as the sails filled in the wind. Out from the lee of the mother craft, and the full force of the crosswind hit the sails, howling through its mast-top horn, and the battle cruiser accelerated into its lethal charge. From every deck and gallery the war cry of the Barakas rose up, urging it on its way.

"Raka ka! ka! ka! Raka ka! ka! ka!"

Now a second Chaka cruiser had been launched, and a third. As all eyes followed the lead craft, the orders echoed and re-echoed along the launch deck, and cruiser after cruiser was unleashed. All the time, the two great mother craft were closing in on each other.

The sightsmen had done their job well. The first two cruisers struck each other head on, their great blades interlocking, mangling each other, sending both craft spinning in a tumble of mutual destruction. A cheer went up from the onlookers, and across the plain, a similar cheer could be heard rising from the decks of Omchaka. The collision had taken place too far away to judge which craft had inflicted the most damage. The cheer was for the first hit of the battle.

Now the strikes were following thick and fast. The sightsmen and the wind masters on both sides were experts at their trades, and the battle cruisers closed in on their moving targets as precisely as if they carried living helmsmen. Soon the central area of the plains between the great mother craft became a graveyard of wrecked battle cruisers, their sails vainly tugging at their beached hulls.

The rate of launching was faster now, as the Chaka commanders piled on the pressure. Clearly their aim was to overwhelm the Baraka fleet with sheer numbers, leaving Ombaraka defenceless during the crucial final phase of the battle, when the two rolling cities were close enough for the attack fleets to inflict damage on the mother craft themselves. All the strategy of battle came down to this single decision: how long to hold back the last, fastest, most manoeuvrable craft in the fleet, the corvettes.

The battle cries never ceased on either side, their steady roar mingling now with the splintering crashes of the cruisers as they piled into each other, or into already-wrecked craft, and spraying yet more wreckage up into the air. Impossible to tell which side was gaining the upper hand, though the Chaka fleet seemed for the moment to be so huge that it covered all the plain.

Still the commands hammered out.

"Go! Go! Go!"

Craft after craft hit the dirt running, as the launch directors sweated to hurl their parrying punches out into the field. Up on the command deck, Raka prowled the observation window, in the midst of a pandemonium of shouting voices.

"Wind veering west two degrees!"

"Chaka launch thirty-one!"

"Hit! Full kill!"

"Closing distance twelve hundred yards!"

"Chaka launch thirty-two! Thirty-three!"

"How many more?" exclaimed Raka.

"Second fleet gone! Corvettes stand by!"

Tanaka, commander of the armed forces, hurried to the warlord's side.

"Do we commit the corvettes, my lord?"

"No! That's what they want!"

"Chaka launch thirty-four! Thirty-five! Thirty-six!"

"Closing distance one thousand yards!"

"We must launch, my lord! We can't block them without the corvettes."

"Damn all Chakas!" exploded Raka. "How many more are they holding back?"

"Chaka launch thirty-seven!"

"We must release the corvettes!"

"We're letting them dictate our strategy," said Raka. "It's what they want."

"Chaka cruiser broken through! Chaka cruiser broken through!"

The cry sent a chill across the whole command deck. This was what they all dreaded: the first craft to evade the defending line of the Baraka battle fleet and come speeding on its way towards Ombaraka itself.

"Track for point of collision!" barked Tanaka. "Sound the danger alert!" And turning back to the warlord, his voice tense with urgency, "My lord—the corvettes!"

"Go, then," said Raka with a heavy heart. "Send out the corvettes."

On the launch decks the teams heard the horns as they sounded a new, shriller note: the danger alert. The war cry faltered as the realisation spread from gallery to gallery: the Chaka fleet had broken through. But there was no time to wonder how or why, because right after the horns came the launch signals, and at last the corvettes were going into action.

"Go! Go! Go!"

Although the children were in the lead corvette, they found they were not to be the first onto the plain. Behind them, one after another, the slim but deadly craft were dropping down and racing away, in rapid-fire sequence, heading arrow-straight for the approaching line of Chaka cruisers. As they were unleashed, the single breakaway Chaka cruiser was already upon them, moving at overpowering speed. It hit the first corvette, sending the lighter craft flying, and roared on to smash like a flying hammer into the lowest deck of Ombaraka. A mighty cheer rose up from Omchaka as the spinning fragments of the crashed cruiser rose high up the walls of Ombaraka and the people ducked for cover.

The crews on the launch decks never flinched. Corvette after corvette went snaking out to meet and halt the advancing Chaka cruisers.

"Go! Go! Go!"

The children waited in the one corvette that had been bypassed, watching the battle, Bowman and Kestrel intent and silent, Mumpo swinging his hooked pole and yelling with excitement.

"Smash! Smash! Hubba hubba! Here they come! Bang-crash-bash! Ya-ha!"

Then a new series of commands could be heard ringing out, and all over Ombaraka the sailmen could be seen furling their sails. Slowly the great rolling city came to a shuddering halt. Raka had chosen his ground for the last stand. Here they would fight to the finish.

For a few long minutes, Omchaka kept rolling towards them. Had they decided to fight the last phase of the battle at close quarters? Then Omchaka, too, could be seen to be furling its sails, and so the two juggernauts came to rest barely five hundred yards apart, to watch their battle fleets' last climactic clash.

On the command deck, Raka was in a frenzy of anguish.

"Do they have any more? I must know if they have any more!"

"No, my lord."

"They've fired their last shots? I can't believe it."

"Hit and kill! Hit and kill!"

"Wind veering southwest three degrees!"

"Three corvettes in reserve, my lord! Do we launch?"

"Do they have any left?"

"All Chaka gantries empty, my lord."

"Then go! Go!"

He threw back his arms, and his eyes sparkled once more.

"They've thrown their last punch too soon! Now we'll see who can break through!"

The war cries on both sides were at their height now, as the enemy tribes, close enough to see each other, competed to drown each other's voices.

"Cha-cha-chaka! Cha-cha-chaka!"

"Raka ka! ka! ka! Raka ka! ka! ka!"

The two battle fleets tangled and clashed, each collision throwing up a great roar from the onlookers. There had been no more breakthroughs on either side, and the Chaka launches had ended when the Baraka reserve corvettes received the order to go.

The children's craft was third and last in line. Kemba's intention was that their destruction would form the grand finale of the battle. The children stayed calm as their sails were at last unfurled and they felt the mast strain in the wind. The pulleys overhead squealed as they were winched to the ground. The sightsman set his course and strapped down the mainsail boom. Kemba gave one last amiable wave.

"Best idea I've ever had," he called down to them. "Give us a good show."

"Go!" came the command. The holding clamps snapped open, and with a wild buck that tumbled all three children into the well, the corvette kicked into action, rocketing out into the open space. The blades on either side began to spin, and the mast-top horn let out its banshee wail.

The crowds ranged all along the decks of Ombaraka greeted the reserve corvettes with a howl of triumph. The last craft in the battle were sure to break through. Then, catching sight of the children in the last corvette, their howl became one of hatred.

"Chaka scum! Chaka spies! Die! Die! Die!"

Then suddenly the chant faded on their lips. Huge doors had swung open on the side of Omchaka, to reveal concealed gantries, cradling an entire new battle fleet.

On the command deck, Raka saw this with cold despair. There was nothing he could do. He had committed his last craft. They were under way and could not be recalled. Ombaraka lay at the mercy of the enemy.

"How many?" he said dully. But he could see for himself, as the gantries rolled out. Eight battle cruisers. At five hundred yards, they would never reach maximum speed, but they would still inflict terrible damage. Safe from attack themselves, the Chaka commanders could take their time releasing them, and he had no choice but to sit here and suffer the blows. Ombaraka would be crippled. It was a disaster.

All his people knew it. A stunned silence fell over the decks and galleries as they watched their own corvettes collide with the last of the Chaka cruisers still in the battle. No cheers for a kill now. Only the wild war cry of Omchaka carried to them on the wind.

Cha-cha-chaka! Cha-cha-chaka!

But then something odd started to happen. The third corvette, the one carrying the Chaka spies, was making a wide curving turn. Astonished, they followed its flight. Two of the children seemed to be working the set of its sails, one

on the mainsail and one on the jib. The third had climbed
to the top of the mainmast, where he was waving a pole. The
wide turn took the corvette away from the battle, in a full
circle, and back again.

In the corvette, racing at giddy speed, Bowman and
Kestrel worked the sails with intense concentration, feeling
the responses of the craft. On their first turn they took care
to keep all four wheels on the ground, but on the second,
they took the turn tighter, letting the craft tip a little. It performed beautifully. Communicating without words, they
shared what they were learning.

Cross now! And over! Hold the turn! There she goes!

As they completed that second long turn, they knew they
had control of the craft. They looked at each other,
exchanging a flash of excitement at the speed of their movement and at their power.

"You all right, Mumpo?" Kestrel called up to the mast top.

"Happy, happy, happy!" Mumpo carolled back, swinging
the hooked pole round his head. "Let's go fishing!"

The first of the hidden Chaka cruisers hit the ground. As
it churned its way into action, set on a course that avoided
the tangle of smashed craft, Bowman and Kestrel swung
round and gave chase. Their course was designed not to
collide with the Chaka cruiser, but to sweep round and run
alongside it.

Round, Kess, round! Now let her run!

The people on Ombaraka watched this manoeuvre in bewilderment. The people on Omchaka were equally bemused, and their triumphant cry fell silent. What was going on? Was the corvette joining the Chaka cruiser in its attack? As the much lighter corvette swung alongside the lumbering cruiser, it certainly looked that way.

Nearer! Nearer! And nearer—

Kestrel was at the prow, calling the turns, and Bowman was on the main boom, running the craft as close as he dared to the Chaka cruiser without getting mangled by its huge spinning blade. Mumpo hung from the top of the mast by his knees, reaching out with his pole, yelling, "Closer! Closer!" Steadily they closed in, until they were so near that they could feel the air-rush of the cruiser's blades.

"Fishy fishy fishy!" cried Mumpo.

"Now!" cried Kestrel.

Bowman jerked the mainsail to tip the craft on to two wheels as it raced along. Mumpo hung out from the mast and hooked the end of his pole into the top rigging of the battle cruiser.

"Pull away! Pull away!" cried Kestrel.

Bowman wrenched the mainsail boom, the corvette righted itself and veered sharply away from the battle cruiser, and Mumpo hung on tight. The Chaka craft lurched onto one side, Mumpo unhooked his pole, the corvette shot away, turning now on its other two wheels, and the battle cruiser came thundering down, to thrash itself to pieces with its own blades.

A wild stamping roar went up from all Ombaraka. The corvette righted itself again, crashing back onto four wheels, sweeping Mumpo vertical once more. He raised his arms like a champion.

"Hubba hubba, Mumpo!" called Kestrel.

And round they raced, back into the attack. The light of battle was in their eyes, and the more they struck, the bolder they became. As the great cruisers were launched, they leaped on them, running them to ground like a hound harrying deer. Twice they missed, but so light were they on the turns that they were back round again for another strike before the heavy cruisers could build up the speed to outrun them. And with every kill, up went the echoing stamping roar from the decks of Ombaraka.

On the command deck, Raka watched in awe, his hands pulling convulsively at his beaded belt.

"These are no Chaka spies," he said softly.

The disaster was turning into triumph before his eyes.

After the fourth of the brand-new battle cruisers had been destroyed, the Chaka high command launched no more. The doors to the secret launch decks closed again, and Omchaka set its sails for a retreat.

Raka of Baraka saw this and ordered the victory call. The high horns began it, and the people of Ombaraka took it up, every man, woman, and child. To the chanting of a thousand voices, Bowman and Kestrel steered the corvette back towards its mother craft, its attack blades still turning. As they came into the lee of the great structure, the sails slackened, and the craft coasted to a standstill. Mumpo came slithering down the mainmast, and the three children embraced each other, still trembling with the tension of the battle.

"Mumpo, you're a hero! Bo, you're a hero!"

"All heroes," said Mumpo, happier than he'd ever been in his entire life. "We're the three heroes!"

As they were hoisted back on board, they were cheered and cheered, all the way over the launch deck and up the walkway and through the pillared halls to the command deck, where Raka was waiting for them.

"After what I have seen today," he declared, "I know that you are not Chakas. And if you're not Chakas, you are Barakas! You are our brothers!"

"And our sister," said Counsellor Kemba, smiling his most amiable smile.

Raka embraced each one of them, shaking with emotion.

"I and all my people are at your service!"

As a special sign of his gratitude, Raka of Baraka ordered that all three children have their hair braided by the Master Braider. After some earnest discussions among his counsellors, it was agreed that the young heroes could have gold threads braided into their hair. This was the highest honour short of the blades worn by the warlord himself, and many eyebrows were raised at its granting. But as Counsellor Kemba pointed out, the children would not be staying long on Ombaraka, and once beyond the care of the Master Braider, the gold threads would soon tarnish.

Mumpo was very excited at the prospect of golden hair; Kestrel and Bowman less so. But they sensed it would be discourteous to refuse. Once the elaborate process had begun, however, they found themselves enjoying it more than they had expected. First, their hair was washed three times, which at last removed from it the mud of the Underlake. Then skilled combers set to work drawing out the strands of hair into hundreds of slender tresses. The combing was both gentle and strong, which was an odd sensation and made their scalps tingle. Then the underbraiders took over, working to the instructions of the Master Braider himself.

Each tress was plaited both with itself and with three

lengths of gold thread to form a fine crisscross braid, ending in a little lumpy golden knot. Unlike Salimba's earlier work on Mumpo's hair, the plaits were worked carefully to hang perfectly straight, and this took a very long time. If the Master Braider saw the beginnings of a kink in a plait, he ordered it undone to the roots, and started again.

When this patient work was almost done, Counsellor Kemba joined them.

"My dear young friends," he said, "Raka of Baraka sends me to invite you to a dinner in your honour this evening. He also wishes to be informed if there is any way he can show his gratitude in a more lasting fashion."

"We would just like to be helped on our way," said Kestrel.

"And what way is that?"

"We have to find the road known as the Great Way."

"The Great Way?" Kemba's pleasant voice suddenly sounded grave. "What do you want with the Great Way?"

Kestrel met Bowman's eyes, and saw there the same suspicion.

"It's just the path we have to follow," she said. "Do you know where it is?"

"I know where it was," replied Kemba. "The Great Way hasn't been used for many, many years. That region is full of dangers. There are wolves there. And worse."

"Wolves don't frighten us," said Mumpo. "We're the three heroes."

"So we have seen," said Kemba with a thin smile. "But nevertheless, I think it would be best if we were to take you south, to Aramanth, which you say is your home."

"No, thank you," said Kestrel firmly. "We have to go north."

Counsellor Kemba bowed in what seemed like assent, and left them to their braiding.

The final results were spectacular. The three children gazed at themselves in the glass and were silent with awe. Their hair now haloed their faces in a shimmer of light, which danced this way and that with every move of their heads. The Master Braider beamed at them with pride.

"I knew the gold would set off your pale skins," he said. "We Barakas need stronger colours, to tell you the truth. Gold would be lost on me."

He fingered his own red, orange, and acid-green plaits.

At the grand dinner, the children's entrance was greeted by a standing ovation. All down the long lines of tables, gasps of admiration could be heard at the gleam of their golden braids in the candlelight. Raka of Baraka beckoned them to sit on his either side. Thinking that he was pleasing them, he announced, "We're sailing south! Kemba has told me that your one wish is to return to Aramanth. So I have given the order to sail south."

"But that's not right," cried Kestrel. "We want to go north."

The smile left Raka's face. He looked across the table to Kemba for an explanation. Counsellor Kemba spread his smooth hands.

"I consider it my duty, my lord, to look after our young heroes in every way we can. The road north is impassable. The bridge over the gorge is in ruins. No travellers dare go that way anymore."

"Well, we dare," said Kestrel fiercely.

"There is another matter." Kemba sighed, as if it hurt him to speak of it. "My lord, as you know, although we have been at war with Omchaka for a long time, we have been spared a greater danger. I speak of—" he hesitated, then murmured low, "the Zars."

"The Zars?" said Raka, in his booming tones. And the word was repeated all down the lines of tables, like an echo. "The Zars—the Zars."

"Were the children inadvertently to wake—"

"Quite, quite," said Raka hastily. "Better to head south."

The twins heard this with dismay.

Leave it for now, said Bowman silently. So Kestrel said nothing more, and Counsellor Kemba, watching them closely, was satisfied.

At the end of the grand dinner, Bowman asked Raka for a special favour. He asked to speak to the warlord alone.

"Certainly," said Raka, who had eaten and drunk well, and was filled by sensations of goodwill. "Why not?"

But Kemba was suspicious.

"I think, my lord—" he began.

"Now, now, Kemba," said Raka. "You worry too much."

He took Bowman off into his private quarters, and Kemba had to content himself with standing close to the door in the next room and listening to every word.

What he heard was not at all what he expected. For a long time, the boy and the warlord sat together in total silence. It even seemed possible that Raka had gone to sleep. But then the counsellor heard the boy's voice, speaking softly.

"I can feel you remembering," he said.

"Yes . . ." This was Raka.

"You're a baby. Your father takes you everywhere. He holds you high, and he smiles. You're only little, but you feel his pride and love."

"Yes, yes. . ."

"You're older now. You're a boy. You stand before your father, and he says, 'Head up! Head up!' You know he wishes you were taller. You wish it, too, more than anything in the world."

"Yes, yes. . ."

"Now you're older still. You're a man, and your father never looks at you. He can't bear to see you, because you're

so small. You say nothing, but your heart cries out to him,
'Be proud of me. Love me.'"

"Yes, yes. . ." Raka was sobbing softly now. "How do you
know these things? How do you know?"

"I feel it in you. I feel it in me."

"I've never spoken of it. Never, never."

Counsellor Kemba, listening at the door, could endure
it no longer. He was unclear quite how it would interfere
with his schemes, but he was sure it was not healthy for the
warlord of Ombaraka to be weeping like a baby. So pre-
tending agitation, he swept in to the private meeting.

"My lord, what has happened? What's the matter?"

Raka the Ninth, Warlord of the Barakas, Suzerain of
Ombaraka, Commander-in-Chief of the Wind Warriors
and Ruler of the Plains, looked up at his chief counsellor
with tears streaming from red-rimmed eyes, and said,
"Mind your own business."

"But my lord—"

"Go and twiddle your hair! Out!"

So Counsellor Kemba retreated. And a little time later,
the orders went out to the helmsmen to set course for the
north, and slowly the great mother craft lumbered round
and began to roll towards the mountains.

As the sun came up on the new day, Kestrel climbed to the

top of the highest watchtower on Ombaraka and looked across the plains. It was a cool clear morning, and she could see for miles. There where the plains ended, she could make out the rising land and the great forest that covered it. And not so far off now, on the horizon, the dark mass of the mountains.

As Kestrel stared at the land, she thought she saw beneath the dust of the plains and between the trees of the forest the outlines of a long-abandoned road, broad and straight, running towards the mountains. She had the map open before her, and there on it was the Great Way, broken by the jagged line called Crack-in-the-land. At the road's end, at exactly the point where the Great Way met the highest mountain, there were written the words that her father had told her said INTO THE FIRE.

The grateful people of Ombaraka gave their heroes a grand send-off—all but Counsellor Kemba, who was nowhere to be seen. Raka embraced them, one by one, with a specially close hug for Bowman.

"If ever you need our help," he said, "you have only to ask."

Salimba came forward with three shoulder bags filled with food for their journey.

"I knew they weren't spies from the first," he said. "Didn't I do his braids?"

Then they were lowered to the ground, and all Ombaraka gathered to chant the victory call once more, as a final tribute. The cries resounding in their ears, the children headed for the nearby foothills and the great forest. They turned back once, to wave farewell to their new friends, and stood for a moment watching as the great rolling city loosed its myriad sails and went creaking and rumbling back over the plains. A gust of wind tugged at their gold-braided hair and made them shiver. The air was colder here, and ahead the land was dark.

CHAPTER SEVENTEEN

THE HATH FAMILY FIGHTS BACK

"WHERE BO?" SAID PINPIN. "WHERE KESS?"

"They've gone to the mountains," said Ira Hath, who did not believe in deceiving a child even as young as two. "Lift up your arms."

"Where Pa?"

"He's gone to study for his exam. Stand still while I do you up. It'll all be over soon."

She examined the child with a critical eye. There had not been enough material in the bedspread to make complete robes for both of them, so for Pinpin she had made just a sleeveless tunic, which she put over her orange smock. Looking at them both now, she felt satisfied that this had been the right decision. To have mother and child in matching stripes would have been too much.

When they were both ready, she picked up the large basket she had packed earlier, took Pinpin's hand, and went out into the passage. As they passed the doorway to the Mooths' room, she heard the door open a crack, and a sharp cry come from within.

"Oh! Look what she's done now!"

Three shocked faces appeared in the crack to watch them make their way to the stairs.

Out in the street, their multicoloured stripy appearance caused a sensation. The block warden, who happened to be passing, at once raised his hand high, blew his whistle, and called out, "You can't do that!"

A man wheeling a cart laden with barrels turned to look, and not watching where he was going, wheeled the cart into a man carrying a basket on his head. The basket went flying, and the barrels tumbled off the cart. Out of the upturned basket fell a mass of small pink crabs, a delicacy much appreciated in White District. Two large women coming the other way, also staring at Ira and Pinpin Hath, fell over the runaway barrels, the larger of the two woman crushing one barrel so completely that it burst open, spilling crude molasses onto the stone street. The block warden, hurrying forward to restore order, stepped into the molasses, strode on through the scurrying crabs, and fell headlong over the smaller of the large women. As he struggled to get up again, his flailing boots smeared her head with molasses, in which several small pink crabs had become stuck.

Pinpin saw all this with delight, as if it was a performance put on specially to entertain her. Ira Hath paid no attention whatsoever. Magnificently indifferent to the stares of her neighbours, the oaths of the warden, and the shrieks of the woman with crabs in her hair, she marched on down the street and turned onto the main avenue to the centre of the city.

As she strode along, her basket in one hand and Pinpin holding the other, she collected a little train of followers. They hung some way behind and spoke to each other in whispers, as if afraid she would hear. Ira Hath found that she was almost enjoying herself. Being stripy gave her a kind of power.

As she passed into Maroon District, and then into her former home territory of Orange, her followers grew in number, until there were fifty or more people of various ranks trailing along behind her. As she entered Scarlet District, she stopped unexpectedly and turned to look at them. They all stopped, too, and looked back at her in silence, like a herd of cows. She knew why they were following her, of course. They wanted to see her punished. Nothing excited people in Aramanth more than seeing fellow citizens humiliated in public.

Something in those rows of sad blank eyes spoke to her at an ancestral level, and the words rose to her mouth unbidden.

"O unhappy people!" she cried. "Tomorrow will bring sorrow, but the day after will bring laughter! Prepare to mingle your colours!"

Then she turned and walked on, and they all came shuffling after her, murmuring among themselves.

Ira Hath walked tall and felt the blood sing in her body. She liked being a wife and mother, but she had just discovered she liked being a prophetess more.

By the time she reached the piazza by the Imperial Palace, every idle person in Aramanth seemed to have joined the crowd. Strictly speaking, of course, there were no idle people in Aramanth, since the city made sure everyone had useful work to do. So the sight of the shuffling procession that trailed the brightly striped mother and child past the College of Examiners was not a pleasing one to the city's governors.

On she strode, through the double row of marble columns, into the arena. Down the nine tiers she went, and the crowd followed her to see what she would do next. In the centre of the great arena, at the foot of the wooden platform of the wind singer, she came to a stop. She hoisted her basket up onto the platform's base. Then she hoisted

Pinpin after it. Then she clambered up herself. Once in position, she took a blanket out of her basket and spread it on the boards, and sat herself and Pinpin down. Out of the capacious basket came a bottle of lemonade and a bag of buns.

The crowd watched, all agape, for her next outrageous action.

"O unhappy people!" cried the prophetess. "The time has come to sit and eat buns!"

Which is what she did.

The crowd waited patiently, knowing there would be developments. After a while, a white-robed senior examiner appeared, followed by four marshals. The examiner, Dr. Greeth, was responsible for the maintenance of order in the city. The sight of him stepping down the nine tiers, flanked by four huge marshals, sent shivers of anticipation through the crowd.

"Madam," said Dr. Greeth in his clear, cutting voice. "This is not a circus. You are not a clown. You will come down from there and dress yourself in your designated clothing."

"No, I won't," said Ira Hath.

Dr. Greeth nodded briskly to the marshals.

"Get her down!"

The prophetess rose to her full height and cried in her

most prophetic voice, "O unhappy people! Watch now, and see that there is no freedom in Aramanth!"

"No freedom in Aramanth?" exclaimed Dr. Greeth indignantly.

"I am Ira Hath, direct descendant of the prophet Ira Manth, and I have come to prophesy to the people!"

Dr. Greeth signalled to the marshals to wait.

"Madam," he said, speaking loudly so that all the people in the crowd could hear him. "You are talking nonsense. You are fortunate enough to live in the only truly free society that has ever existed. In Aramanth, every man and woman is born equal, and has an equal chance to rise to the very highest position. There is no poverty here, or crime, or war. We have no need of prophets."

"And yet," cried the prophetess, "you fear me!"

This was a clever move, as Dr. Greeth at once realised. It would not look good if he were to overreact.

"You are mistaken, madam. We don't fear you. But we do find you a little noisy."

The crowd laughed. Dr. Greeth was satisfied. There was no need to use force—it would only bring the woman sympathy. Better to leave her on her perch until she grew cold and hungry and came down of her own accord.

In the meantime, to reassert his authority, he ordered the marshals to disperse the crowd.

"Back to your work!" he cried. "Let's leave her to prophesy what she's going to eat for dinner."

Hanno Hath, shut away in the Residential Study Centre, did not learn of his wife's rebellion until the midday meal. The serving girls passed on the gossip in excited whispers as they spooned vegetable stew into the candidates' bowls. A wild woman dressed as a clown was sitting on the wind singer, they said, telling everyone to be unhappy. Hanno recognised his wife's style at once, and felt a rush of pride and concern. He pressed the serving girls for more details. Had the authorities tried to force the wild woman off the wind singer?

"Oh, no," said the girl on the rice pudding. "They come and have a good laugh like the rest of us."

This both reassured Hanno and hardened his resolve. The High Examination was now only two days away, and his own small act of rebellion was well advanced. Little by little, the other candidates had fallen in with his plan, until only one, a factory cleaner called Scooch, remained unconvinced. One accidental result was that the atmosphere of the Study Course had been transformed. The candidates who had stared so numbly at their revision books, and had listened to the Principal's lectures with defeat in their eyes, were now applying themselves eagerly to their exercises.

Principal Pillish, too, saw this with satisfaction. It seemed to him that the candidates were helping each other overcome their negative approach to examinations, and this augured very well for the results. He observed that the gentle soft-spoken Hanno Hath was the centre of this new enthusiasm. Curious to know what it was he had told his fellow candidates, he called Hanno into his study for a private talk.

"I'm impressed, Hath," he said. "What's your secret?"

"Oh, it's very simple," said Hanno. "We have the time here to think about the real value of examinations. We've realised that what an examination does is test the best in us. So if we give it our best, well—whatever the result, we should be content to be judged by it."

"Bravo!" cried Principal Pillish. "This is a real turnaround. I don't mind telling you, Hath, that your file has you down as incurably negative in your attitudes. But this is excellent! Give it your best—quite so. I couldn't put it better myself."

What Hanno Hath did not feel obliged to explain to the Principal was just how he and the other candidates proposed to give their best. The idea had come to Hanno while listening to Miko Mimilith talk about the different fabrics he handled. "If Miko could only sit an exam on fabrics," he had thought, "he would have no fears." This had been followed at once by a further thought. "Miko's knowledge of fabrics is his special expertise and his passion. Why is he tested on other subjects, at which he will only fail? Each of us should be tested on what we do best."

He had said as much to his new friends on the Study Course.

"That's all very well," they said. "But it's not going to happen."

The High Examination contained more than a hundred questions, of which they would be lucky to get even one on fabrics or cloud formations.

"Ignore the questions on the paper," said Hanno. "Write about what you know best. Give them your best."

"They'll just fail us."

"They'll fail us anyway, even if we try to answer their questions."

They all nodded. That was true enough. They were on the Study Course precisely because they'd always failed before. Why should it be any different this time?

"So what's the point?" said Hanno, gently persisting. "It's like giving tests in flying to fish. Let's each of us do what we're good at."

"They'll hate it."

"Let them. Do you want to sit in that arena and feel sick with panic for another four hours?"

That was what did it. Every one of them dreaded, almost more than the results, the long humiliation of the exam itself. Every hated detail had burned itself into their memories. The slow walk to the numbered desk. The scrape of a thousand chairs as they were pulled out. The rustle of a thousand exam papers as they were turned over. The smell of the fresh print. The dancing black letters on the paper, forming words that made no sense. The scratch-scratch-scratch of pens all around, as the clever candidates began their answers. The pad-pad-pad of soft shoes, as the supervising examiners passed down the rows. The panic need to begin writing, something, anything. The deep dull certainty that nothing you wrote would be right, or good, or beautiful. The slow drag of the hands on the clock. The spreading paralysis of despair.

Anything, anything, but that.

So one by one they joined Hanno Hath's secret rebellion. In their exercises, they practised writing papers on subjects of their own choosing. Monographs were in preparation on drainage systems, the growing of cabbages, and rope-jumping games. Miko Mimilith was working on the definitive classification of woollen weaves. Hanno Hath was tackling some problems in old Manth script. Only little Scooch wrote nothing. He sat hunched at his desk, staring at the wall.

"You must know something about something," Hanno said.

"Well, I don't," said Scooch. "I don't know anything about anything. I just do what I'm told."

"Isn't there something you like to do when your work is finished?"

"I like to sit down," said Scooch.

Hanno Hath sighed.

"You have to write something," he said. "Why don't you just describe a typical day in your life?"

"How do you mean, describe?"

"Just start at the beginning, when you get out of bed, and write down what you do."

"I eat breakfast. I go to work. I come home. I eat supper. I go to bed."

"Right. Now all you have to do is add a little more detail. Maybe put down what you have for breakfast. What you see on your way to work."

"It doesn't sound very interesting to me."

"It's more interesting than looking at a wall."

So Scooch settled down to describe his typical day. After an hour or so of steady work, he reached midmorning in his description and made a surprising discovery. When it was time for the candidates' own midmorning break, he hurried over to Hanno Hath to tell him about it.

"I've found something I know about," he said. "I'm going to write about it in the High Examination."

"That's wonderful," said Hanno. "What is it?"

"Tea breaks."

Scooch beamed at him, his face glowing with pride.

"I didn't realise till I started writing about my day, but what I love most in all the world is tea breaks."

He passed the next half hour explaining to a patient Hanno Hath how he looked forward to his tea break from the moment he started work. How his anticipation mounted as the time approached. How the laying down of his broom and the picking up of his flask of tea was a moment of almost perfect joy. How he breathed in the steam that rose from the flask as he removed its stopper and poured the hot brown tea into his mug. How he unwrapped his three oat biscuits from their slippery greaseproof paper wrapping, and how, one by one, he dipped them into the hot tea. Ah, the dipping of the biscuits! This was the heart of the tea break, the time of tension and gratification, the exercise of skill, and the encounter with the unknown. Sometimes, when he judged it right, he raised the sweet sodden biscuit to his mouth and consumed it intact, allowing it to crumble and melt on his tongue. Sometimes he dipped it for too long, or raised the biscuit too abruptly, or at too sharp an angle, and a large fragment fell off and sank to the bottom of the mug. What made the tea break so intense an experience was not knowing when or whether this would happen again.

"Really, you know," said Hanno Hath thoughtfully,

"someone should find a way to make a biscuit that goes soggy when dipped in tea, but doesn't break."

"Make a biscuit?" said Scooch, astonished. "You mean, invent a different sort of biscuit altogether?"

"Yes," said Hanno.

"Well, boggle me!" said Scooch, and he began to think. To be an inventor of biscuits! That would be something.

In this way, as in many others, with a mounting eagerness, inspired by Hanno Hath's gentle leadership, the candidates in the Residential Study Course prepared for the day of the High Examination. For the first time in their lives, whether it was wanted or not, they would be giving their best.

Ira Hath and Pinpin remained on the wind singer all night. It turned out that Ira had planned for this and had brought extra food and blankets in the deep basket. She had even brought nightclothes for Pinpin, and her special pillow.

When they were found to be still there in the morning, another crowd gathered to laugh and jeer.

"Let's hear you prophesy, then!" they cried. "Go on, say, 'O unhappy people!'"

"O unhappy people," said Ira Hath.

She spoke rather more quietly than they liked, and some-how it didn't sound so funny anymore. Then again, soft and sad, she said, "O unhappy people. No poverty. No crime. No war. No kindness."

This wasn't funny at all. The people in the crowd shuffled their feet and avoided each other's eyes. Then for a third time, most quietly of all, Ira Hath said, "O unhappy people. I hear your hearts crying, for want of kindness."

No one ever said such things in Aramanth. The people heard her in shocked silence. Then they began to leave, in ones and twos, and Ira Hath knew she had proved herself a true prophetess, because none could bear to hear her speak.

The Board of Examiners raised the matter at their morning meeting. Dr. Greeth continued to argue against intervention.

"The woman can't stay there much longer. Better to let everyone see how futile this kind of behaviour is. She'll realise it herself soon enough, and what will she do then? She'll climb down."

Dr. Greeth was rather pleased with this turn of phrase. It seemed to him to make the point with economy and precision. But the Chief Examiner didn't smile.

"I know this family," he said. "The father's an embittered failure. The mother is mad. The older children—well, one way or another they won't trouble us again. That leaves the infant."

"I'm not quite clear," said Dr. Greeth, "whether you are disagreeing with me or not."

"I agree with your approach in principle," replied Maslo Inch. "In practice, we must have her out of there before the High Examination."

"Oh, she'll be gone long before then."

"And then there is the matter of reparation."

"What exactly do you propose, Chief Examiner?"

"The conduct of this family has been an insult to the city of Aramanth. There must be a public apology."

"She's a high-spirited woman," said Dr. Greeth doubtfully. "A willful woman."

"High spirits can be brought low," said the Chief Examiner, smiling his cold smile. "Willful spirits can be broken."

CHAPTER EIGHTEEN

CRACK-IN-THE-LAND

NOW THAT THE TWINS WERE ON THE GROUND, the Great Way, which Kestrel had seen so clearly from the high watchtower of Ombaraka, seemed to have hidden itself again. The low rising hills were scattered with mounds and ditches, and there were clumps of scrubby trees here and there, but no obvious broad avenue between them. Only the jagged mountains could still be seen on the horizon ahead, and it was towards these that they directed their steps.

Mumpo groaned as he walked. He had chewed too much tixa at the time of the battle, and now the inside of his head hurt and his mouth was dry, and he had that feeling where you want to be sick but never quite do it. Bowman and

Kestrel were concerned at first, and very sympathetic. However, his complaining went on so long that after a while they became irritated, and Kestrel reverted to former habits.

"Oh, shut up, Mumpo."

After that, as well as groaning, Mumpo started to cry. When he cried, his nose ran, and it was even harder to be sympathetic to him, because his upper lip was shiny with nose dribble. Anyway, both Bowman and Kestrel had other matters on their minds. As the trees became more frequent, and their path lay more and more through shadowy glades, Kestrel was searching for signs of the Great Way, and Bowman was looking about him, fearful of possible danger. He knew he had an overactive imagination, and he didn't want to alarm the others if there was nothing there, but it seemed to him that they were being followed.

Then he saw something, or someone, ahead. He froze, pointing silently so the others could see. Through a clump of trees they could make out a huge figure, standing on some high perch and staring towards them. Bowman and Kestrel had the same thought at the same time: giants. The Old Queen had said there were giants on the Great Way. For several long moments, they didn't move, and the giant didn't move. Then Mumpo sneezed, suddenly and loudly, and said, "Sorry, Kess."

The giant showed no signs of having heard. So they approached, cautiously at first. As they cleared the clump of trees, their fears evaporated.

They were looking at a statue.

The figure was at least twice life-size, and very old and very weather-beaten. It represented a robed man, raising one hand to point south—one arm, rather, for the hand was gone. As was the other arm, and much of the face. The figure stood on a high pedestal of stone, its edges worn smooth by wind and rain.

Not far off there was another pedestal with another statue. Now that the children understood what they were, they could make out more and more, forming a broad double line through the trees.

"Giants," said Kestrel. "To guide travellers down the Great Way. There must have been statues all down it, once."

Confident now that they were on the right path, they pressed on towards the mountains. But soon Mumpo was snivelling and groaning again.

"Can't we sit down? I want to sit down. My head hurts."

"Best if we keep moving," said Bowman.

Mumpo started to howl.

"I want to go home," he cried dismally.

"I'm sorry, Mumpo," said Bowman, trying not to be too hard on him. "We have to go on."

"Why don't you ever wipe your nose?" said Kestrel.

"Because it just goes on running," said Mumpo miserably.

When they had reached the forest proper, and there were tall trees on either side, they saw that they were indeed following what once had been a road. Some young saplings had seeded in the open space, but the really big old trees rose up high on either side of a broad avenue, just as they must have done in the far-off days of the Great Way. Satisfied that they were making progress, Kestrel said they could stop for a short rest and eat their food. Mumpo at once collapsed in a heap. Bowman divided up the bread and cheese, and they ate hungrily, in silence.

Kestrel watched Mumpo as they ate, and saw how his good spirits returned as his stomach was filled. It reminded her of Pinpin.

"You're just like a baby, Mumpo," she said. "You cry when you're hungry, like a baby. You sleep like a baby."

"Is that wrong, Kess?" said Mumpo.

"Do you want to be like a baby?"

"I want to be whatever you want me to be," said Mumpo simply.

"Oh, honestly. It's no use talking to you."

"Sorry, Kess."

"I really don't know how you managed to stay in Orange all these years."

Bowman said quietly, "That's because we've never asked him."

Kestrel stared at her brother. It was true: she knew next to nothing about Mumpo. At school, he had always been the one who was odd, the one to avoid. Then when he had become her unwanted friend, she had found his affection irritating, and had not wanted to do anything to encourage it. In the course of their journey together, she had come to think of him as a kind of wild animal that had attached itself to her and become almost a pet. But he was not an animal. He was a child, like herself.

"What happened to your father and mother, Mumpo?"

Mumpo was surprised at her question, but very happy to answer her.

"My mother died when I was little. And I haven't got a father."

"Did he die, too?"

"I'm not sure. I think I just haven't got one."

"Everyone's got a father. At least for a while."

"Well, I haven't."

"Don't you want to know what happened to him?"

"No."

"Why not?"

"I just don't."

"If you haven't got a family," said Bowman, "how can you have a family rating?"

"How can you go to school in Orange District," said Kestrel, "even though—"

She caught Bowman's glance, and broke off.

"Even though I'm so stupid?"

He didn't seem at all offended. "I've got an uncle. It's because of my uncle that I go to school in Orange District, even though I'm so stupid."

Bowman felt a wave of sadness pass through him, and he shuddered as if it were his own.

"Do you hate school, Mumpo?" he asked.

"Oh, yes," replied Mumpo simply. "I don't understand anything, and I'm always alone. So I'm always unhappy."

The twins looked at him and remembered how they had laughed at him along with the others, and they felt ashamed.

"But it's all right now," he said. "I've got a friend now. Haven't I, Kess?"

"Yes," said Kestrel. "I'm your friend."

Bowman loved Kestrel for saying that, even if she didn't mean it.

Love you, Kess.

"Who's your uncle, Mumpo?"

"I don't know. I've never seen him. He's very important, and has a very high rating. But I'm stupid, you see, so he doesn't want me in his family."

"But that's horrible!"

"Oh, no, he's very good to me. Mrs. Chirish is always telling me so. Only, if I was in his family, it would make his family rating much lower. So it's better that I lodge with Mrs. Chirish."

"Oh, Mumpo," said Kestrel. "What a bad, sad place Aramanth has become."

"Do you think so, Kess? I thought only I thought that."

Bowman wondered at Mumpo. The more he knew of him, the more, in a strange way, he admired him. There seemed to be no malice in him, or vanity. He accepted what each moment brought him, and never troubled himself with matters that were outside his control. Despite the unhappiness of his lonely life, he seemed to have been born incurably good-hearted: or perhaps the one had somehow led to the other, and the many cruelties he had known had taught him to be grateful for even the smallest kindness.

They had eaten now, and rested, and the day was wearing on, so they rose and continued on their journey. Mumpo was in much better heart, and it was in a new spirit of determination and fellow feeling that they marched up the ruins of the Great Way towards the mountains.

Their road ran straight enough, but all the time it was climbing, ascending the foothills of the larger mountain range ahead. Little by little, the trees grew taller on either side and closer together, and as the sun dropped in the sky, the shadows deepened around them. They began to see or to imagine shapes moving between the trees, and the glint of watching eyes. They kept close together, and walked faster, and it seemed that the shapes loped alongside them, always just out of sight.

When dusk began to gather, they realised they would have to pass at least one night in the forest. They kept moving, but now as they went they looked about them for a suitable place to make camp. Mumpo was becoming tired, and cared very little where he lay down, so long as it was soon.

"What about here? Here's good."

"What's good about it?"

"Between these big trees, then."

"No, Mumpo. We need somewhere where we can't be seen."

"Why? Who's looking for us?"

"I don't know. Probably nobody."

But Mumpo got nervous after that, and kept jumping and looking round. Once he saw something, or thought he saw something, in the trees, and started to run round and round in a panic. Bowman had to catch him and hold him until he became quiet again.

"It's all right, Mumpo."

"I saw eyes watching us! I did!"

"Yes, I've seen them, too. So whatever it is, we mustn't let it hurt Kess."

"You're right, Bo." He became calmer at once. "Kess is my friend."

He still went on looking nervously into the trees, but after that, whenever he saw a shape moving, he shook his fist at it and cried, "Come any nearer, I'll bash you!"

So they trudged on into the twilight, determined to cover as much ground as they could. And just when they had decided the time had come to stop, whether there was a suitable camping place or not, they saw looming ahead of them between the trees two tall stone pillars.

The pillars stood on either side of the old Great Way, marking the beginning of a long stone bridge across a ravine. On the far side, two more pillars stood where the land began again—far away, two hundred yards or more. The bridge was in ruins. Its two walls, each one capped with a parapet, crossed the ravine on two lines of immense stone arches, twenty yards apart: but the entire middle of the bridge, what had once been the roadway, was gone. How had these twin rows of soaring arches survived without the support they had once given each other? For the gorge they had been built to cross was stupendous.

The three children came to a stop by the pillars and gazed into the canyon. The ground dropped away before them in a series of steep rock faces, down and down into the twilight shadows to a river far below. They could see it glinting as it rushed along, passing between the two centre arches that held the high bridge. The farther side of the canyon rose up before them, higher than any sea cliff, its fissures sprouting grasses and scrubby bushes, and crazed and riven with fault lines. To either side of them, the jagged edge of the gorge ripped through the forest as far as the eye could see, like a great knife wound in the world.

"Crack-in-the-land," said Kestrel.

There was no way across the great rift except by the bridge, and the more they looked at the bridge, the less they wanted to cross it.

"It's crumbling," said Bowman. "It won't hold us."

Eroded by a hundred winters, the masonry had crackled and broken away, leaving sloping shoulders of stone that looked friable and treacherous. One of the walls had collapsed in the middle, but the other, cut from a more enduring stone, stood unbroken, all the way across the gorge.

Kestrel went up to the parapet and felt its surface. It was firm to the touch. The top of the wall was about two feet wide, and it was flat. She looked along its length, all the way to the far pillars. It ran straight and level all the way.

"We can walk on the wall," she said.

Bowman said nothing, but he was filled with terror at

the narrowness of the parapet, and the dizzying drop below.

"Just don't look down," said Kestrel, who knew what he would be thinking. "Then it'll be no different from walking along a path."

I can't do it, Kess.

"What about you, Mumpo? Can you walk on the wall to the other side?"

"If you go, Kess," said Mumpo, "I'll go, too."

I can't do it, Kess.

But even as he was sending his sister this fear-filled thought, there came a shuffling sound behind them, and an icy chill went through him. He turned slowly, dreading what he knew he would see. There they were, in a line, holding hands all across the Great Way. They advanced slowly and carefully, snickering as they came, like children playing a secret game, except that their laughter was deep and old.

"You have come a long way," said their leader. "But here we are again."

Mumpo began to whimper with fear. Kestrel took one look at the line of old children, another at the long parapet, and said, "Come on! Let's go."

She jumped up onto the parapet and set off towards the far side. Mumpo followed her, calling out, "Don't let them touch me, Kess!"

Bowman hesitated a little longer, but he knew he had no

choice. So he drew a long breath, and climbed up onto the parapet. Moving with tense and careful steps, he followed after the other two.

For a few yards, the bridge wall ran over the broken edge of the gorge, and the drop below wasn't far at all. But suddenly the land fell away in a sheer cliff below them, and after that it was as if they were walking in midair. The daylight was now fading fast, but not fast enough, and when Bowman looked down, as he had sworn he would not, he could see the gleam of the river running like a silver thread so far below that it made his head go faint, and his body started to shake.

Kestrel stopped to look back, and saw that the old children had clambered up onto the parapet and were following them.

"Just keep walking," she said. "Remember, they're old, and can't go as fast as us. We'll be on the other side long before them."

She pressed on, drawing the other two after her by sheer determination. Bowman, looking back, saw that she was right, and they were crossing the long bridge much faster than the old children. Several of them were now on the parapet, coming one behind the other, picking their way with slow care.

Kestrel stepped steadily on, one foot in front of the

other, not looking down, not thinking about the gorge below, thinking, Halfway there, not much longer now, when she saw on the far side a sight that made her heart jump. Beside the pillars that marked the end of the bridge stood more old children, dozens of them. And as she came to a stop, and stared, they climbed up onto the parapet ahead and began to shuffle towards her.

Bo! They're at the other end!

Bowman looked, and saw, and understood, in a single flash of knowledge. This time there was no escape. The old children were advancing slowly from either end. Once they reached the middle, there was no way of fighting them off, because every touch brought weakness. He looked over the side, at the immense drop into the gathering darkness, and wondered what it would feel like to fall and fall, and then smash! to hit the rocks. Would the dying be quick?

Bo! We have to fight!

How?

I don't know. But I'm going to fight them.

He felt the familiar fury in her thoughts, which was oddly reassuring. He tried to think what they could do, but all the time the old children were shuffling nearer and nearer. At this point, Mumpo realised what was happening and began to panic.

"Kess! Bo! They're coming to get us! Don't let them

touch me! What shall we do? I don't want to be old!"

"Don't jump about, Mumpo! Stay still."

"It's all right, Mumpo. They won't get past us."

Remember, said Kestrel, *they're old and weak, and they can come only one at a time. All we have to do is keep them out of reach.*

"Without touching them," said Bowman, answering aloud.

"Keep them away from me!" cried Mumpo, jerking from side to side in his fear. He tried to grab hold of Kestrel, and was threatening to unbalance them all.

"Stop it, Mumpo!"

How can we calm Mumpo down?

Feed him, replied Bowman.

Kestrel then realised she was still carrying her nut-socks round her neck, and that in one of the socks there was one mudnut remaining. She unhooked it and reached it out to Mumpo.

"Here you are, Mumpo."

As she swung it towards him, she felt the weight of the mudnut, and letting it swing back, she set it circling round and round at the end of the sock. Her eyes followed the swinging weighted end.

"Bo!" she cried out. "Have you got any mudnuts left?"

Bowman felt the nut-socks round his neck. One mudnut left in each. He had distributed the last two that way, for balance.

"Two," he said.

"Here's how we keep them away from us," said Kestrel, and she swung her weighted nut-sock through the air before her.

"Mudnuts won't hurt them."

"They don't have to. All we have to do is knock them off balance."

"Or us."

"Remember, we're young and bendy. They're old and stiff."

Not at all convinced, Bowman tried swinging his nut-sock round and round, and nearly fell off the wall. Heart pounding, sweat streaming down his body, he righted himself.

"It won't work. I can't do it."

"You've got to," said Kestrel.

"I'm hungry," said Mumpo. In all this talk of mudnuts, he had forgotten his fear.

"Shut up, Mumpo."

"All right, Kess."

All this time, the two leading old children were still creeping towards them across the parapet, from either end of the bridge. Others followed steadily behind them. The ones on Bowman's side were the nearest and would have to be fought off first.

"Swing it round, Bo," called Kestrel. "Get your balance."

Bowman looked down and saw beneath him now only inky blackness. I wouldn't mind, if there wasn't that great drop below, he thought. And as he stared down, a simple idea popped into his head. It's all dark down there. It can be anything I want. So he stopped imagining the great drop, and built a new picture in his head. There's no Crack-in-the-land, he told himself. Just a little way below me there's soft meadow grass. He added some details to this picture: clover, and poppies, and, to be real, a clump of stinging nettles, and he found to his surprise that his fear of falling was gone. That left the old child, shuffling ever closer on the wall.

He swung his nut-sock round, holding it above his head so that it made horizontal circles in the air. He swung it faster, giving it extra power each time it passed in front of him. He imagined the position of the old child's head, and he swung the mudnut through the air just where it would soon be.

Soft grass, soft meadow grass, he said to himself. Soft cushiony grass.

"Be careful, boy," said the old child, in his creaky voice. "Here, take my hand."

He reached out his withered hand and snickered. But he wasn't close enough yet.

Kestrel was facing the other way, her nut-sock in her hand, watching the leading old child approaching from her side.

It's going to be you first, Bo. Can you do it?

I'll try.

Love you, Bo.

No time to answer, not even in the silence of his head. The old child was close now, his hand patting the air between them. Bowman swung his mudnut, still holding his arm back, and it hissed through the air some way from his attacker.

"Why struggle?" said the old child. "It's as the Morah wills. You know that."

Bowman said nothing. He flexed his legs and tested his balance on the narrow parapet. He swung the weighted nut-sock faster and faster, and gauged the distance between them.

"You mustn't be afraid to be old," murmured the old child. "It's only for a little while. And then the Morah will make you young again, and beautiful."

He kept shuffling forward as he spoke, and now Bowman calculated he was within range. But he had to be sure.

"There, there," said the old child. "Come and let me stroke you."

Bowman swept his arm forward over his head, swung the mudnut at full power, and aimed for the grizzled head.

Wheee!

It whistled harmlessly past, meeting no resistance. Bowman tottered and almost fell. The old child had ducked.

"Oh, dear, dear," the deep voice sniggered. "Be careful, boy. You wouldn't want to—"

Bowman swung again, made bold by anger, and hammered the weighted sock *smack!* into the old child's face, catching him full on the cheek, just below the ear.

"Yow! Yow-ow-ow!"

Clutching at his face, the old child rocked on the wall and lost his balance. His arms reached for support, but there was nothing. He beat the air, as if to hold himself up, but even as he did so, he fell.

"Aaa-aaah . . ."

The thin voice, keen with terror, shrieked as he fell, and went on shrieking, down and down and down. And still they could hear that ghastly scream, dropping and dropping, until at last it ceased.

Hubba hubba hubba, Bo! cried Kestrel.

Nut-sock flying, she ran at her own attacker, and swept him, too, off the parapet and into the great gorge.

This galvanised the old children, and uttering creaking cries of vengeance, they pushed in on Bowman and Kestrel from either side. But only one could come forward at a time, and as Kestrel had foreseen, their reactions were slower and their joints were stiffer, and the twins sent them tumbling, one after another, into the inky darkness.

Kestrel exulted as she swung her weapon.

"Come on, you wrinkly old pocksicker! You want to practise skydiving too?"

"Hit him, Kess!" cried Mumpo, bouncing with excitement. "Knock him off!"

Kestrel lunged forward and struck, and another old child fell shrieking into the void. Mumpo called after him.

"You're going to go smash! Smish-smosh-smash and bashed flat, yah-de-dah stupid stinky no-friends!"

After seven of the old children had been sent tumbling from the wall, they stopped shuffling forward, and murmured among themselves. Then turning with nervous care, they faced the other way and shuffled back to their companions on either side of the gorge. They had retreated.

The twins saw this, and raised their arms in the air, and cheered in triumph. Bowman especially was flushed with a fierce and unaccustomed pride.

"We did it! We beat them!"

"They won't come near us again!" cried Mumpo.

But the old children hadn't gone far. They climbed down from the parapet at either end, and there they stayed. Mumpo may have believed that their victory made them safe, but Kestrel and Bowman knew otherwise. They knew that on the land, where the old children could cluster round them as they had done before, a swinging nut-sock would never save them.

Once again, they were trapped.

"Chase them, Kess!" cried Mumpo. "Bash them again!"

"I can't, Mumpo. There's too many."

"Too many?"

He looked one way across the long bridge, peering into the night, and then the other.

"We have to stay here," said Kestrel. "At least until morning."

"What, all night?"

"Yes, Mumpo. All night."

"But, Kess, we can't. There's no room to sleep."

"We're not going to sleep, Mumpo."

"Not sleep?"

To Mumpo, sleeping was as necessary and as unavoidable as eating. He wasn't so much dismayed as bewildered. How could he not sleep? Sleep wasn't something you chose. Sleep came upon you, and closed your eyes for you.

The twins knew this as well as Mumpo.

"Come on, Mumpo," said Bowman. "We'll sit either side of you, and if you want to sleep, you can."

They sat down on the wall in a row, and Bowman and Kestrel held hands round Mumpo, who sat between them, and they both leaned inwards, to hold him in a double hug, just like a wish huddle. That way if he fell asleep they could stop him from rolling off the wall. Mumpo felt the close warm embrace of the twins, and was deeply happy.

"We're the three friends," he said. And so great was his trust that he actually did fall asleep, sitting on two feet of stone wall, balanced half a mile above the granite gorge.

The twins did not sleep.

"We can't get away from them, can we?" said Bowman.

"I don't see how."

"One of them said to me, Don't be afraid to be old. The Morah will make you young again."

"I'd rather die!"

"We'll go together, won't we, Kess?"

"Always together."

They fell silent. Then, after a while, "What about Ma and Pa and Pinpin?" said Bowman. He was imagining what they would think if they never returned. "They wouldn't know we were dead. They'd go on waiting for us."

Somehow this picture of his parents still hoping, after they were dead, upset him more than the prospect of dying. Because they were in a kind of a wish huddle, he turned his dismay into a wish.

"I wish Pa and Ma could know what's happening to us."

"I wish we could escape the old children," said Kestrel, "and find the voice of the wind singer, and get safely home."

After that they were silent. The only sounds were Mumpo, snuffling in his sleep, and the sighing of the wind through the great gorge below.

And distant thunder.

"Did you hear that?"

A red flash lit up the sky and faded away.

"Is it a storm?"

Again the roll of thunder. Again the burst of red light. This time they saw it: a jet of fire, far off, streaking skywards and then curving down to earth.

"It's coming from the mountains."

"Look, Kess! Look at the old children!"

Crash! went the thunder, and *flash!* went the fireball, and as the arc of burning red was traced across the sky, and another, and another, the old children on both sides of the gorge were calling, and running about, and watching the falling fire.

Now the thunder was rolling all the time, and the fireballs were shooting skywards in all directions. Some of the burning fragments were falling close by. The twins saw one pass within a few yards of them and drop down and down, a glowing ember, into the ravine below. Another fell to earth on the ground ahead, and burned for a moment before fading into the night.

The old children were going wild. At first the twins thought it was fear, but then they saw how they were reaching their arms to the sky, and hurrying towards the fireballs as they sank to earth.

"They want to be hit!"

As Kestrel spoke these words, a fireball landed directly on one of the old children, and at once exploded in a gush of orange flame. The brilliant light faded as quickly as it had come, leaving behind—nothing.

The old children became frantic, running about, stretching up their arms, crying, "Take me! Take me!"

And here and there, more by luck than by judgement, a fireball would fall on one of them, and he would be consumed.

The sky was now bright with fire, and the thunder was unceasing. So many fireballs rose up that they could distinguish their source, which was the highest of the mountains in the northern range. The twins gazed at it, too awed by the spectacle to be frightened, and Mumpo slept stolidly on.

"That's where we have to go," said Kestrel, looking at the mountain. "Into the fire."

The fireballs fell all around them, and the children never moved, because they had nowhere to go. Somehow they knew they would be safe. This wasn't for them, this shower of death, they were only accidental witnesses. This was for the old children.

"Take me!" the old children cried, reaching for the fire. "Make me young again!"

But when the flame took them, it left nothing.

Then the thunder began to fade, and the sky grew darker,

as the fireballs came less and less frequently. The last few rose only a little way into the night, and fell far off. The remaining old children, crying pitifully, ran off towards them, as if they could cover the many miles before the flaming fragments fell to earth. And after a while, the mountain was silent, and the twins realised they were alone again.

They woke Mumpo gently, not wanting him to get up with a bounce and fall off the parapet. In fact, he remained half asleep, and did as he was told without really knowing where they were going. So feeling their way with care, they crossed to the other side of the gorge, and stepped down from the narrow parapet to the safety of solid ground.

Here Mumpo simply curled up and went back to sleep. The twins looked at each other, and realised how exhausted they were. Kestrel lay down.

"What if they come back?" said Bowman.

"I don't care," said Kestrel, and she, too, fell asleep.

Bowman sat down on the rough scratchy ground and decided he would keep watch over the others. However, within moments he too was asleep.

CHAPTER NINETEEN

MUMPO GOES WRONG

WHEN THE TWINS AWOKE, IT WAS FULL DAYLIGHT. There were no signs of the old children of the night before. They were lying close to the edge of the great gorge that they had seen before only in the half light of dusk. Now as they rose and stretched their aching limbs, they saw the fearsome depth of the gorge, and the fragile thread of wall by which they had crossed it, and they were amazed.

"Did I really walk on that?" said Bowman.

Kestrel was looking down at the great stone arches that carried the bridge across the gorge. She could see now what had not been obvious the night before, that the supporting stonework was crumbling at many points. One of the columns that held up the arches was so worn at its base by the floodwaters of the river that it seemed to stand on a pin-point. But Kestrel said nothing to Bowman about this, knowing that they would have to return this way.

Mumpo now awoke, and announced that he was hungry.

"Look, Mumpo," said Kestrel, showing him the spectac-ular sight of Crack-in-the-land. "We crossed that great bridge!"

"Did we bring anything to eat?" said Mumpo.

Bowman found the nut-sock that he had used as a weapon against the old children, and pulled out the mudnut. It was heavily bruised, but better than nothing.

"Here you are."

He tossed it towards Mumpo, but Mumpo missed it. It rolled over the sloping ground to the edge of the gorge. He chased after it, and saw where it disappeared over the edge. Kneeling on the edge, he peered down.

"I see it!" he cried. "I can get it."

"I've got another one," said Bowman.

"Let him get it if he can," said Kestrel. "We need all the food we've got."

They joined Mumpo at the edge, and saw where the mud-nut was caught in a tussock of springy grass growing from the rock face. Just below it was a clump of bushes. Bowman backed away, made giddy by looking down the immense drop. Mumpo lay on his stomach and reached over the edge for the mudnut. He could almost touch it, but not quite. So he started to wriggle forward.

"Careful, Mumpo."

But Mumpo was hungry, and his only thought was for the mudnut that lay before his eyes. He wriggled a little farther, and his fingers touched it. But still he couldn't grasp it.

"Just a bit more," he said, and wriggled again. His hand reached for the mudnut, just as his body started to slither over the edge.

"He-e-elp!" he cried, realising he couldn't stop himself.

Kestrel threw herself onto his legs, and wrapped herself tight around them.

"That's better," said Mumpo, and dangling over the edge of Crack-in-the-land, his mind was back on his breakfast.

"Climb back!" called Kestrel. "Back!"

"I'll just get the—"

His fingers were closing over the mudnut, when a withered bony hand shot out of the bush below, and seized his wrist.

"Aah! Aah! Help me!"

Mumpo jerked in terror, and Kestrel nearly lost hold of his legs.

"Bo! What's happening?"

Bowman forced himself to look over the edge, and saw there one of the old children, half supported by the bush, gripping tight to Mumpo's arm.

"Bash him, Mumpo!" Bowman screamed. "Bite him!"

"What is it?" cried Kestrel, struggling to hold Mumpo, feeling the extra weight pulling him down.

"Help me," came Mumpo's pitiful voice, changing as he spoke, growing deeper. "Help me. . . ."

"It's one of the old children," said Bowman. He unhitched his second nut-sock, and trying not to look down at the giddy-making drop, he swung it over the edge. The weighted end brushed the old child harmlessly on the shoulder. At once he turned to look up at Bowman, and his wrinkled face contorted with hatred and rage.

"Babies!" he hissed. "Silly little babies!"

That made Bowman look at him properly. He saw the thinning grey hair, the wizened cheeks, the scrawny neck—and he felt the hard dry longing in him to hurt and to destroy. He raised the nut-sock high and he swung it hard, and he brought it down on the old child's upturned face.

"Aaah!" cried the old child, and released his grip on Mumpo's arm. Losing his hold, he slipped down into the bush. The bush juddered under his weight and gave way, and down he fell.

"Aaa-aa-aa-aa . . ."

They heard his cry all the way to the bottom, and they heard the distant sound as he struck the rocks.

Kestrel dragged Mumpo back from the edge, and then let

go of him. Holding him made her feel weak. He lay there, not moving, groaning a little.

"Are you all right, Mumpo?"

His reply came in a deep cracking voice.

"I hurt all over."

He tried to stand, but the effort was too much for him. He sat down again, breathing heavily.

"I've gone wrong, Kess."

Kestrel and Bowman stared at him, trying to conceal their horror at what they saw. Mumpo's braided hair had gone grey, with the golden threads still plaited into it. His skin had gone wrinkly and baggy. His body was bent. He had turned into a little old man.

"It'll be all right, Mumpo," said Kestrel, fighting back an impulse to cry. "We'll make you all right again."

"Am I ill, Kess?"

"Yes, a little. But we'll make you well again somehow."

"My body hurts all over."

He started to cry. Not the noisy howls of the Mumpo they knew, but a silent weary weeping, a few thin tears creeping down the deep wrinkles that had formed in his face.

What can we do?

We have to go on, Bowman replied. Aloud, he said to Mumpo, "Can you walk?"

"I think so."

He got up, more carefully this time, and took a few steps.

"I can't go fast."

"That's all right. Just do your best."

"Could you help me, Bo? If I could lean on you just a little, I could go faster."

"You mustn't touch us, Mumpo. Not until you're better."

"Not touch you? Why not?"

They realised then that he hadn't understood what had happened to him.

"So we don't catch your sickness."

"Oh, I see. No, we don't want that. Will I be better soon?"

"Yes, Mumpo. Soon."

So they turned their backs on Crack-in-the-land, and set off up the Great Way to the mountains.

It was pitifully slow going. Try as he might, Mumpo couldn't walk at a normal pace. He shuffled along, and then he had to stop and rest for a few minutes. Then he shuffled along again, making no complaint, so clearly trying as hard as he could. But it was plain to both the twins that they would never make it to the top of the mountain like this.

Mumpo was not their only concern. The forest on either side was changing. The route they were following, the overgrown avenue that had once been the Great Way, was itself clear of trees, but it was flanked by an ever-denser wall of deepening forest. And through the trees, just out of the light, there sometimes seemed to be shapes accompanying them, loping silently alongside, never running ahead, never falling behind. Bowman sensed their presence out of the corners of his eyes, but whenever he turned to look, there was nothing there.

Then there were the shadows overhead. They could see now that they were birds, circling high above the trees. At first they paid them no attention; but all the time they were descending, gliding noiselessly on great outreached wings. For a while there were no more than five or six of them, but when Bowman next looked up, he counted thirteen. When he looked up again, barely half an hour later, there were too many to count: a streaming flock of ominous black shapes trailing away into the high distance. Dim tales surfaced in his mind of wild animals following travellers, watching for stragglers, waiting for their strength to fail. He pressed on faster, increasing the pace.

"This is too hard for Mumpo," said Kestrel. "We have to slow down. We should rest."

"No! We mustn't stop!"

Kestrel looked round sharply, hearing the fear in his voice.

"It's—all right," said Mumpo. "I'll—keep—up." But he could hardly find the breath to speak these few words.

Bo, we can't do this.

What else can we do?

So they struggled on. The slower they went, the bolder the birds became. They were sailing lower now, at treetop level, their great black wings casting shadows on the ground. They looked like eagles, except that they were black, and far bigger. Hard to judge just how big they were, up there above the trees.

Then Mumpo stumbled on some loose stones, and fell. He lay there, making no attempt to get up. Kestrel knelt down beside him to make sure he wasn't hurt, but he was only exhausted.

"He has to rest, Bo. Whether we want it or not."

Bowman could see that she was right.

"He'll feel better after he's had something to eat."

He swung down his nut-socks and took out his last remaining mudnut. He was reaching it out to Kestrel to give to Mumpo, when he felt a sudden rush of wind, a swish of darkness, and a sharp, painful blow to his hand.

Bowman cried out more in surprise than pain, and clutched his hand. Blood trickled out between his fingers. The black eagle was already powering away, beating its immense wings, the mudnut clutched in the razor-sharp talons that had sliced his skin in four clean shallow lines. He looked up in sheer shock at the size of the bird. There were three more of them, hovering low above them, waiting for more food to come out of the sock. Their wingspan was so huge that the three of them, side by side, shaded the whole broad avenue.

Mumpo lay staring up at the giant eagles, his eyes wide with terror, his heart pumping. Instinctively, Kestrel had put her arms over him, as if to protect him. The birds were dropping ever lower, looking for food.

"Throw it away, Bo!" shouted Kestrel.

Bowman hurled the nut-sock as far away as he could. At once, a giant eagle swooped, and snatched up the sock, and sailed up to the treetops. And the others, so many of them, went on circling silently overhead, watching, waiting.

Because the children's eyes were on the sky, they didn't see the first beast come padding silently out from between the trees, or the second. The beasts could smell Bowman's blood: the smell of wounding, and weakness. They came quietly out of the forest, one by one, and stood there, yellow eyes staring. It was Mumpo who saw them first.

He screamed.

Bowman turned quickly—and froze. All round them, some twenty yards away, stood a ring of huge grey wolves. Lean and shaggy-coated, as big as deer, their immense jaws hung open, their tongues lolling out as they panted softly and stared.

"It's all right, Mumpo," said Kestrel, hardly thinking what she was saying, just to stop his screaming.

The black eagles circled lower once more, expecting a

kill. Their great wings, overlapping each other, cast all the broad avenue now into shadow, as if night were falling. The wolves padded nearer, and stopped again. Waiting to see if their prey would turn and fight.

Mumpo's scream became his familiar fearful whimpering, only now he sobbed with an old man's voice.

"Don't let them get me," he croaked.

Now they could feel the rush of the air as the eagles swept by overhead, and they could smell the hot wet smell of the wolves' pelts. Motionless, huddled together in their terror, the children saw the wolves bare their teeth, slick and sharp and creamy-white, and pad closer still.

Then there came a sound from the trees, a long baying call. At once the wolves came to a stop. The great eagles, who had been dropping lower with each circling pass, began to climb again. The baying call sounded once more, mournful and strong, and the wolves turned and looked expectantly into the forest.

Out of the trees, stepping slowly, came a huge grizzled old wolf, the biggest of them all. His every movement spoke of power and authority, but he was old now, and with each breath there came a low sighing rumble from his broad chest. As big as a stag, but lean and sinewy for all his age, he came stepping out of the trees, and his yellow eyes were on Bowman all the way.

Bowman never flinched. The other wolves parted to make

way for their leader, and the father of the pack padded forward until he was towering over the boy. Then his long shaggy body rippled, and he sank down onto his haunches; and from there into a prone position. He laid his head on his outstretched paws, and his eyes gazed steadily at Bowman. The other wolves followed their leader's example, until the entire pack was lying down, all round the three children, panting softly.

Bowman then realised he knew what it was he must do. He held out his bleeding hand, and the father of the wolves lifted his grey muzzle, and smelt it. Then out came the long pink tongue, and licked away the blood.

Bowman sat himself slowly down on the ground, with his legs crossed, and the wolf rested its head in his lap. Its eyes looked up at the boy, and as much as man and beast can, they understood each other.

"They've been waiting for us," said Bowman, wondering how he knew the wolf's mind.

"What for?"

"To fight the Morah."

As he spoke this name, a ripple ran through the wolves, like a cold wind passing, making their shaggy fur shiver. The father of the pack rose up onto his haunches, and all the others followed suit. The old wolf then lifted up his head high and gave another mournful baying call.

The great eagles circling overhead heard the call, and they

began to descend, lower and lower, until they were passing so close that their wing tips seemed to brush the children's heads. Then one by one they landed, to stand round the wolves in a second guardian ring.

Bowman looked into the black eyes of the eagles and the yellow eyes of the wolves and saw their pride and their courage.

We have waited a long time. Now we will face the ancient enemy at last.

"They'll help us," he said. He rose to his feet, and all the wolves rose.

"Now it's time to go."

Kestrel and Mumpo obeyed him without question, accepting that he knew things they could never know. The eagles unfurled their wings and took to the air; and children and beasts continued up the Great Way towards the mountains.

Mumpo moved slowly, his weary old bones dragging him down. The twins kept to his pace, knowing how afraid he was of being left behind. But after a little while, the time came when he knew he could go no farther. He sat down on the ground, and began to cry.

"Don't leave me," he said as he wept.

The father of the wolves saw and understood. Shortly a strong young wolf was loping forward to lie beside Mumpo.

"Climb onto his back, Mumpo. He'll carry you."

They dared not help him, but after an awkward scramble,

Mumpo got himself up onto the wolf's back, and there gripped on tight to the shaggy coat. The journey was now resumed at a good steady pace, and they began to make progress towards the distant mountain.

In time the twins, too, became tired, and the wolves took them on their backs. Now for the first time they were free to leave the open track of the Great Way, and follow the wolf trails through the trees. And so, all three riding, they covered the ground far more swiftly, while the great eagles flew overhead, and their escort of wolves ran on either side, and all they could see around them were the shadowy vaults of the forest.

They were now on the higher slopes of the mountains, where the air was cold, and a mist lingered in the topmost branches of the tall pines. The trees became sparser, and when they looked back they could see the great number of wolves that had joined them, streaming away behind them as far as the eyes could see, while overhead flew hundreds and hundreds of eagles.

Ahead now loomed the mountain towards which they had been journeying. It seemed so immense, its flattened peak so impossibly high, that they couldn't see how they could ever reach it, even at the speed of the running wolves. What was worse, it proved to be even farther away than they supposed, for as they came over a ridge, they saw a tree-covered valley dip away before them and realised they hadn't even begun to ascend the main peak.

The trail curved here as it descended, and passed out of sight round the ridge. The wolves carrying the children ran slower now, and then walked, while the eagles above began dropping down, circling to land. As they reached the bend in the trail, the wolves came to a complete stop and lay down. It was evident that they wanted the children to dismount. As they did so, the eagles landed in their hundreds, all over the ground and in the trees.

Kestrel looked to Bowman to know what they were to do next, but he had no idea. It was Mumpo who now took the lead.

To the surprise of the twins, as soon as he was standing, he started to move, shuffling down the trail as fast as he was able, impelled by some inexplicable urgency.

"Mumpo! Wait!"

He didn't hear them. He was reaching his arms forward as he went, as if to come all the sooner to whatever it was that drew him on. Bowman turned to look at the great army of the wolves. They sat or lay, tongues out and panting, eyes on the father of the pack. He for his part sat with raised head, sniffing the wind, waiting. Bowman smelt the air.

"Smoke."

"We can't lose him."

So they set off after Mumpo, who was now out of sight.

And as they, too, rounded the bend in the trail, they saw before them an extraordinary sight. There below them lay the Great Way once more, broad and open, and down it were moving many figures, Mumpo now among them. Like Mumpo, they had their arms outstretched, and they were stooping, and they hobbled as they went. Mumpo was some way ahead of them, and almost running. He groaned and panted as he ran, calling out in his old man's voice.

"Take me!" he cried. "Take me!"

He was running towards the source of the smoke, where the Great Way ran into the mountainside, into a rift as wide as the road that was filled with fire. The flames climbed high and became smoke, and the smoke streamed out into the open air above. Down the Great Way towards this gate of fire, ahead of Mumpo and behind him, moved the other stooping figures, their arms outstretched like his, not all children, but all old; and from their mouths came the same cry, as they neared the flames.

"Take me! Make me young again!"

Mumpo was truly running now, jerkily and with difficulty, but as if his life depended on it.

"Mumpo! No!"

Kestrel started after him, but he was too far ahead, and he didn't seem to hear her. He was running directly towards the fire. The other old people were all doing the same: the nearer they got to the flames, the faster they hurried, as if eager for death. When they reached the fire, they let their out-reached arms drop, and they walked into the flames without visible fear or pain. What happened to them then, Kestrel couldn't see, because they were lost in the brightness of the fire.

Bowman caught up with her and stood by her side. In silence, they stared at the towering crack in the mountain and the belching smoke. They stared as Mumpo ran stumbling and calling towards the flames.

"Take me! Make me young again!"

Then the pitiful cry fell silent, and his clumsy gallop was slowed to a hobbling walk, and he, too, was swallowed by the fire.

For a moment longer, the twins were silent, in shock. Then Kestrel felt for her brother's hand.

We must go into the fire.

We go together, he said, knowing this was how it had to be.

Always together.

So hand in hand they walked down the last of the Great Way towards the flames.

CHAPTER TWENTY

INTO THE FIRE

AS THEY APPROACHED THE GREAT RIFT IN THE MOUNTAIN, the twins felt the fierce heat of the fire, and smelt its acrid rising smoke. Why did the old people have no fear? How could they step so eagerly into its very heart and never cry out? But on they walked towards the fire, only revealing their fear by the tightness with which they held hands.

When the glare was too bright, they closed their eyes. The heat was strong, but not burning. The sounds of the outer world, of the mountains and the forest, were slipping away into silence. Even their own shoes, resolutely treading towards the furnace, seemed now to make no sound.

No going back now. Just a few more steps . . .

All at once, the heat faded away, to be replaced by a soft

coolness that seemed to lick about them. The brightness was still dazzling, blinding their closed eyes with blood-red light. But even without seeing it, they knew they had entered the fire, and were being bathed in cool flame.

On they walked, unharmed, and the dazzling light became less intense, and the cool caress fell away. Then little by little they sensed that the light was fading. Opening their eyes, they saw that the flames were fainter now. And within a few more paces, they were out of the fire entirely, and into a realm of shadow. Though where they were was hard to say.

As their eyes adjusted to the darkness, they made out the walls of a broad passage, with doors at its far end. The walls were timber panelled, and the floor was tiled. They seemed to be in the hallway of a grand mansion.

Looking back, they had another surprise. There was the fire behind them, but it was no more than a coal fire, burning in a well-kept grate, within a carved stone fireplace. Had they just walked out of that?

The long hallway ran from the fireplace at one end to the doors at the other. It had no windows. There was only one way to go.

Still hand in hand, beyond amazement, they made their way down the hallway to the closed double doors at the far end. Bowman tried the handles and found the doors were not locked. He eased one open a crack and looked through. Another hallway.

This hallway, an extension of the first, had many rooms opening off it on either side. It was candle-lit, and more ornately decorated. The dark wood panelling was carved in patterns of leaves and flowers. There were tapestries hanging between the many doors, faded scenes of hunting and archery. Down the centre of the passage ran a finely woven carpet.

The twins made their way down this carpet, looking through the open doors to the right and left as they went. They caught glimpses of darkened sitting rooms, the furniture all draped in dust sheets.

They moved as quietly as they could, fearful of what they might find. Although there was nothing to tell them so, they were directing their steps towards the far end of the hallway, which as before was closed with double doors. As they drew closer, they saw that unlike the other rooms they were passing, which were dark, there was a glow of light beneath the end doors.

They heard nothing as they went but the beating of their own hearts. The mansion, if mansion it was, seemed to be deserted. Yet candles burned in sconces along the passage walls, and the carpet over which they walked was well swept.

When they reached the end doors, they stood close by

them and listened. There were no sounds. Softly, Kestrel turned one handle and opened one door. The hinges gave a slight creak. They froze. But nothing happened, no footsteps, no calling voices. So she opened the door all the way, and they entered the room beyond.

It was a dining room, and it was laid for dinner. A handsome dining table stood in the middle of the room, gleaming with silver and crystal. Places were set for twelve. The candles on the two branched candelabra were burning, as were the candles in the great chandelier that hung above. There was water in the crystal water jugs and bread in the silver bread baskets. Coal fires burned in two elegant fireplaces, one on each side of the room. Portraits hung on the windowless walls, haughty images of lords and ladies of the distant past. There was only one other door, and that was facing them, at the far end. It was closed.

None of this was as the twins had imagined. They had hardly known what to expect, except that it would make them feel fear. This strange deserted grandeur was frightening, but not because it felt dangerous. The fear lay in not understanding. Because nothing they were now seeing made any sense. Anything could happen. And there was nothing they could do to prepare themselves for it.

Stepping softly, they crossed the room, past the brocaded chairs lined up before the long glittering table, to the far door. Once again Kestrel paused, listened, and heard nothing. She opened the door.

A lady's dressing room, lit by two oil lamps. Tall closets, their doors open, filled with beautiful gowns. Stacks of drawers, also pulled open, in which lay chemises and stockings and petticoats, all beautifully pressed and folded. And shoes, and slippers, and boots, in numberless array. On a dressmaker's dummy hung a ball gown in the process of being made, its seams held together by pins. Bolts of fine figured silk lay partly unrolled over a daybed, and on an inlaid table were arranged all the tools of the dressmaker's art, the scissors and needles, the threads and buttons and braids. There was a tall pier glass, in which they caught sight of their own reflections, pale-faced and nervous, eyes wide, hand in hand.

Two doors led out of the dressing room, and both were open. One was to a bathroom: unlit and empty. The other led to a bedroom.

They stood very still in the dressing room doorway and looked into the bedroom. A lamp burned here, too, on a low table beside a bed. The room was large and square. Trophies hung from its panelled walls: swords and helmets, flags and pennants, as if this were the mess room of a regiment, proud of its battle history. But instead of leather club chairs and tables spread with newspapers, there was only the high ornate canopied bed, set right in the middle of the polished floor. The canopy was of gauze, suspended from a centre ring in the ceiling, spread out like a diaphanous skirt to cover the entire bed. On the bedside table, beside the softly glowing lamp, stood a glass of water and an orange on a plate. Beside the orange, a little silver knife. And in the bed, just visible through the gauze, beneath lace-edged linen sheets and embroidered coverlets, propped up in a sitting position by a mound of pillows, lay an old, old lady, fast asleep.

Very slowly, hardly daring to disturb the still air in which the old lady slept, the twins entered the bedroom. The wide boards made no sound beneath their feet, and they forced themselves to breathe in low even breaths. So, little by little, they came up to the bedside, and stood gazing at the old lady through the gauze; and still she slept.

Her face was calm and smooth in sleep, the outline of the bones showing clear through the papery skin. She looked as if she had been beautiful once, many years ago. Bowman gazed on her, and felt an almost unbearable longing, though for what he did not know.

Kestrel's eyes were darting round the room, to see if there was a cupboard or box that might contain the voice of the wind singer. It wasn't big, it could be anywhere: in this room, or one of the other rooms, or in some place they had not yet entered. For the first time Kestrel allowed herself to believe, with a deep dark lurch of fear, that they might fail. They might never find it. Her brother sensed the terror in her mind. Without taking his eyes off the sleeping old lady, he spoke silently to his sister.

It's there. In her hair.

Kestrel looked, and saw it. Holding back the old lady's fine white hair was a silver clasp, in the shape of a curled-over letter *S*: the shape of the outline etched on the wind singer, and drawn on the back of the map. An intense relief, as sudden as the terror, streamed into her, bringing with it a renewal of strength and will.

Can you get it without waking her?

I'll try.

Bowman seemed to have lost his usual timidity, or to have forgotten it in his fascination with that old, old face. Gently he reached out one hand, and with sure, untrembling fingers took hold of the silver clasp. Holding his breath, so that his whole body was still, he drew the clasp slowly, slowly, out of the thinning white hair. Still the old lady slept on. Now, with the faintest shudder, the clasp came free, and in the glinting of the lamplight Bowman saw that across the curve of the *S* ran many fine threads of taut silver wire. He released his held breath, and lifted the clasp away. As he did so, he felt a sudden tug. A single white hair was snagged in the clasp, and as he lifted it, the hair strained tight, and snapped.

Bowman froze. Kestrel reached for the silver clasp that was the voice of the wind singer and took it from his outstretched hand.

Let's go!

But Bowman's eyes were on the old lady. Her eyelids were flickering and opening. Pale, pale blue eyes gazed up at him.

"Why do you wake me, child?"

Her voice was low and mild. Bowman tried to look away from those eyes, but he could not.

Bo! Let's go!

I can't.

As Bowman gazed into those watery blue eyes, he saw them change. In her eyes there were other eyes, many eyes, hundreds of eyes, staring back at him. The eyes drew him in, and in each he saw more eyes, and more, so that there was no end to them. As he looked, he felt a new spirit flood his body, a spirit that was bright and pure and powerful.

We are the Morah, said the million eyes to him. We are legion. We are all.

"There, now," said the voice of the old lady. "Not afraid anymore."

As she spoke the words, he knew they were true. What was there to fear? So long as he looked into the million eyes, he was part of the greatest power in existence. No more fear now. Let others fear.

From far off he heard the sound of distant music: drums, pipes, trumpets. The unmistakable sound of a marching band, accompanied by the tramp of marching feet.

"Bo!" cried Kestrel aloud in her fear. "Come away!"

But Bowman could not remove his gaze from those pale blue eyes in which he was joined to the legion that was the Morah; nor did he want to. The sound of marching feet was coming nearer, led by its jaunty band.

"They're coming now," said the old lady. "I can't stop them now."

Kestrel took his arm and pulled at it, but he was unexpectedly strong, and she couldn't move him.

"Bo! Come away!"

"My beautiful Zars," murmured the old lady. "They do so love to kill."

To kill! thought Bowman, and he felt a thrill of power course through him. To kill!

He looked up, and there before him on the wall hung a fine curving sword.

Tramp! Tramp! Tramp! came the sound of the approaching marchers.

"Take the sword," said the old lady.

"No!" cried Kestrel.

Bowman reached up and took the sword from the wall, and the handle felt good in his right hand, and the blade felt light but deadly. Kestrel stepped back from him, frightened, and it was well that she did, for all at once he turned, smiling a smile she had never seen before, and slashed with his sword across the space where she had stood.

"Kill!" he said.

Oh my brother! What has she done to you?

Tramp! Tramp! Tramp!

The beat of the drums, the blare of the trumpets. Kestrel looked and in her terror saw that the bedroom walls were fading away into darkness. The dressing room door, the trophy-laden walls, were disappearing, until all that was left was the canopied bed, and the table beside it, and the lamp, reaching out its soft light in a circle of illumination. Beyond that, a black void.

Tramp! Tramp! Tramp!

"No more fear," said the old lady. "Let others fear now."

Kestrel was backing away from Bowman, terrified, even as she called out to him.

My Bo! My brother! Come back to me!

"Kill!" he said, slashing the air with his sword. "Let others fear now!"

"My beautiful Zars march again," said the old lady. "Oh, how they love to kill."

"Kill, kill, kill, kill!" said Bowman, singing the words to a jaunty tune, the tune played by the marching band. "Kill, kill, kill!"

My dear one, called Kestrel, her heart breaking, *don't leave me now. I can't live without you—*

And now at last, out of the darkness they came. In the lead, twirling a golden baton, high-stepped a tall beautiful girl in a crisp white uniform. Long golden hair flowed freely over her shoulders, framing her lovely young face. She looked no older than fifteen, and as she marched and twirled her baton, she smiled. How she smiled! The white jacket was square-shouldered and tight at the waist, with big golden buttons. She wore spotless white riding britches and gleaming black boots. On her head, set at a jaunty angle, was a white peaked cap braided with gold, and over her shoulders flowed a long white cape lined with gold. She gazed straight ahead of her, into the high distance, and she smiled as she marched.

Behind her, out of the darkness, came a line of bandsmen, all uniformed in white. They, too, were young, boys and girls of thirteen, fourteen, fifteen, and every one of them was beautiful, and every one of them was smiling. They marched briskly, keeping excellent time, playing their instruments as they came. Behind them were more bandsmen, followed by a rank of drummers. And behind them, singing as they smiled and swung along, came rank upon rank of youthful soldiers.

Kestrel heard the singing voices, and slowly the shape of the words penetrated her shocked senses. These beautiful boys and girls, this army of white-and-golden youth, were singing the same song as Bowman, the song that had only one word.

"Kill, kill, kill, kill! Kill, kill, kill!"

The tune was martial but melodic, and the melody, once heard, was impossible to forget. It swung up and down, and back up to its climax; and then round it came again, relentless.

"Kill, kill, kill, kill! Kill, kill, kill!"

The ranks of soldiers came on, line after line, out of the darkness. How many were there? The numbers seemed limitless.

"My beautiful Zars," said the old lady. "Nothing can stop them now."

The baton-twirling bandleader now came to a stop but continued marching on the spot. Behind her the band, still playing, formed up in broad ranks, also marching on the spot. And behind them, the soldiers. The singing ceased, but the music and the steady tramping went on, though now the great army did not advance. At the rear, far away in the darkness where the lamplight didn't reach, more lines of soldiers were coming forward all the time to join the waiting ranks. All were young, all were beautiful, and all were smiling.

Kestrel was backing farther and farther away all the time, in the direction of the passages and the fire. She still clutched the silver voice tight in one hand, but she had forgotten it entirely. She was weeping, also without knowing it. For her eyes were on her beloved brother, who she loved even more than she loved herself, and her young heart was breaking.

My brother! My love! Come back to me!

Bowman didn't hear her, or look at her, he was so changed. He was moving into position in front of the great army, and his sword was sweeping the air, and on his face was the same terrible smile that was on all their faces. Then in the ranks behind, even as she wept, Kestrel saw another familiar face transformed. It was Mumpo, wearing the white-and-gold uniform of the Zars, and he wasn't old anymore, and he wasn't dirty. He was young, and handsome, and smiling with pride. As she stared at him, he caught her eyes and waved at her.

"I've got friends, Kess!" he called to her joyously. "Look at all my friends!"

"No!" screamed Kestrel. "No! No! NO!"

But her screams were drowned as Bowman raised his

sword high, and with a long rippling flash all the Zars drew their swords, and the army began to march. The beautiful baton twirler came high-stepping behind Bowman, and the bandsmen and the drummers played, smiling into the distance, and the soldiers sang as they marched.

"Kill, kill, kill, kill! Kill, kill, kill!"

Kestrel turned, and weeping, she ran for her life.

When the column of Zars reached the canopied bed, they parted to either side of it. Their drawn swords flashed as they marched, slicing the orange on its silver plate, slashing the canopy to ribbons, sending fragments of gauze floating in the air. One fragment landed in the bowl of the lamp and caught fire. In a moment, the whole bed was ablaze. Still the Zars marched on, unswerving, their handsome young faces briefly illuminated by the burning bed. And in the bed, the old lady lay motionless, raised on burning pillows, and watched the army pass with pride.

Kestrel ran weeping down the Halls of Morah, the silver voice in her hand. Behind her came the Zars, destroying everything in their path. The elegant clothes laid out in the dressing room, the dining table laid for a company that never came, all fell to the flashing swords and turned to dust.

Oh my brother, my dear love, my own!

Kestrel cried out in her heartbreak as she ran in her

terror, until she saw before her the stone fireplace, where burned the fire in its grate. Behind her the marching tramp of a million feet, the singing of a million voices. No time to question or to understand. Without slowing down in her headlong flight, she hurled herself into the fireplace, and—

Silence. Cool columns of flame. Dazzling brightness. Panting, shaking, she forced herself to stop. The eerie cold of the fire cleared her head, and she knew this was not what she wanted to do. Why was she running from her twin? For her, there was no life without him. If he was changed, then she would change, too.

Not like this, she thought. We go together.

She turned, and there in the white light she saw her beloved brother coming towards her, at the head of the army of the Zars. He was moving slowly, and the sound of the music seemed far away, but he was still singing softly, as were they all, a smiling whisper as they came.

"Kill, kill, kill, kill! Kill, kill, kill!"

Kestrel raised her eyes to meet his, and opened her arms wide, so that his sword, which rose and fell before him as he marched, would strike her across the breast.

We go together, my brother, she said to him. *Even if you have to kill me.*

His eyes found her now. He was still smiling, but the words of the song faded on his lips.

I won't leave you, she said to him. *I'll never leave you again.*

He was closer now, the sword still rising and falling before him.

I love you, she said to him. *My beloved brother.*

Now the smile, too, was fading, and the sword rising and falling more slowly. He was very close to her, and could see the tears on her cheeks.

Kill me, dear one. Let's go together.

His eyes filled with confusion. His sword was raised now, and he had reached her. One more downward stroke would cut her through. But the blow never fell. He stopped and stood there, motionless.

The beautiful bandleader came high-stepping right past them without so much as a sideways glance. So, too, the lines of bandsmen and drummers, playing away, smiling into the chill of the flames. Bowman's eyes were locked on Kestrel's, and she could see him returning, the brother she had lost, like a diver rising from the deep.

Kess, he said, recognising her. And the sword fell from his hand. He took her in his arms and hugged her, as the army of the Zars marched singing past them.

Oh, Kess . . .

He was shaking now, and weeping. She kissed his wet cheeks.

There, she said. *There. You've come back.*

CHAPTER TWENTY-ONE

THE MARCH OF THE ZARS

SEIZING HIS SISTER'S HAND, BOWMAN RAN THROUGH the cool white flames, and Kestrel ran with him. There was no time to talk of what had happened. They overtook the leader of the band, who still paid them no attention, as if the fire through which they passed held everything in suspension. Then suddenly they were out of the fire, and there were the forest-clad mountains rising on either side, and the wind in their faces, and the broad sweep of the Great Way before them, and dark clouds above.

Not clouds: Kestrel looked up and saw them. The eagles were circling in their hundreds, darkening the sky. She pulled Bowman off the road, into the trees.

"They're going to attack!"

The great eagles swept lower and lower, the beat of their powerful wings shivering the branches of the trees. And there, standing silently between the trees, yellow eyes on the gate of fire, were line upon line of grey wolves.

The beautiful young bandleader came strutting out of the fire, her baton flying high, and after her the band, playing their jaunty music. As the columns of the Zars followed them eight abreast onto the Great Way, the eagles folded their wings and dropped like thunderbolts, screaming out of the sky. They spread their wings again at the last moment as the giant talons struck. The claws took hold, and up they powered, white-and-gold bodies twitching beneath, to release their victims high above the tallest treetops. Never once did the raptured Zars utter a single cry; never once did their comrades look up or show fear. Eagle after eagle, wave after wave, ripped into the marching column, but each hole they tore in the ranks was immediately filled from behind, and still the Zars marched on. Their long swords were out, flashing and deadly, and many an eagle made its dive and never rose again. But more terrifying than the blows the Zars struck was their disregard of the blows they received. Not for one instant did they cease to smile as their comrades were hurled into oblivion. Not once did they miss a step. And still, unending, they marched out of the tunnel, a long unbroken line of white and gold.

Now the eagles were peeling away, and it was the turn of the wolves. The old wolf lifted up his head and gave a savage cry. From out of the trees, howling with blood lust, the first lines of wolves fell on their enemy. The great jaws ripped into the Zars, rending bloody holes in the column, but the long swords were fast and deadly, and not one of the beasts rose up to attack again.

And so the battle raged. Now the eagles returned to the attack, and now the wolves: but always the marching lines reformed from behind, and the shining white-and-gold soldiers marched steadily onwards to the music of the band, tramping over the bodies of eagles and wolves, and the bodies of their dead and wounded comrades alike.

Tramp! Tramp! Tramp!

"Kill, kill, kill, kill! Kill, kill, kill!"

They never even stopped singing.

Bowman watched them with horror and fascination.

"They're marching to Aramanth," he said. And turning to Kestrel, with fierce urgency, "Do you have the voice?"

"Yes. I have it here."

"We must go! We must get to Aramanth before them!"

He was ready to go there and then, to try to outrun the tireless Zars all the way home, but Kestrel held his arm.

"Look! There's Mumpo!"

In the midst of the battle, radiant with returned youth,

his white-and-gold uniform spattered with blood, Mumpo marched with the Zars, smiling at the carnage on all sides.

"Go!" cried Bowman. "We must go!"

"We can't leave him," said Kestrel.

As he marched past, she dashed into the fray and caught hold of his arm, and dragged him out to the side. Half-hypnotised by the music and the marching, he didn't at first realise what was happening.

"Kess! Look at all my friends, Kess!"

Kestrel and Bowman took him between them and ran with him deeper into the trees. As they ran, a detachment of Zars broke away from the column in pursuit.

They ran until they were exhausted. Then Kestrel rounded on Mumpo.

"Listen to me, Mumpo. The Zars aren't your friends, they're your enemies. We're your friends. Either you go with them, or you go with us."

Mumpo stared at her in confusion.

"Why can't we all go together?"

"Can't you see—" In her frustration, she almost shook him.

"It's all right, Kess," said Bowman. He took Mumpo's hands in his, and spoke to him softly.

"I know what it feels like, Mumpo. I felt it too. It feels like you're not alone and afraid anymore. Like no one can ever hurt you again."

"Yes, that's right, Bo."

"We can't give you that feeling. But we've stood by you, and you've stood by us. Don't leave us now."

Mumpo looked into Bowman's gentle eyes, and slowly the dream of glory faded.

"Am I to be alone and afraid again, Bo?"

"Yes, Mumpo. I wish I could tell you we'll keep you safe, but I can't. We're not as strong as they are."

Kestrel watched her brother speaking, and she marvelled at him. He sounded older, sadder, surer. Mumpo, too, she saw it now, had been changed by all that had happened to him. He was confused, but he was no longer foolish.

"You were my first friends," he said simply. "I'll never leave you."

The twins took him in their arms, both together, and there was just time for a hug of comradeship before they saw the glint of white uniforms approaching through the trees. The Zars had not just followed them, as they very soon saw: they had encircled them. A dozen and more now closed in on the spot where they stood.

"Climb!" said Kestrel.

She jumped up into the spreading branches of the tree above and started to climb. Bowman and Mumpo followed her. They climbed up and up, until they came out onto the topmost branches. From here they could see the Great Way, and the still-raging battle. The eagles were fewer now, and the wolves almost all exhausted. On a high rock, the grizzled father wolf stood, his long baying howl sending the last lines of wolves into the attack.

From their high tree, the children watched helplessly as the wolves made their charge. The few remaining wolves stood tall and proud among the trees, waiting their turn, and when the order came, they knew they too would meet their death at the edge of those merciless swords. But in they went, crying their deep-throated war cries, to bring down as many Zars as they could before falling themselves. Against any natural enemy, the power and the savagery of the wolves would have been devastating. But the Zars were numberless, and no matter how many were brought down, there were always more.

"Stop!" cried Kestrel from the high branch, in pity and horror. "Stop! It's no good!"

But if the old wolf heard her, he paid her no heed. He shook his shaggy mane, and called once more, and the very last line of wolves threw themselves into the battle. As he watched them fall, one after the other, the pride of the mountains laid low, he stilled his aching heart.

We face the ancient enemy at last. What can we do but die?

Then he lifted his old head high, and howled his own war cry, his death cry, and gathering all the power remaining in him, he hurled himself into the fray. One down, his killer teeth ripping, tossing, two down, turn on a third, and for a second he saw the bright gleam before the blade passed through his shoulder and into his bursting heart.

And still the Zars marched singing onwards. Behind them they left a grisly litter of corpses, above them the great eagles still swooped and struck, but the column swung gaily along, unbroken, the only sign of their losses the blood that spattered their billowing white cloaks.

Meanwhile, below the children, their pursuers surrounded the base of the tree. Laughing like young people at play, they threw off their caps and their cloaks and began to climb.

They were astonishingly agile, and seemed able to cling to the side of the broad trunk itself. Soon the leader, a sunny-faced boy who could not have been older than thirteen, had reached the higher branches, and was gazing up to where the children were perched.

"Hallo!" he called up to them in a friendly voice. "I'm coming to kill you!"

And as he began the next stage of his climb, he hummed the tune of the marching song under his breath.

"Kill, kill, kill, kill! Kill, kill, kill!"

Behind him came a lovely ash-blonde girl, catching him up fast.

"Leave one for me!" she called to her comrade. "You know how I love killing!"

The children shuffled farther out along their branch. That way, the Zars would have to come after them one at a time. Kestrel looked down. Too far to jump. Bowman looked up, knowing there was now only the one way of escape. He called, a long wordless cry, and they heard him, and came beating fast across the sky towards them, the great eagles.

The leading Zar was just one layer of branches below them now, and as they watched, he came climbing up to support himself on their branch.

"Doesn't take long, does it?" he said, smiling. And drew his long sword.

"Leave one for me!" called the girl below. "I want the girl."

"I want the girl for myself," said the young Zar, stepping out onto their branch. "I've never killed a girl."

A flash of darkness, a shuddering blow, and he was seized by the talons of a diving eagle and ripped into the air. Before the children could quite absorb what had happened, there were three eagles hovering above them, and they knew what they had to do. Bowman raised his hands high.

"Hands up!"

Mumpo copied Bowman's gesture. An eagle dropped down, gently clasped his wrists in its great claws, and carried him up and away. Bowman followed. Kestrel hesitated, staring at the girl Zar coming along the branch towards her, her sword snicking the air. She raised her arms, too, seeing the eagle approaching. The sword flashed, forcing the eagle to swerve, just as Kestrel sprang off the branch into nothingness. Her arms outreached, she fell, and the eagle fell with her, its wings hissing. Then she felt its sudden rushing closeness, and the swooping claws closed about her wrists, and she was falling no more.

The great wings beat strongly, carrying them over the marching ranks of Zars, and on down the Great Way. The wind on her face, the wide wings above shielding her from the sun, Kestrel allowed herself to feel hope. She looked back and down. The Zars seemed small and far away now, though the end of the marching column was still not in sight. Then she became aware that her eagle was straining to maintain its height. Ahead she could see Bowman's eagle was already flying more slowly and losing altitude. Big though the eagles were, the children were too heavy for them to carry far. What now? If they were put down, the Zars would overtake them soon enough.

She looked back to see how much of a lead they had, and there behind her, keeping pace with them, were three more eagles. As she watched, she saw them separate and glide silently into position.

It happened so quickly she had no time to be afraid. One moment she became aware that an eagle was passing beneath her. The next moment she felt the talons holding her wrists open wide, and she was dropping like a stone. And barely a moment later, the eagle below had banked, turned on its back, and its talons had locked onto her wrists. The great wings beat once, and she was in flight again, sailing up over the trees.

Twisting about, she was able to watch the entire manoeuvre take place with Mumpo. He lost control when he was let go, and thrashed his arms in the air, but the eagle waiting for him was still able to catch his wrists and swing him the right way round.

Bowman was already on to his second eagle, streaming through the air on her left. She turned and looked back, and there in the far distance she could see the column of the Zars, marching steadily down the Great Way, harried by the few eagles now left to fight the lost battle. Turning again, she saw ahead the jagged rift called Crack-in-the-land, and the high arches of the ruined bridge that was its only crossing. There were no more eagles to carry them when these three tired, and Aramanth was still far away. She knew they had only the one chance.

"Bo!" she called out. "We have to smash the bridge!"

Bowman, too, had been looking ahead, and he

understood all that his sister was thinking. He tugged on his eagle's legs, and the great bird, glad to rest, circled down to the ground.

They landed on the south side of the ravine, near the high pillars that marked the start of the bridge. Once they were safely on the ground, the eagles took off again to return to the battle, as if it were understood that all must die before it was over.

Bowman started gathering up stones at a frantic pace.

"We have to make an avalanche," he said. "We have to bring down the bridge."

He rolled stones down the slope, following them to the very edge of the gorge to watch where they fell. When at last one of the stones rattled against the base of the most fragile supporting column far below, he marked the spot.

"Mumpo, give me your sword!" he cried.

Mumpo drew his sword from its scabbard, and Bowman drove it firmly into the ground.

"All the stones we can find, here!" he said, and he started to form a pile of stones against the blade.

Mumpo meanwhile was unbuckling his sword belt, and unbuttoning his gold buttons, and peeling off his white jacket. Off came the high black boots and the white riding britches with the gold braid down the outside seam. Underneath were his old faded orange clothes. When all of the uniform of the

Zars was off, he pulled the boots back on, because he had left his own shoes behind. Then he took the little pile of white bloodstained clothes and threw them into the ravine.

"That's over now," he said.

Then all three of them worked as fast as they could, building their mound of stones. They laboured on as the light faded in the sky, until the pile was higher than their own heads. And all the time, the marching Zars were getting nearer. Every now and again, some of the stones broke free from the pile, and skittered down the slope into the gorge. Each time Bowman ran ahead to follow the stones' fall. Each time he came back saying, "More! We need more!"

The sun turned red and began to set. Across the great ravine the vanguard of the Zars was near enough now for them to make out the baton-twirling bandleader, high-stepping at the front. There was no way of knowing whether they had gathered enough stones to do what they wanted, but Bowman knew that now they had run out of time.

"Let's do it!"

All three of them positioned themselves against the high mound of stones and braced themselves. The sounds of the band came floating through the sunset air towards them, and with it that ceaseless beat of marching feet.

Tramp! Tramp! Tramp!

"Now!" said Bowman, and he pulled away the sword, and

they all pushed. A part of the pile slithered and went crashing down into the ravine.

"Push! Harder! We have to get it all moving at once!"

They pushed again, straining with all their might, and suddenly the pile gave way. With a slow rumble, it started to slide. The thousands of stones they had gathered poured down the slope, gathering speed, throwing up a cloud of dust and other fragments, until they leapt out into the emptiness of Crack-in-the-land. Down fell the spill of rubble, down and down in a ribbon of smoky debris, as the children watched and listened, holding their breath. The shadows in the gorge were too deep now to see where their avalanche fell, but after a longer time than they had thought possible, at last they heard it: the fusillade of cracks and rattles as the stones struck—what? The supporting columns? The sides of the gorge? Then there followed the sound of more falling fragments, but they had no way of knowing whether this was the avalanche they had triggered from above, or the breaking masonry of the tall slender arches. They watched the upper sections of the bridge, that same narrow parapet on which they had fought the old children, but nothing was moving. And on the far side of the gorge, the Zars were in view now, their white-and-gold uniforms glowing red in the low rays of the setting sun.

"It didn't work."

This was Kestrel, gazing at the bridge.

"We must go," she said. "We have to keep ahead of them."

"No," said Bowman, his voice steady and low. "They'll overtake us long before we get to Aramanth."

"What else can we do?"

"You go on, with Mumpo. I'll stay here. Only one of them can cross the bridge at a time. I can hold them."

Now the Zars had reached the edge of Crack-in-the-land. The bandleader was marching on the spot, the golden baton still rising and falling, and behind her the band was formed up, still playing. Then even as Kestrel was finding words to tell her brother there had to be another way, the bandleader caught her baton, pointed it forward, and stepped up smartly onto the parapet of the bridge. Behind her, while the band played along the lip of the gorge, came the Zars, in single file.

Bowman stooped and picked up the sword.

"No!" cried Kestrel.

He turned and gave her a curious smile, and spoke in a voice she had never heard him use before: quiet, but very strong.

"Go on to Aramanth. There's no other way."

"I can't leave you."

"I've felt the power of the Morah. Don't you see?"

He turned and ran towards the bridge. The bandleader was already halfway across, high-stepping as calmly as if she was still on the Great Way itself, and behind her came the long line of smiling Zars. Bowman raised the sword high as he ran, and he shouted, a wordless howl of fury, unaware that as he cried out, the tears were streaming down his cheeks.

Kestrel started to run after him, calling with all her might.

"Don't go! Don't go without me!"

Only Mumpo stayed staring at the slope, and so it was he who saw the first signs of what was about to happen.

"The bridge!" he called out. "It's moving!"

Bowman had just reached the start of the stone parapet when the central arch gave a slow ripple, like a tree in a strong wind, and there came the sound of cracking masonry. Then, still slowly, the thin line that joined one side of the ravine to the other snapped like an overstretched string, and the wall and the parapet shivered and started to fall. It fell first from the children's end, unravelling faster and faster towards the middle, where the Zars were high-stepping across. Then the parapet on which they marched was curling down and away, and the bandleader was falling, and the line of Zars was falling, out of the region of sunset light and into the well of darkness. They neither cried out nor made a sound. And behind them as they fell, their comrades marched on, to fall in their turn.

Bowman had come to a stop, staring in shock at the sight.

Kestrel now joined him and put her arms round him. Hugging each other, they watched as the Zars marched on, now in their column formation, eight abreast, over the edge of the gorge, to plunge to their doom. Line after line, to the beat of the band, over they went.

"We stopped them, Bo. We're safe."

Bowman stared at the fallen bridge.

"No," he said. "We're not safe. But we've got time now."

"How can they cross Crack-in-the-land, with the bridge gone?"

"Nothing can stop the Zars," said Bowman.

Mumpo came to join them, awed by the sight of the Zars marching so blithely to their deaths.

"Don't they mind dying?" he said.

"Don't you remember how it felt, Mumpo?" said Bowman. "So long as one Zar lives, they all live. They live through each other. They don't care how many die, because there are always more."

"How many more?"

"There's no end to them."

This was the horror the Old Queen had seen. The Zars could be slain, they could be defeated, but they could never be stopped. There were always more.

"That's why we have to get to Aramanth before them," said Bowman.

He turned as if to set off then and there. But his last charge, in which he had expected to die, had drained him of all his remaining strength; and after taking a few steps, he folded slowly to the ground. Kestrel dropped to his side, alarmed.

"I can't go on," he said. "I have to sleep."

So Kestrel and Mumpo curled up on either side of him, where he had fallen, and the three of them slept in one another's arms.

CHAPTER TWENTY-TWO

THE HATH FAMILY BROKEN

ON THE DAY BEFORE THE HIGH EXAMINATION, Principal Pillish assembled all the candidates on his Residential Study Course to give them his customary day-before talk. He was proud of this talk, which he had given many times, and knew by heart. He believed it steadied the nerves of the candidates in a specially valuable way. It was true that year after year every member of his little group went on, without exception, to fail the High Examination. But who was to say they would not have failed even more dismally, but for his day-before talk?

The truth was, Principal Pillish had a secret dream. He was an unmarried man, devoted to a job that offered little in the way of rewards. His secret dream was that one year, one of his failing group of candidates would surprise him, and all Aramanth, by winning top marks in the High Examination. In his secret dream, this happy candidate would then come to him, Principal Pillish, with his wife and children accompanying him, and weeping tears of joy, would thank him for transforming his life. Then the candidate's wife would bow humbly before him and kiss his hand, and the candidate's children would step forward to present him, shyly, with a little posy of flowers they had picked themselves, and the candidate would make a clumsy but heartfelt speech, in which he would say that he owed it all to those few shining words in that precious day-before talk. After that, felt Principal Pillish with a sigh, he could retire happy, knowing his labours had not been in vain.

This year, he told himself as he surveyed the faces of his candidates, this year, surely, there really was a chance. Never before had he known such high morale. Never before had he reached this stage in the study course without a single nervous breakdown. This year, surely, at long last, he would have his winner.

"Candidates," he began, beaming at them to infuse them with vital confidence. "Candidates, tomorrow you sit the High Examination. You are nervous. That is natural. All candidates are nervous. You are not at a disadvantage because you are nervous. In fact, your nervousness will help you. Your nervousness is your friend."

He beamed at them again. He believed this to be one of the transforming insights of his day-before talk. In his secret dream, the successful candidate would say to him, "When you told us, 'Your nervousness is your friend,' I saw everything differently. It was as if a blindfold was removed from my eyes, and everything became clear."

"An athlete is nervous before the start of the race," he went on, warming to his theme. "That nervousness brings him to the highest pitch of readiness. The starting signal is given, and off he goes! His nervousness has become his power, his speed, his victory!"

He had hoped at this point to see an answering glow of excitement in their eyes. Instead, they seemed to be smiling. This was unusual. By this stage in the Study Course, in all former years, the candidates wore a sullen defeated look, and avoided meeting his eyes. This year they were positively cheerful, and somehow he had the feeling that they weren't really listening to him.

He decided to break off from his day-before talk, if only briefly, to check their responses.

"Candidate Hath," he said, picking out the one on whom his highest hopes rested. "Do you feel well prepared for tomorrow?"

"Oh, yes, I think so," said Hanno Hath. "I shall give my best."

"Good, good," said Principal Pillish. However, there was something about Candidate Hath's reply that didn't feel quite right.

"Candidate Mimilith. How are you feeling?"

"Not so bad, sir, thank you," said Miko Mimilith.

There it is again, thought Principal Pillish. Something isn't right here. Instinctively he turned to the weakest candidate on the course.

"Candidate Scooch. One day left. Raring to go, I trust?"

"Yes, sir," said Scooch cheerfully.

This was downright odd. What is it that's wrong here? Principal Pillish asked himself. Back came the answer: They're not nervous.

At once he was overcome with a sensation of outrage. Not nervous! What right did they have not to be nervous? What use was his day-before talk if they weren't nervous? It was disrespectful. It was insolent. It was—yes—it was ungrateful. And worst of all—yes, this was undoubtedly true—if they were not nervous, they would perform poorly in the High Examination, and that would damage their family ratings. Nervousness was their friend. It was his duty, as their teacher and guide, to reintroduce nervousness to this inappropriately confident group. He must do it for their sake, and for the sake of their families.

"Candidate Scooch," he said, no longer smiling. "I'm

delighted that you feel so eager for the fray. Why don't we sharpen our mental swords for battle by trying a few questions here and now?"

He reached for one of the study books and opened it at random.

"What is the chemical composition of common salt?"

"I don't know," said Scooch.

Principal Pillish turned pages at random.

"Describe the life-cycle of the newt."

"I can't," said Scooch.

"If sixty-four cube-shaped boxes are stacked in a cube-shaped pile, how many boxes high is the pile?"

"I don't know," said Scooch.

Principal Pillish closed the book with a sharp snap.

"Three typical questions from the High Examination, Candidate Scooch, and you can't answer any of them. Does that make you feel just the smallest bit nervous about tomorrow?"

"No, sir," said Scooch.

"And why is that?"

"Well, sir," said Scooch, unaware that Hanno Hath was trying desperately to catch his eye, "I won't be answering those sorts of questions, sir."

"What then, Candidate Scooch, will you be writing about on your examination paper?"

"Tea breaks," said Scooch.

A faint pink mist seemed to form before Principal Pillish's eyes. He felt for the edge of the table beside him.

"Tea breaks?" he repeated faintly.

"Yes, sir," said Scooch, all unaware of the effect he was producing. "I think I may be a bit of an expert on tea breaks. Not everybody has them, it turns out. I've been talking it over with the other fellows on the course. How can mortal man last from breakfast until lunch, sir, without a little something that's both restful and stimulating? For the first part of the morning you can look forward to it, sir, and for the second part of the morning you can remember it—"

"Be quiet," said Principal Pillish.

He glowered at the assembled candidates. His secret dream, which had seemed so close, lay shattered at his feet. His heart was filled with bitterness.

"Does anyone else propose to write about tea breaks?"

No one answered.

"Will someone please tell me what's going on?"

Hanno Hath raised his hand.

Principal Pillish listened to Hanno Hath's explanation in the privacy of his office. Hanno delivered a passionate defence of his novel system, but none of it made any sense. When Hanno said, "You might as well test fish for flying,"

Principal Pillish passed a hand over his brow and said, "The candidates on my course are not fish." When Hanno was done, the Principal sat in silence for a while. He felt betrayed. He had not understood the flow of eager words, but he had heard, loud and clear, the underlying note of rebellion. This was not a case of laziness, or exam nerves. This was mutiny. Under the circumstances, his duty was clear. He must inform the Chief Examiner.

Maslo Inch listened to the whole unhappy tale, and then shook his head slowly from side to side, and said, "I blame myself. The man's a rotten apple, and now he's infected the whole barrel."

"But what should I do, Chief Examiner?"

"Nothing. I will deal with him myself."

"The difficulty is, he's not sorry. He thinks he's right."

"I'll make him sorry."

The Chief Examiner spoke these words with such forceful conviction that Principal Pillish's wounded pride was soothed somewhat. He wanted to see Hanno Hath's smile crumple into an expression of fear and need. He wanted to see him humbled. For his own good, of course.

This new development decided the matter for Maslo Inch. He sent for the captain of the marshals, and gave him his orders. That night, two hours after sundown, a troop of ten specially picked men moved quietly into the arena and surrounded the wind singer, where Ira Hath was sleeping with Pinpin in her arms.

They achieved complete surprise. Ira Hath knew nothing until she felt her arms gripped tight, and awoke to find the warm weight of her child being lifted away from her. She started to cry out, but a strong hand clamped over her mouth, and a blindfold was pulled tight around her eyes. She could hear Pinpin calling pitifully, "Mama! Mama!" and she kicked and struggled with all her might, but the men who held her knew what they were doing, and she could not free herself.

Then Pinpin's cries faded out of hearing, and, exhausted and gagging for breath, she fell still. A voice close to her ear said, "Are you done?"

She nodded.

"Do you come with us, or do we drag you?"

She nodded again, meaning she would come. The rough hand was removed from her mouth. She drew a long gasping breath.

"Where's my daughter?"

"Safe enough. If you want to see her again, you do as you're told."

After that Ira Hath knew she had no choice. Still blindfolded, she let them lead her down from the wind singer and out of the great arena. They went across the plaza, and into a building, through doors and down corridors, into one room and then another, until she and her escort at last came to a stop.

"Let her go," said a voice she recognised. "Take off the blindfold."

There in front of her, seated at a long table, was Maslo Inch. And on her right, not quite close enough to reach out and touch, stood her husband.

"Hanno!"

"Silence!" barked the Chief Examiner. "Neither of you will speak until I've said what I have to say."

Ira Hath was silent. But her eyes met Hanno's, and they spoke to each other in looks, saying, *We'll get through this together somehow.*

A warden entered the room carrying a small pile of neatly folded grey clothes.

"Put them on the table," said Maslo Inch.

The warden did as he was told, and left.

"Now," said Maslo Inch, looking up at them with steady eyes. "This is what you will do. Tomorrow is the day of the High Examination. You, Hanno Hath, will sit that examination, as is your duty to your family, and you will acquit yourself as best as you can. You, Ira Hath, will attend the High Examination, as a dutiful wife and mother, to show support for the head of your family. You will of course be wearing your designated clothing."

He nodded at the pile on the table before him.

"When the examination is over, and before the people leave the arena, I will call upon each of you to make a short public statement. Your statements are written here. You will learn them by heart overnight."

He held out two sheets of paper, and the captain of the marshals passed them on to Hanno and Ira.

"You will be spending tonight in detention. You will not be disturbed."

"Where's my daughter?" broke in Ira Hath, unable to stop herself.

"Your child is in safe hands. The good woman who has charge of her will bring her to the arena tomorrow, where she will watch the progress of the High Examination from the infants' enclosure. If you demonstrate to me by your behaviour tomorrow that you are fit guardians for an impressionable child, she will be returned to you. If you do not, she will be made a ward of the city, and you will never see her again."

Ira Hath felt hot tears rise to her eyes.

"Oh, monster, monster," she said in a low voice.

"If that is your attitude, ma'am—"

"No," said Hanno. "We understand. We'll do as you say."

"We shall see," said Maslo Inch evenly. "Tomorrow will tell."

Left alone in their detention room, Ira and Hanno Hath fell into each other's arms and broke into bitter sobs. Then after a while Hanno wiped away his wife's tears and his own, and said, "Come, now. We must do what we can."

"I want Pinpin! Oh, my baby, where are you?"

"No, no. No more of that. Just one night, that's all."

"I hate them, I hate them, I hate them."

"Of course, of course. But for the moment, we must do as they say."

He unfolded his sheet of paper and read the statement he was to learn and repeat in public:

My fellow citizens, I make this public confession of my own free will. For some years now I have not striven to do my best. As a result, I have failed my family and myself. To my shame, I have sought to blame others for my failure. I now see that this was childish and self-centred. We are each of us responsible for our own destiny. I am proud to be a citizen of Aramanth. I promise today to do all in my power, from now on, to make myself worthy of that honour.

"I suppose it could be worse," said Hanno with a sigh, after he had finished reading it.

Ira Hath's statement ran:

My fellow citizens. You may know that recently I have lost two of my children. The strain of this loss led to a mental breakdown, in the course of which I acted in ways of which I am now ashamed. I ask for your forgiveness and under-

standing. I promise in future to behave with the modesty and decency that befits a wife and mother.

She threw the paper to the floor.

"I won't say it!"

Hanno picked it up.

"It's only words."

"Oh, my babies, my babies," cried Ira Hath, starting to weep again. "When will I hold you all in my arms again?"

CHAPTER TWENTY-THREE

THE SCOURGE OF THE PLAINS

WHEN THE LIGHT OF DAWN WOKE THE THREE CHILDREN, the first sound they heard was the music of the band, and looking across the great gorge, they saw the Zars still marching, and still falling. Horrified, they went to the edge of the gorge and looked down. There far below, the river bed was white, as if with a drift of snow, except that in the white there glittered points of gold. Into this whiteness fell the beautiful young Zars, and little by little the whiteness was reaching farther and climbing higher. There would come a time, who knew how soon, when the Zars would walk across a mountain of their own dead to the other side.

Without further words, the three friends turned and

rejoined the Great Way, and strode off in the cool of the morning towards Aramanth.

The silver voice of the wind singer hung round Kestrel's neck, inside her shirt, tied by a gold thread she had unplaited from her hair. It lay against her bony chest, made warm by her own warmth, and as they walked she felt it tickling her skin. Already, because they were on the homeward journey, her thoughts were reaching ahead to Aramanth, and her father and mother and little sister. This gave needed strength to her legs, for Bowman was keeping up a relentless pace.

"We must get to Aramanth first," he said.

The Zars were no longer pursuing them, but as they hurried on down the Great Way, they faced a different problem, about which none of them spoke. It was a sign of the great change that had taken place in Mumpo that he, too, said nothing, though the ache in his stomach was growing stronger with every hour. They were hungry. They had eaten nothing for a day and a night, and now half another day. Their food bags were empty, and the trees they were passing bore no fruit. Here and there a wayside stream provided water, but even this refreshment would end, they knew, when they reached the great desert plains. How far did they then have to go? They couldn't tell, because they had been carried across the plains by the thousand sails of Ombaraka.

They guessed three days, maybe more. How could they make the long crossing without food?

The Great Way was broad, and sloped gently downwards, and now they could see the plains lying before them as they went. By noon, their hunger was slowing them down, and feeling their growing weakness, they began to be afraid. Even Bowman was becoming weary. So at last he gave in, and called a rest stop. Gratefully they sank to the ground, in the shade of a broad-leafed tree.

"How are we going to get home?" said Kestrel. She realised as she spoke that she was turning to her brother now, as their natural leader.

"I don't know," he answered simply. "But we will get home, because we must."

It was no answer, but it comforted her.

"Maybe we could eat leaves," she said, tugging at the branch above.

"I know!" said Mumpo. He reached inside his pocket, and brought out the last of the tixa leaves he had carried with him all the way from the Underlake. He divided them into three portions, and gave a share to each of the others.

"It's not real food," he said, "but it makes you not mind about food."

He was right. They chewed the tixa leaves, and swallowed the sharp-tasting juice, and though it did nothing to fill their empty bellies, it made them feel it didn't matter.

"Tastes bitter," said Kestrel, pulling a face.

"Bitter bitter bitter," said Mumpo in a singsong voice.

Up they got and on they went, loping and rolling, and all the insuperable problems ahead seemed to dwindle away. How would they cross the great plains? They would fly like birds, carried effortlessly on the wind. They would drift like clouds over the land.

As they danced down the Great Way, borne in the arms of tixa, they found themselves speaking their fears out loud, singing them, laughing at them.

"Ha ha ha, to the Zars!" sang Mumpo.

"Ha ha ha, Zar Zar Zar!" sang the twins.

"Mumpo was an oldie!" chanted Kestrel.

"Oldie, oldie, oldie!" they all sang.

"What was it like being old, Mumpo?"

Mumpo danced an oldie dance for them, moving with exaggerated slowness.

"Slow and heavy," he sang as he pranced gravely before them. "Slow and heavy and tired."

"Tired, tired, tired," they sang.

"Like when we were all covered with mud."

"Mud, mud, mud!"

"Then the mud fell off, and—" He sprang into the air and waved his arms wildly. "Zar, Zar, hurrah!"

"Zar, Zar, hurrah!" they echoed.

Linking arms, all three fell into the high-stepping march of the Zars, making their own band music with their mouths.

"Tarum-tarum-taraa! Tarum-tarum-taraa!"

In this fashion, marching and singing, they came out of the forest and onto the plains. Here they came at last to a stop. Then, as they gazed across the arid wastes at the distant horizon, the effects of the tixa wore off, and they knew once more that they were hungry, starving hungry, and far, far from home.

It would have been easy then to lie down and sleep and never get up, because their singing and dancing had taken the very last of their strength. But Bowman wouldn't allow it. Stubbornly, relentlessly, he insisted their journey must go on.

"It's too far. We'll never get there."

"It doesn't matter. We have to go on."

So they went on, keeping the sun on their right side as it slowly descended in the sky. A keen wind was whipping up, and they went slower and slower, but they didn't stop. They stumbled in their weariness, but on they trudged, driven by Bowman's will.

Dusk was falling, and heavy dark clouds scudding across the sky, when Kestrel at last came to a stop. She drew the gold thread over her head and handed the silver voice to Bowman, saying quietly, "You go on. I can't."

Bowman took it and held the fine silver clasp tight in his hand, and his eyes met hers. He could see there her shame that she could do no more, but deeper and stronger than the shame, the weariness.

I can't do it without you, Kess.

Then it's over.

Bowman turned and saw Mumpo watching him, waiting for what he would say that would make them believe there was hope—and he had no words left. He closed his eyes.

Help me, he said silently, not knowing to whom or what he was appealing.

As if in answer, there came a half-familiar sound: a distant creaking and groaning, carried on the wind.

He opened his eyes, and all three of them turned to look. There, rising slowly above the swell of the land, was a pennant snapping in the wind, silhouetted against the twilight sky. Up over the rim of land rose the masts and sails, the lookout towers and the topmost decks. Then the main decks, crowded on all sides by full-bellied sails, and the whole vast bulk of the mother ship grinding slowly towards them, rolling out of the dusk.

"Ombaraka!" cried Kestrel.

Energised by hope, the children set off running towards

the immense moving city, waving their arms and calling out as they ran, to attract the attention of the lookouts. They were seen. The great craft lumbered to a slow halt. A boarding cradle was winched down. They clambered into it, hugging each other, weeping tears of relief. Up creaked the cradle, past the lower decks, to judder to a halt at the command deck. The gates were thrown open, and there before them stood a troop of heavily armed men, their hair shaved close to the skull.

"Baraka spies!" cried their commander. "Lock them up! They'll hang at first light!"

Only then did they realise they were prisoners of Omchaka.

The children were thrown into a cage that was just big enough for the three of them to sit in, side by side, their knees drawn up to their chests. Once locked in, the cage was winched several feet into the air, and there they were left to dangle, twisting in the wind, jeered and spat at by the guards set to watch over them.

"Baraka scum! Got up like dolls!"

"Please," pleaded the children. "We're hungry."

"Why waste food on you? You'll hang in the morning."

The Chaka people seemed to be fiercer than the Barakas, perhaps because of their way of shaving their heads; but in all other respects they were strikingly similar. The same sand-coloured robes, the same warriorlike swagger, the same festoons of weapons. When the children were heard crying, they laughed and reached up to poke them through the bars.

"Snivelling girlies!" they taunted. "You'll have something to cry about in the morning."

"We won't live till morning," said Kestrel in a faint voice. "We haven't eaten for days."

"You'd better live," cried the biggest of their guards. "If I find you dead in the morning, I'll kill you."

The other guards laughed tremendously at this. The big guard went red.

"Well, what's your brilliant idea, then? Do you want to tell Haka Chaka there'll be no public hanging?"

"Kill them again, Pok! That'll scare them!"

They laughed even more. The big guard they called Pok scowled and fell to muttering to himself.

"You all think I'm so stupid, well, you're the stupid ones, not me, you'll see all right, just you wait. . . ."

As night descended and the wind grew stronger, the guards decided to take it in turns to stand watch. Big Pok volunteered to go first, and the others departed. As soon as they were alone, Pok approached the cage and called up in a hoarse whisper.

"Hey! You Baraka spies! Are you still alive?"

No answer came from the cage. Pok groaned aloud.

"Please talk to me, scum. You're not to die."

Kestrel spoke in a tiny croaking voice.

"Food," she said. "Food . . ."

The word faded on her lips.

"All right," said Pok nervously. "Just wait there. I'll get you food. Don't do anything. I'm going to get you food. Don't die, all right? Promise me you won't die, or I won't go."

"Not long now . . ." said Kestrel faintly. "Slipping away . . ."

"No, no! That's what you're not to do! Don't do that or I'll—I'll—"

Realising he had no effective way to threaten them, he resorted to pleading.

"Look, you're going to die anyway, so it doesn't matter to you, but it does matter to me. If you die on my watch, they'll blame me, and that's not fair, is it? You've got to admit, it wouldn't be my fault, but I can tell you now how it'll be. 'Oh, Pok again,' they'll say. 'Trust Pok to make a mess of it. Poor old Pok, thick as a rock.' That's what they say, and it isn't fair."

Silence from the children. Pok panicked.

"Just don't die yet. That's the thing. I'm going. Food's on its way."

He galloped off. The children stayed still and quiet, in case someone else was watching, although by now the night was very dark, and the roaring wind kept the people indoors. Shortly, Pok reappeared, his arms full of bread and fruit.

"Here you are," he said, panting, poking loaves through the bars. "Eat it up! Eat it up!"

He watched anxiously, and when he saw the children begin to eat, he let out a sigh of relief.

"There! That's better. No more dying, eh?"

The more the children ate, the happier Pok became.

"There! Old Pok's not made a mess of it after all! You'll be chirpy as sparrows in the morning, and Haka Chaka can have a fine hanging. So all's well that ends well, as they say."

The food brought strength back to Bowman, and with strength came hope. He began to think of how to escape.

"We're not really Baraka spies," he said.

"Oh, no," said Pok. "Oh, no, you can't fool me that easily. Even old Pok can see you're not Chaka, and if you're not Chaka, you're Baraka."

"We're from Aramanth."

"No, you're not. You've got Baraka hair."

"What if we were to unbraid our hair?" said Kestrel. "What if we were to shave it all off, like you?"

"Well, then," said Pok uncertainly. "Well, then, you'd be . . . You'd look like . . ."

He found the whole idea deeply muddling.

"We'd look like you."

"That's as may be," he said. "But you can't shave your hair off tonight, and in the morning you're going to be hanged. So that's that."

"Except you wouldn't want to hang us and find out afterwards it had all been a mistake."

"Haka Chaka gives the orders," said Pok contentedly. "Haka Chaka is the Father of Omchaka, the Great Judge of Righteousness, and the Scourge of the Plains. He doesn't make mistakes."

The children did sleep that night, for all the cramped conditions in the cage and the howling of the wind. The food in their bellies and the weariness in their bones were stronger than their fear of the morning, and they slept deeply until the light of dawn awoke them.

The wind had fallen, but the sky was leaden grey, heavy with an approaching storm. A squad of Chaka guards marched up and formed a circle round the cage. The cage was winched down onto the deck, and the gate unlocked. The children stumbled out. The squad formed up around them, and they marched across a causeway to the central square of Omchaka. Here a great crowd was waiting, packed tight round the sides of the square and hanging from the rails of the decks above. As soon as the children came in sight, the crowd began to hiss and call out insults.

"Hang them! Baraka filth! String them up!"

In the centre of the square there stood a newly built scaffold, from which hung three rope nooses. Behind the scaffold stood the commanders of the Omchaka army and a line of drummers. The children were led to the scaffold and stood on a bench, each one before a rope noose. Then the drummers beat their drums, and the Grand Commander cried out, "All stand for Haka Chaka, Father of Omchaka, Great Judge of Righteousness and Scourge of the Plains!"

No one moved, since they were all standing anyway, and into the square strode Haka Chaka, followed by a small entourage. He was an old man of imposing stature, his grey hair shaved close to his skull. But it was not at him that the children gazed in amazement. Behind him, hair also shaved, walked Counsellor Kemba.

"He's a Baraka!" cried Kestrel, pointing at him accusingly. "His name's Kemba, and he's from Ombaraka!"

Kemba smiled, seemingly unconcerned.

"They'll be saying you're a Baraka next, Highness."

"They can say what they like," said Haka Chaka grimly. "The talking will end soon enough."

He gave a sign to the men holding the three children, and the nooses were placed round their necks. Mumpo didn't cry, as he would have done once, but he did make a small choking noise.

"I'm sorry, Mumpo," said Kestrel. "We've been no good for you after all."

"Yes, you have," he said bravely. "You've been my friends."

Haka Chaka climbed up onto a high speaking platform to address the crowd.

"People of Omchaka!" he cried. "The Morah has delivered our enemies into our hands!"

All at once Bowman saw the way out.

"The Morah has woken!" he called out.

A surprised silence fell over the crowd. From the grey sky above came the low rumble of the approaching storm. Kemba's eyes turned on Bowman, burning intensely.

"The Zars are on the march!" cried Bowman.

This caused consternation in the crowd. A buzz of agitated chatter broke out on all sides. Haka Chaka turned to his advisers.

"Can this be true?"

"They're marching after us," cried Bowman. "Wherever we are, they'll find us."

Now on all sides there were voices raised in fear, intensified by the sudden gusts of wind that rattled the rigging above.

"Nothing can stop the Zars!"

"They'll kill us all!"

"Tell the sailmen! We must set sail!"

"Fools!"

It was Kemba who took control of the panic. He spoke loudly, but in tones that were calm, even soothing.

"Can't you tell a Baraka trick when you see one? Why would the Morah have woken? Why would the Zars march? He lies to save his own miserable skin."

"I woke the Morah myself," said Bowman. "The Morah said to me, 'We are legion.'"

These words chilled the hearts of the crowd. Kemba looked at Bowman with hatred, but mingled with the hatred was fear.

"He lies!" he cried. "These are our enemies! Why do we listen? Hang them! Hang them now!"

The crowd fell on this proposal, echoing it wildly, their newly aroused fear streaming out of them as hate-charged anger.

"Hang them! Hang them!"

The nooses were pulled close around the children's necks. Two guards stood at either end of the high bench, ready to knock it away from the children's feet. Haka Chaka raised his arms to still the baying of the crowd.

"What have we to fear?" he cried. "We are Omchaka!"

A great cheer greeted this call.

"Let Ombaraka tremble! This is how we deal with all ene-mies of Omchaka!"

But in the moment of silence before he dropped his arms, which was to be the signal for the hanging, a new sound came to them, carried by the storm wind: the tramp-ing of marching feet, the music of a marching band, the singing of a multitude of young voices.

"Kill, kill, kill, kill! Kill, kill, kill!"

The people of Omchaka looked at each other in silent horror. Then the one word that all dreaded now formed on their lips.

"The Zars! The Zars!"

Counsellor Kemba was galvanised into action.

"Highness," he said urgently. "Release the spies! Put them in a land-sailer and send them south. The Zars will follow them. Omchaka must set course for the east at once."

Haka Chaka understood, and the orders were given. As the crowd broke up and the people of Omchaka hurried to their action stations, Kemba approached the children and addressed them in a savage whisper.

"Forty years of peace and you ruin everything! My life work destroyed! My only consolation is that you won't escape the Zars, nor will your precious Aramanth!"

The children were released, and bundled into a land-sailer—not one of the sleek manoeuvrable corvettes, but a heavy low-bottomed provisions craft, with a single fixed sail. It was winched hurriedly over the side while the great city of Omchaka echoed with frantic activity. On every deck the sailmen were unfurling sails and yelling out instructions, and the ever-strengthening wind was bellying out the myriad canvases and tugging the immense mother craft into juddering movement.

As the little land-sailer banged onto the ground, the Zars could be seen far off, marching in their column, eight abreast, led by the band, high-stepping across the plains. The storm wind sweeping down from the north caught the sail and jerked the land-sailer out of the lee of Omchaka. Here, hit by the full force of the wind, the craft picked up speed. And all at once, with a roll of thunder across the iron sky, the storm overtook them, bringing with it drenching rain.

Faster and faster ran the land-sailer, crashing over the stony ground, and the children could do nothing but cling tight to the mast and hurtle through the storm. The wind became a gale, the rain became a torrent, through which they could see nothing. Again and again, lightning crackled across the livid sky, and the long booming explosions of thunder rolled over their heads. Water was filling up the well of the craft, slopping over their feet, but all they could do was hold tight as they charged on, bucking and bouncing, out of all control.

Then one wheel struck a rock, and two of its spokes snapped. For a few moments longer the wheel spun on, then the rim buckled, and almost at once the wheel imploded. The craft lurched to one side. The pitiless wind hammered into the sail, spinning them round, and a second wheel burst into fragments. The land-sailer went over onto its side, skated a little way under its sheer momentum, and then skidded to a stop.

Still the storm raged around them. They could do nothing, so they huddled together in the shelter of the broken hull, and waited for the pelting rain to pass. Bowman felt the silver voice of the wind singer, still hanging round his neck, and he thought how close they had come to death, and it seemed to him that someone or something must be looking after them. Someone or something wanted them to make their way home, though who or what it might be, he had no idea.

"We're going to do it," he said.

Kestrel and Mumpo felt it too. They couldn't be far from Aramanth now.

In time, the heavy rain gave way to intermittent showers, and the wind dropped. The children crawled out from under their shelter, and looked around them in the light of the brightening sky. The storm was passing to the south, and there on the near horizon, unmistakable even through the veil of falling rain, rose the high walls of Aramanth.

"We're going to do it," said Bowman again, exultantly.

Tramp! Tramp! Tramp!

Through the showers, soaked but smiling, singing as they marched, came the unstoppable Zars.

"Kill, kill, kill, kill! Kill, kill, kill!"

Without another word, the children set off at a run towards the city walls.

CHAPTER TWENTY-FOUR

THE LAST HIGH EXAMINATION

TODAY WAS THE DAY OF THE HIGH EXAMINATION. The unseasonal rain storm had delayed the start of the session, which was most unusual, but now the rows of desks that filled the arena terraces had been wiped dry, and the examination was well under way. Seated at the desks were the heads of every family in the city, at work on the papers that would determine their family rating for the coming year. Each circular terrace held three hundred and twenty desks, and there were nine terraces. Nearly three thousand examinees all sitting in utter silence, but for the scratching of pens on paper, and the soft padding of the examiners as they patrolled the arena.

All round the main terraces, and crowded into the steeply

raked stands on either side, sat the families of the examinees. Everybody except those engaged in essential occupa-
tions had to be present on the day of the High Examination,
partly to lend support to their family head, and partly to
demonstrate that the examination ranked the family as well
as the individual. The families sat in segregated sections
according to their colours—the few whites and the many
more scarlets at the palace end; the broad middle taken up
by orange on one side and maroon on the other; the end by
the statue of Creoth a sea of grey. Maslo Inch, the Chief
Examiner, sat on a podium raised on a stone plinth, on
which was carved the Oath of Dedication.

I VOW TO STRIVE HARDER, TO REACH HIGHER,
AND IN EVERY WAY TO SEEK TO MAKE
TOMORROW BETTER THAN TODAY.
FOR LOVE OF MY EMPEROR
AND FOR THE GLORY OF ARAMANTH.

He looked at his watch and noted that one hour had passed.
Rising, he stepped down from the podium and made a slow
circuit of the arena, letting his eyes roam at random over the
bowed heads of the examinees. For Maslo Inch, the High
Examination was always a time for satisfying reflection, and
today, after the recent disturbances, more so than ever.

Here were the people of Aramanth, ranked and ordered, going about the business of being tested in a manner that was fair and just. None could complain of favouritism, or of secret grudges against them. All sat the same exam, and all were marked in the same way. The able and the diligent came to the fore, as was right and proper, and the stupid and the idle slipped down the rankings, as was also right and proper. Of course it was unpleasant for those who performed poorly and had to move house to a poorer district, but it was fair, because always it meant that some other family that had worked hard and done well was being rewarded. And never forget—in his mind he rehearsed his end-of-exam speech—never forget that next year, at the next High Examination, your chance will come round again, and you can win back all you have lost. Yes, all things considered, it was the best possible system, and no one could deny it.

His wandering eyes fell on the group from the Residential Study Course, who sat together because they were subject to extra supervision. He saw on their faces the looks of panic and despair that he saw every year, as they struggled with questions for which they had failed to prepare themselves, and he knew that all was as it should be. Why is it, he thought, that some people never learn? All it takes is a little effort, a little extra push. And there in the midst of them sat Hanno Hath, with his head in his hands. Truly that man was a disgrace to Aramanth. But he was under control now.

His eyes swept across the arena to the area where the families from Grey District sat. There was the Hath woman, sitting dressed in grey, her hands folded in her lap, as docile as you could wish. His eyes moved on to the infants' enclosure, where that dependable woman Mrs. Chirish sat with the Hath child in her lap. He had expected the child to cause trouble, but it seemed to be quiet, no doubt awed by the great studious silence that hung over the arena.

Well, that's a good job well done, said Maslo Inch to himself. The pride of the Hath family was well and truly broken.

High in the tower above the Imperial Palace, the Emperor stood moodily eating chocolate buttons, looking down on the deserted streets of the city. He had watched the examinees and their families arrive earlier, and had sensed their feelings of anxiety and dread. He hated the annual day of the High Examination. He had heard the thousands of voices chanting the Oath of Dedication, and when it came to the part that said "for love of my Emperor," he had blocked his ears. But for the last hour, all had been silent. It was as if the city had died.

But now he began to imagine he could hear a new sound: far away, faint, muffled, but—could it be a band playing? He strained his ears to catch it more clearly. Who

would dare to play music on the day of the High
Examination?

Then as he stared down at the streets below, he saw the
strangest sight. A manhole opened up in the road, and a muddy
child burst out, followed by two more. They looked around
them, seemed confused for a moment, and then set off at a run
towards the arena. The Emperor watched them run, and it
seemed to him he knew one of them. Wasn't it the girl—?

Suddenly out of the manhole popped a handsome young
lad in a white-and-gold uniform. After him came another,
and another. Then from behind them, down the long street,
came a whole column of them, led by a marching band. The
Emperor's eyes stood out in his head, and he was rooted to the
spot. He needed no telling. This was the army of the Zars.

More and more of them came marching out of side
streets and clambering out of sewers to join the main column. And now as they marched they started to sing, a song
made of only one word:

"Kill, kill, kill, kill! Kill, kill, kill!"

The Emperor knew he must stop them. But how? He
couldn't even move. He took a handful of chocolate buttons
from the bowl, unaware that he was doing so, and ate them
without tasting them, and wept as he ate.

The children raced past the statue of Creoth, burst through

the pillared entrance to the arena, and came to a stop, panting, on the topmost terrace. Somehow, urgent though the danger was, the sight of the thousands of examinees bent over their desks in silence awed them, and for a few crucial moments, regaining their breath, they hesitated.

In these few moments, Maslo Inch had seen them, and was outraged. Nothing was permitted to break the sacred silence of the High Examination. He did not recognise the three bedraggled urchins, with their ridiculous stringy hair and their muddy feet. It was enough that they were intruders. He signed sharply to his assistants to deal with the matter.

The children saw the scarlet-robed examiners moving grimly towards them. Down in the centre of the arena, the wind singer stood turning silently this way and that in the breeze. Bowman drew the silver voice out of his shirt, and unlooped the string from round his neck. He spoke silently to his sister.

Stay close. If they get me, you take it.

The children spread out, staying in reach of each other, and started down the terraces towards the wind singer. By now the examinees were beginning to notice the disturbance, and a buzz of low voices came from the stands. This is intolerable, thought Maslo Inch to himself, moving instinctively back to his podium.

The examiners closed in on the children from above and

below, thinking at first that it would take no more than stern whispers to remove them. But as they came close, the children suddenly bolted in three different directions, sprinting round the terraces, past the examinees.

"Get them!" roared the Chief Examiner to the marshals, no longer caring that the examination would be disrupted. "Stop them!"

As he shouted, he heard an impossible sound from outside in the street: a marching band, and marching feet.

Tramp! Tramp! Tramp!

Bowman zigzagged through the desks, knocking over piles of papers here and there, jumping down from terrace to terrace. To his left he saw Kestrel, keeping up with him. He raced past Hanno Hath without even noticing, but his father recognised him, and, his heart pounding with joy, he rose up in his seat—

A marshal caught Kestrel, but she buried her face in his arm and bit him so hard that he let her go. No one was working at their papers now: all heads were raised, gazing in astonishment at the children and the pursuing marshals.

In the Grey stand, Ira Hath rose to her feet, staring. She was almost sure—only their hair was so different—but surely it was—

"Hubba hubba, Kestrel!" she yelled, wild with excitement. And Hanno Hath, on the far side of the arena, also standing, his heart hammering, cried out, "Hubba hubba, Bowman!"

Turning to wave to him, Bowman ran into two marshals, and between them they caught him fast by the neck and legs.

"Kess!" he yelled, and threw the silver voice high in the air.

She heard, and saw, and was there, scrabbling for the voice where it had landed, racing down the next terrace towards the wind singer, Mumpo by her side.

In all this excitement, Mrs. Chirish let go of Pinpin, who at once seized the opportunity to jump off her lap and run away.

"Hey!" cried Mrs. Chirish. "Stop that child!"

But Pinpin was gone, wriggling under benches and between legs, towards the funny brown figures she had instantly recognised as her brother and sister.

Kestrel hurled herself down from the last terrace and ran for the wind singer, with two big marshals close behind her. She got as far as the base of the wooden tower, when their hands closed about her and dragged her down.

"Mumpo!" she yelled, and threw the silver voice towards him. Maslo Inch saw it as it fell, and suddenly and completely understood what was happening. He strode across the floor to seize it. Mumpo got there just before him.

"Give that to me, you dirty little brat!" commanded the Chief Examiner in his most authoritative voice, seizing Mumpo in his powerful hands. But as he spoke, his eyes met

Mumpo's, and something happened inside him that he couldn't control. He gave a low gasp, and felt a hot rush in his throat and face.

"You!"

He let go, and Mumpo broke away and raced towards the wind singer, the silver voice in his hand. Outside, the marching Zars were closer now, and the crowd in the arena could hear the band, and were straining to see who it was that dared to play music on this day of days. Bowman and Kestrel, each held tight by their captors, watched as Mumpo reached the wind singer, and started to climb.

Go, Mumpo, go!

Agile as a monkey, Mumpo shinned up the wooden tower, the silver voice in his hand. But where was it to go?

"In the neck!" shouted Kestrel. "The slot in the neck!"

Now the music of the Zars was coming clear from the street, and the *tramp! tramp! tramp!* of their marching feet. Mumpo searched frantically for the slot, his hands feeling the rusty metal of the wind singer's neck.

Hanno Hath watched him, his heart in his mouth, willing him with all his being.

Go, Mumpo, go!

Ira Hath watched him, trembling uncontrollably.

Go, Mumpo, go!

All at once his fingers felt it, higher up than he had

expected. The silver voice slipped into the slot with a slight springy *click!* just as the leading Zars burst through the pillars, their swords drawn and flashing, their song on their lips.

"Kill, kill, kill, kill—"

The wind singer turned in the breeze, the air flowed into its big leather funnels, and found its way down to the silver voice. Softly, the silver horns began to sing.

The very first note, a deep vibration, stopped the Zars dead in their tracks. They stood as if frozen, swords raised, faces bright and smiling. And all round the arena, a queer shivery sensation ran through the people.

The next note was higher, gentle but piercing. As the wind singer turned in the wind, the note modulated up and down, over the deep humming. Then came the highest note of all, like the singing of a celestial bird, a cascade of tumbling melody. The sounds seemed to grow louder and reach farther, taking possession of the arena terrace by terrace, and then of the stands, and then of the city beyond. The marshals holding Bowman and Kestrel released their grip. The examinees looked at the papers on their desks in bewilderment. The families in the stands stared at each other.

Hanno Hath left his desk. Ira Hath left the Grey stand. Pinpin crept out from the lowest benches and toddled into the open space and started to chortle with joy. And all the time, the song of the wind singer was reaching deeper and deeper into the people, and everything was changing. Examinees could be heard asking each other, "What are we doing here?" One examinee took the papers off his desk, tore them up, and threw the pieces into the air. Soon everyone was doing it, laughing like Pinpin, and the air was thick with flying paper. The families in the stands began to intermingle, and there was a great mixing of colours, as maroon flowed into grey, and orange embraced scarlet.

The Emperor up in his tower heard the music of the wind singer, and opened his window wide, and hurled out his bowl of chocolate buttons. They scattered as they fell, and landed all round the column of the frozen Zars. Then the Emperor turned and strode out of one of his many doors and down the stairs.

In the arena, Ira Hath moved wonderingly down the tiers, through the crowd, where people were now swapping clothes, trying out combinations of colours, and laughing at the unfamiliar sight. She saw Hanno coming from the other direction, his arms outstretched. She reached the centre circle and took Pinpin in her embrace, and hugged her and kissed her, and turning found her dear Bowman before her, his arms reaching for her, his lips kissing her cheeks. Then Hanno joined them, and Kestrel was in his arms, and there were tears streaming down his kind cheeks, and that was when Ira Hath, too, started to weep for pure joy.

"My brave birds," Hanno was saying as he embraced them all, kissing them over and over again. "My brave birds came back."

Pinpin jumped and wriggled in her mother's arms, beside herself with excitement.

"Love Bo!" she cried. "Love Kess!"

"Oh, my dear ones," said Ira Hath, as she put her arms round them all. "Oh, my heart's darlings."

Not far away, unnoticed in the confusion and the laughter of the crowd, Maslo Inch made his way to Mumpo, and slowly sank to his knees before him.

"Forgive me," he said, his voice trembling.

"Forgive you?" said Mumpo. "Why?"

"You're my son."

For a few long moments, Mumpo stared at him in astonishment. Then, shyly, he held out one hand, and the Chief Examiner took it, and pressed it to his lips.

"Father," said Mumpo. "I've got friends now."

Maslo Inch began to weep. "Have you, my boy?" he said. "Have you, my son?"

"Do you want to meet them?"

The Chief Examiner nodded, unable to speak. Mumpo led him by the hand to where the Hath family stood.

"Kess," he said. "I have got a father, after all."

Maslo Inch stood before them, his head lowered, unable to meet their eyes.

"Look after him, Mumpo," said Hanno Hath in his quiet voice, his arms still tight round his children. "Fathers need all the help their children can give them."

The Emperor passed between the double row of pillars onto the top terrace, and stood gazing at the chaotic scene in the arena. The song of the wind singer flowed on, and he felt its warming loosening power like sunshine after a long winter. He spread his arms wide, and smiled happily, and called out, "That's the way! Ha! A city needs to be noisy."

As for the Zars, from the moment that the wind singer had begun to sing, they had started to age. Standing still as statues, the beautiful features of the golden youths crinkled and sagged, and their fanatic eyes grew dim. Their backs began to stoop, and their golden hair thinned and went grey. Years passed by in minutes, and one by one the Zars crumpled to the ground, and there they died. Time and decay, held at bay for so long, now overwhelmed them. The flesh rotted on their bodies, and turned to dust. Out in the streets of Aramanth, the wind that sang in the wind singer blew the dust from their bones, and swirled it away into gardens and gutters, until all that was left of the invincible army of the Morah was a long line of skeletons, swords at their sides, glinting in the sun.

THE WIND ON FIRE TRILOGY
BOOK ONE: THE WIND SINGER
BY WILLIAM NICHOLSON

"The song of the wind singer will set you free.
Then seek the homeland."

In this masterful fantasy trilogy, William Nicholson ranges from delightfully inventive characters and societies reminiscent of *The Wizard of Oz* to social and theological insights comparable to those of Lois Lowry in *The Giver* or Philip Pullman in the His Dark Materials trilogy. In the first volume, Nicholson raises some provocative questions relevant to our own society about the destructiveness of competition and ranking, but makes his points with humor and suspense. The second volume becomes more serious as the children grow into thoughtful teens with romantic interests, and the plot explores the contradiction of freedom and social order; but always within the framework of an action-filled story. And the third volume brings it all to a soaring and mystical conclusion, with a satisfying epilogue to complete the stories of Hanno and Ira; Bowman, Kestrel, and Sisi; Mumpo and Pinto; Creoth and Mist; and all the other entrancing characters in this awe-inspiring trilogy.

BOOK ONE:
THE WIND SINGER

In the walled city of Aramanth, the citizens'
lives are ruled by frequent exams and family
rankings that determine their jobs, their social
status, the quality of their dwellings, and even
the color of their clothes. Everyone vows to
strive harder and reach higher, every day, and
the people are full of anger and envy—except
the family of twins Bowman and Kestrel, who
believe in ideas and dreams, and that everyone
should be rewarded not for test scores, but for
what they are good at. Hanno Hath, the kindly
librarian father, and his wife, the prophetess
Ira, cherish the twins and their little sister,
Pinto; and they all resist the domination by test
scores, at first privately, and then in open
rebellion.

Running away from a bad day at school, Kestrel
climbs the wind singer, a mysterious wooden
structure at the center of the town. At the top
she finds an empty slot where the missing voice
mechanism fits—the voice that, according to

legend, protected Aramanth from the fierce Zar soldiers long ago. Shouting out her frustration in all the bad words she knows, Kestrel is arrested by Maslo Inch, the Chief Examiner, and sentenced to undergo the sinister Special Teaching. She escapes by climbing a tower and at the top finds the Emperor, an ineffective old man who gives her a map and explains that she must go on a quest to bring back the device that activates the wind singer's voice, the only thing that will liberate their society.

Kestrel and her twin, Bowman, set out, followed doggedly by the class reject, lonely and stinky Mumpo. After encounters with the humble and kindly Mud People and the warlike Ombaraka, a town on wheels that sails across the desert, and pursued by the terrifying old children from Special Teaching, they eventually find the voice of the wind singer in the halls of the Morah. But in taking it, they rouse the merciless Zars, who begin to march in neverending ranks toward Aramanth as the three children race to return the voice to the Wind Singer in time.

Discussion questions

The theme of *The Wind Singer* is the injustice and lack of freedom in a society governed by official ranking. Here are some questions to help you clarify your own thoughts about this important idea.

1. The subjects of the examinations in Aramanth are calculation, grammar, general science, and general art. Hanno Hath says, "Whatever brilliance I have remains undetected in exams." What kinds of brilliance and ability are not measured by these four subjects? Who decides what the subjects of tests should be?

2. Principal Pillish tells the examinees that the High Examination "does not favour only those with natural aptitude. It favours those who work hard." Is this true, both in the book and in your own experience? He also instructs them to "Read. Remember. Repeat." Is this real learning? What would be a better way to teach?

3. "Each of us should be tested on what we do best," Hanno tells his fellow examinees. What would be the results of this method? Are there some things people need to learn even if they don't do them well? What would you like to be tested on? How do you know what you are good at until you are tested on it?

4. The people of Aramanth are told that they are free because they own the power to better themselves. But do they really? Why or why not? They are also told that there is no poverty in their society, but the people of grey district are kept poor deliberately. Why?

5. Before Aramanth was subject to the ratings system, they depended on debates and elections to guide their city. Which do you think is better? What are the problems of each method? Give examples from your own experience.

6. Kestrel says, "I'm already at the bottom of the class. What more can you do to me?" The High Examiner takes her up on this challenge. What does our own world do to someone who chooses to be at the bottom of the class? In desperation, Kestrel runs away from the constant testing. Does this solve her problems? What is the real solution to an unfair situation in society?

7. The Emperor tells Kestrel that testing has led to envy and fear. Is this always true? How else is rank or competency established, other than by testing? Would competition exist without ranking? What would be the shape of a group (or an art or a sport) without competition?

8. Research the history of Civil Service examinations, or testing for competency and promotion within government. Talk with someone who has taken such a test in this country. Does he or she feel the exam was fair in the way it tested ability to do the job?

And here are some questions about other people and ideas in *The Wind Singer*:

I. Kestrel relieves her feelings by making a song of all the bad words she knows (page 38). These are, of course, made-up swear words. Try saying them aloud and then making up some of your own. What qualities give a swear word shock value? Why do they need to be rude to be satisfying?

2. Ira Hath is a reluctant prophetess to her people. What is a prophet or a prophetess? Research the stories of some other prophets and prophetesses (Cassandra, Elijah, Muhammad) to see why Ira is unwilling to take on this role. What is the mark of a true prophetess (page 241)?

3. Mumpo lives in the present and is simple in his feelings and reactions. Is he stupid or wise? What qualities in his character are revealed to Bowman only gradually as he gets to know the other boy (p. 249)? How are these qualities shown in his actions?

4. Chewing tixa leaves helps Bowman, Kestrel, and Mumpo through some bad times, but gives them only false energy and courage. The men of the Mud People find relief from their hard work in tixa, but have hangovers the next day. Does tixa's harm outweigh its benefits?

5. The Ombaraka are essentially a gentle people, but eager for war. Are you satisfied with Kemba's explanation of this contradiction (page 195)? Do you think their solution—to fight by means of war machines without killing each other—is a good one? Are there flaws?

6. What becomes of the old children who are hit by the fireballs or the other old people who go into the fire? (Hint: Mumpo is the evidence.)

A TALK WITH
WILLIAM NICHOLSON

Well before he wrote the Wind on Fire trilogy, William Nicholson enjoyed a brilliant career in film. Nicholson began his writing career producing documentaries for the BBC. He went on to become screenwriter of such movies as *Nell* and *Gladiators*—for which he garnered an Academy Award nomination. Nicholson then became a director himself, with his 1998 film *Firelight*. With so much success in the movie industry, what made him decide to turn his attention to writing children's literature?

"I was at the point where my only other work was screenplays, and I was very grateful for that, but for a writer there is a downside to it. Your work is always at the mercy of several people, which can be frustrating. So I began looking for a corner I could call my own—a place where I could go out to play. And that became The Wind on Fire trilogy," he explains.

It was only natural for him to write about fantasy, as he wrote his first novel when he was just sixteen years old. The story was heavily influenced by James Bond stories. Although the novel was never published, Nicholson realized that he had a flair for fantasy.

The Wind on Fire trilogy was initially supposed to be one book, *The Wind Singer.* "I really wanted to see what people would think of it first." He didn't have to worry—as it turned out, two of Britain's top children's book editors immediately began vying for the rights.

According to Nicholson, the key to creating an exciting fantasy begins with the characters. And talking to Nicholson for even just a few minutes, you can see how close he is to characters like Bowman, Kestrel, Mumpo, and Pinto. More than once, he refers to them as "my children." He talks a lot about their character development. "Character development—how the characters grow throughout the story—is the key to creating a gripping fantasy," he says.

Another key element that makes this series so engaging is that all three books are filled with powerful themes, which Nicholson, with his classical Roman Catholic education, calls "theology." Thought-provoking themes, such as family unity, the concept of slavery vs. freedom, the validity of our existing testing system, and conformism vs. individuality resonate throughout.

Nicholson's engagement with issues such as these has garnered the trilogy an adult following. But what Nicholson finds most gratifying is the response of young fans. The books have been a tremendous hit in Great Britain, and Nicholson is deluged with fan mail. Kids send him games, draw pictures, make up recipes for "mudnuts," tell him, "This is the best book I've ever read in my life." "They pick up on different things, too," he observed. The eight-year-olds, like his daughter, enjoy the talking cats and flying hermits, while the fourteen-year-olds are deep into the philosophical aspects.

When we asked the consummate screenwriting professional if he had made a Hollywood deal for the trilogy, the answer surprised us. Speaking passionately, Nicholson replied, "I have had a lot of offers to make the trilogy into a movie, and I have refused every one of them.

I have said that I don't want it to be a movie until everyone has read my books in paperback. Books are not merely 'movies in waiting.' A book is a meeting place between the writer's world and that of the reader. An important part of this process for any reader is bringing your own experiences to the book. In a movie, everything is set out for you and you're unable to see it in any other way."

It took Nicholson five years to complete the highly acclaimed trilogy, as he balanced his publishing and movie careers. After having spent so much time on the project, we asked Nicholson if, now that the trilogy is over, it's been hard letting go of his "children." "Yes, of course, because they are all little bits of me, every one of them," he said. "But the end of the trilogy is also an exhilarating time, because of the enormous creative satisfaction I've gotten from writing it. As I was finishing *Firesong* [the final volume], I had the sensation of simply discovering the story, as if it was already written and waiting for me. That's a truly wonderful feeling for any writer to have."

ABOUT THE AUTHOR

William Nicholson had a brilliant career well before he wrote The Wind on Fire trilogy. He was first a writer and producer of more than forty documentaries for the BBC, then the Academy Award—nominated screenwriter of such movies as *Shadowlands, Sarafina!, Nell, First Knight,* and *Gladiators,* and finally a movie director himself, with 1998's *Firelight.* Nicholson lives in a fourteenth-century farmhouse in East Sussex, England, with his wife, Virginia, and three children, a boy and two girls ranging in age from 8 to 13.

Online Resources for Fantasy Lovers

Fantastic Fiction
www.fantasticfiction.co.uk
Comprehensive bibliographies of science fiction, fantasy, and horror authors.

Fluent in Fantasy
www.genrefluent.com
Many reviews and links by young-adult librarian and genre expert Diane Herald.

Locus
www.locusmag.com
The award-winning journal of science fiction and fantasy, with interviews, reviews, and recommended reading lists.

Mythopoeic Society
www.mythsoc.org
A prestigious society devoted to the study of mythic fantasy, especially the works of Tolkien, C. S. Lewis, and Charles Williams. Links to mythic chat groups and the Elvish Linguistic Fellowship.

The SF Site: The Home Page for Science Fiction and Fantasy

www.sfsite.com/home.htm

Information on authors, awards, and forthcoming books, plus links to bibliographies and audiobooks.

Uchronia: The Alternate History List

www.uchronia.net

An annotated bibliography of novels, essays, and short stories about alternate histories or "what ifs."

World Fantasy Convention

www.worldfantasy.org

Information about past and future World Fantasy Conventions and their awards